WHERE THE WOODS END

CHARLOTTE SALTER

DIAL BOOKS FOR YOUNG READERS

DIAL BOOKS FOR YOUNG READERS
PENGUIN YOUNG READERS GROUP
An imprint of Penguin Random House LLC
375 Hudson Street
New York, NY 10014

Copyright © 2018 by Charlotte Salter

Salter, Charlotte, author.
Where the woods end / Charlotte Salter.
New York, NY : Dial Books for Young Readers, 2018
Summary: Twelve-year-old Kestrel lives in a seemingly endless forest, and in order to escape she will need to defeat her Grabber, a creature that builds its body to reflect her greatest fear.
LCCN 2017043434 | ISBN 9780735229235 (hardcover)
Subjects: | CYAC: Monsters–Fiction. | Fear–Fiction. | Forests and forestry–Fiction.
LCC PZ7.1.S254 Wh 2018 | DDC [Fic]–dc23 LC

Printed in the United States of America
1 2 3 4 5 6 7 8 9 10

Design by Cerise Steel
Text set in Ashbury

For everyone who has ever been followed by a monster

KESTREL'S NOTEBOOK.
DO NOT TOUCH!!!!

Grabbers:

1. A grabber chooses a victim from the village.

2. It stalks them for days, or weeks, or even years.

3. They build a ~~bodie~~ body from things they find + steal. They take the form of whatever their victim is most scared of.

4. THEN THEY ATTACK.

5. Get them where they're weak, e.g. the heart.

People eaten: ~~||||~~ ~~||||~~ ~~||||~~ ~~||||~~ ~~||||~~ ~~||||~~ |||

Grabbers killed by Kestrel: ~~||||~~ ~~||||~~ ~~||||~~ ||

THE HUNGRY HOUR

The endless forest was as dark as the back of a wolf's throat, and it was filled with countless horrors.

Cats with too many eyes. Dogs with teeth as long as knitting needles. Ravenous birds with razor-tipped feathers.

And that was only the beginning. Every night, all of the people who lived in the forest's only village slammed their doors, pulled the sheets up to their chins, and crossed their fingers that they would survive till morning.

Well. All except one.

Kestrel had been lurking in the branches of a moonlit tree since sundown. It was the Hungry Hour, the time before sunrise when the forest was darkest and most dangerous. Here she was, a ready-made monster meal, completely and utterly alone.

So why had nothing tried to kill her yet?

"Help," she said unconvincingly.

Kestrel sighed and wriggled her nose to try and get some blood back into it. She was hanging upside down, her knees hooked over a branch, swinging gently like a sock on a wash line. It was part of her research on bats. She wanted to know what was so good about being upside down all the time, but so far it had only made her feel sick.

She'd write it down later—*right side up is BETTER*—adding another tiny bit of knowledge to everything she knew about the forest. The more she knew, the better she'd be able to work out its secrets.

And the more she knew about its secrets, the sooner she'd be able to escape.

Kestrel touched the hard leather book stuffed under her shirt. It had belonged to her grandma, Granmos. It was crammed full of Granmos's terrifying descriptions of the most dangerous places in the forest, notes on the monsters that lived there, and some truly unique, stomach-churning recipes. Kestrel had added her own carefully written additions, such as *ghosts are scared of cheese* and *don't touch those weird yellow frogs ever again, I MEAN IT.* She was proud of her notebook.

Then she checked the rest of her arsenal. There was a slingshot up her sleeve. Her favorite weapon, a spoon with a sharpened handle, was wedged in her boot. Lastly, there was reeking pork fat in her pocket and a necklace of tasty chicken bones hanging around her neck, which she had stolen from Mardy Banbury, the evilest hag in the village.

Kestrel wasn't sure what made someone a hag, but Mardy was probably it. Unless you counted Kestrel's mum.

She looked toward the village, thinking longingly of the warm gutter where she sometime slept, or the dark, dry burrow she hid in when her mother was in a bad mood. But she couldn't leave without catching the awful creature that had been running around the village at night, hissing at people through the shutters.

"Look at me, completely and utterly alone like a snack on a stick," she said loudly. "I hope nothing tries to eat me."

But the animals knew that Kestrel was undelicious and as stubborn as a badger, and they kept their distance.

Instead, Kestrel was answered by the kind of laughing, creaking silence that only the forest could make. The trees scratched the inky sky like a creature with thousands of long, bony fingers and overgrown nails. The wolf fire, a huge pyre that kept the ravenous beasts away, flickered in the distant village. It helped keep the village safe, but it made the shadows bigger, too.

Kestrel saw something out of the corner of her eye. It was a tiny, fleeting movement, and most people wouldn't have noticed it, but her eyesight was formidable and she was quicker than a greased fox. In one fluid movement the slingshot was in her hand, fitted with a stone.

"Come out," she said boldly, tightening her fingers around the stone. Her heart started to thump, but she made herself ignore it. "I'm ready!"

Nothing happened, and she slowly lowered the slingshot. Kestrel cautiously hoped it was because everything near the village was terrified of her. She was scary, but she wasn't as good at hunting as her grandma, who had taught Kestrel everything she knew. Even her dad was a great hunter. He set incredible traps and hadn't let a villager get eaten by a wolf in five years. He was so good that the villagers called him the Trapper.

Kestrel secretly thought it was a terrible name, like something you'd call a dog, but she liked hearing it anyway.

Kestrel pulled the notebook from her pocket and pretended to read, so it wouldn't look like she was lying in wait. She could see every shadow of the forest in her peripheral vision. She turned the book around as her grandma's scrawled sentence crawled around the corner of the page, turning into a tight spiral and bumping into a recipe for snail cake.

The reeking monster-fat candle inside her storm lantern suddenly guttered. A group of giant moths, which had been hopefully bumping into it, spiraled into the air and disappeared.

They knew that something was wrong.

Kestrel shoved the notebook back under her shirt, hand

on spoon, as her heart did a horrible little dance in her chest. She thumped her ribs, shutting it up.

The first thing Granmos taught her was that fear is bad. Being scared is more dangerous than having snakes in your bed or spiders in your tea. It stops you breathing properly, it makes your heart thump so loudly any creature can hear it, and it makes your skin so cold you can't move. All those things mean it's easier for you to get caught and eaten.

When she thought of her training, Kestrel felt a familiar queasiness in her stomach. It was the same queasiness she always felt when her grandma called her name, ready for the next session.

But that was all over now.

"Don't let them know you're scared," she muttered, clinging to her grandma's mantra. "Shut it away and deal with it later."

Bit by bit, her racing heart slowed. Kestrel glared through the trees. She'd spent ages practicing looking dangerous, and there were lots of small rabbits who were, indeed, completely terrified of her.

There was another *crack*, closer by this time. Something was in the forest with her, and it wasn't Finn, the only other person who might be hanging around here in the dead of night. It wasn't Pippit, either. Pippit was never quieter than an explosion.

Something was watching her. She could feel its eyes drilling into her.

Kestrel gritted her teeth and looked down.

The creature was sitting on the branch right underneath her, watching her greedily. Its eyes were as flat as black buttons, set in a smooth brown skull with no nose. It was at least her size, with gangly arms and legs and two long, flat wings folded against its back. It froze with a claw stretched toward her, as though it had been caught doing something wrong.

Kestrel recognized it from her notebook: It was a treecreeper. Treecreepers liked to sneak up on their prey. They made their victims jump so they fell out of trees, then they picked at the body for dinner.

Kestrel thought quickly.

"I know what you've been up to," she said imperiously. She secretly felt unnerved by its unblinking stare. "You've been creeping around the village and scaring people. Big mistake."

The treecreeper hissed and tilted its head to get a better look at her. It opened its mouth, revealing three rows of tiny peg teeth on its upper and lower jaws.

Kestrel clamped a hand over her nose. The treecreeper stank of rotting potatoes.

"*Kessstrelll,*" it rasped. Kestrel's blood turned to icy slush. She hadn't expected it to know her name. She scrolled through her mental list of creatures that had something against her.

"Hunnnterrr," it belched. The noise escaped from its throat with no input from its tongue or teeth, as though the word had come right from its stomach.

Kestrel's eyes flicked over its body, looking for a weak spot. She decided to aim her slingshot right between the treecreeper's eyes. She calculated the distance and the force she'd need. She imagined the stone smacking the treecreeper right in the forehead.

The treecreeper twitched, raising a hand to its head. Kestrel caught her breath.

Gotcha, she thought.

She pointed her stare at the treecreeper and thought very hard of the snail cake recipe, imagining the crunchy sponge and the slimy icing in as much stomach-churning detail as possible. She visualized picking a slice up with her fingers, the frosting oozing between her fingers as she raised it to her mouth.

The treecreeper shuddered, turning a bit green.

"Did you enjoy that?" she said, feeling triumphant. "That's right, I know what your trick is. You're just a stupid mind reader."

"Twelllve," the treecreeper rasped, desperately trying to claw the situation back.

"I'm not impressed," Kestrel replied. She began to inch along the branch until she was right above its head. "Just 'cause you can read minds doesn't mean you're dangerous. You haven't even tried to eat me yet."

The treecreeper paused with its mouth open, as though nobody had ever challenged it before. Kestrel noticed that there was a gaping darkness behind its teeth. She stared down its throat and tried to remember what else her grandma had told her about treecreepers.

"You're not even moving your mouth in the right way," she said. She was thinking out loud now. "I don't think you're any more dangerous than a squirrel. In fact . . ." an idea squeezed through. "I don't think you're much bigger than one, either."

She grinned and flexed her fingers, getting ready to jump. If her grandma was watching now, Kestrel knew she'd be pleased.

"Granmossss?" the treecreeper said, and a smile cracked across its face, like it knew the next thing it said would strike her to the core. *"Murderrrrrr."*

Kestrel threw a punch, hissing like a cat. The treecreeper jerked out of the way just in time.

"It's rude to go in people's heads," Kestrel said dangerously. "Didn't you ever get taught that?"

They stared at each other. Waiting. Then the treecreeper twitched, and Kestrel leaped.

They both screamed as Kestrel hit the treecreeper spread-eagle. It was horribly light and fragile, with paper-thin skin.

They tumbled to the ground, slamming against the branches of the tree as they fell. They crashed into the dead leaves a few feet from each other, Kestrel's slingshot flying from her pocket and landing in a deep puddle.

The treecreeper groaned. It was huge, but it didn't look any more terrifying than a crumpled kite now that it was on the ground. Kestrel plunged her hand into the puddle, ignoring the small horrors that might be lurking there, and grabbed her slingshot. She aimed an acorn at the treecreeper, which looked at her pitifully with its big, watery eyes.

"Mercyyyyy," it croaked. It was a pathetic monster, really, with fragile bones and dry, thin skin that looked about as tough as moths' wings. Kestrel pressed her lips together, but her hand was beginning to drop.

Then the treecreeper leaped at her. Kestrel was faster, and the stone punched the treecreeper in the side of the head, making a big hole through which she could see the moon. The treecreeper gurgled in surprise, reaching out for her with its big, hooked claws, but it was already deflating as though it had been filled with nothing but air. Kestrel stepped back as it slumped at her feet. Then it lay still.

She bent down and prodded it with her finger. She'd stayed up all night for *this*?

"Yeah, take that!" she said anyway, shaking a fist. "And tell all your creepy friends I'll turn 'em into stew if they mess with me!"

With that she plunked herself down in the leaves and folded her arms, waiting for the onslaught. The forest breathed out again. Cold air began to seep through Kestrel's holey shirt and under her skin.

"I guess you're all afraid of me," she said after a minute. She didn't want to admit that she was secretly relieved.

After a minute, she pulled the notebook out again to add some notes about the treecreeper. With half an eye still on the forest, she flicked through the pages.

Kestrel was used to feeling disappointed by the notebook. Every time she looked at the maps, she hoped that she'd notice something she'd never seen before. A big red arrow that said *this is the way out,* maybe.

Kestrel's grandma had been born outside the forest. Kestrel remembered her describing it when she was little, when Kestrel still sat on her lap, cocooned in Granmos's huge coat made of rags. Outside, there were huge, churning expanses of water filled with shells, which were like leaves made of stone. There were enormous open fields, and sometimes not a tree in sight. There were even *other villages.* Her grandma had run away into the forest when she was young, and the forest had—Kestrel never forgot this description—*closed behind her like a purse.* Granmos knew that the forest was more than just a big bunch of trees; it was a huge, clever animal that swallowed the unwary and wouldn't let them out.

Granmos became the most fearsome hunter in the forest's history, and eventually got married and had her dad. Kestrel was determined to leave the forest and find the place her grandma had come from. Together she and Finn were exploring every single place Granmos had described in the notebook, following each scrawled and twisting map. Kestrel wanted to see the bright fields of water. She wanted to collect piles of shells and roll through long, tickly grass. It would be nothing like the scrubby, spiky patches of grass in the forest that sometimes tried to eat you.

She was sure that one day they'd find the path Granmos had wandered down, and they'd be able to leave.

Well, if her mother ever let her. But that was a different story.

Kestrel traced her finger over a drawing of a shell, smooth and shiny from the path her finger had taken again and again. She dragged her eyes away, flipped the page, and paused. There was nothing left in the middle but a jagged line of paper hanging from the spine. The page had been ripped out by a set of claws. On it, half torn away, was one huge word written in thick black ink:

GRABBER

Kestrel shifted uncomfortably. Suddenly the forest seemed an awful lot darker. Even the trees were shivering, as though they were horrified by the word in the notebook.

Kestrel got up. She didn't feel like writing notes now. She

grabbed the lantern and her bag of missiles, which she'd hidden in the roots of a nearby tree, and started pacing. As she turned she saw a grinning face out the corner of her eye. Without thinking she grabbed her spoon and pointed it at the creature's neck, a snarl rising in her throat. But it was only a scarecrow planted behind the trees.

Kestrel lowered the spoon, then quickly looked around to check that nobody had seen her mistake. Some of the villagers thought that if you built a scarecrow that looked like you, your grabber would be confused and eat the scarecrow instead. It would have taken a lot of bravery for someone to put it there; the villagers only came into the forest in large groups, and even then, only rarely.

But the villagers would do almost anything to keep themselves safe from their grabbers. You were as good as dead once your grabber came after you. Any other kind of death was a relief.

There was a soft chittering sound high up in the trees. Kestrel swung the lantern and saw a giant moth, its wings the color of an old carpetbag, swoop away. She forgot all about the scarecrow. She loved hunting moths.

"Come back!" she yelled, and all her worries fell away like an old cloak.

If you got lost in the forest you could stumble in circles for days, not finding the way home even if it was right next to you. Sometimes the trees even seemed to shift behind your back. But Kestrel had spent so long sprinting, climbing, and swinging through the trees that they didn't dare try to confuse her. She could slip through gnarled roots like a fox, find rabbit holes to hide in within seconds, and climb a trunk so fast she'd be doing acrobatics in the branches by the time a squirrel caught up with her. She knew which streams were poisonous and which just looked bad, and she knew exactly where to find a long, sharp stick to fight with.

Kestrel skidded to a halt and rooted around in her bag for stones as the moth disappeared into a high tree. Her hand went right through the bottom of the bag. She turned it upside down and looked at it properly for the first time. There was a neat slit in the fabric where someone had taken to it with a pair of scissors.

One of the village kids had found her burrow, where she hid her stuff, *again*. She'd thought the bag felt too light. What else had they done? Poured sour milk in her boots like last time? Thrown away all the objects, the trinkets and things from outside the forest, that she'd carefully collected?

"Well done," she said aloud, squashing the shame burning behind her eyelids. "A hole in my bag. Original!"

There was a low, rumbling growl in the trees. Kestrel stopped, then very slowly lowered the slingshot. She knew what was making that noise.

"Hullo, dog," she said, turning around with her hands raised. "Good doggy. Good boy."

The dog was, in fact, the complete opposite of anything someone might describe as "good." It was large and black with bristly fur and shining teeth, and an expression that suggested it had recently swallowed a wasps' nest. It was also standing so close that she could feel its breath on her face. It wasn't technically a real dog, but that hadn't stopped it so far.

The dog growled again. Kestrel wished she'd spent more time with the treecreeper, which at least had never bitten her.

"My mother wants me back, right?" said Kestrel. "I'm coming, I promise. I just need to finish—"

The dog leaped at her. Kestrel shouted as it barreled straight into her chest with all the force of a cannonball. She hit the ground with a loud *oomph* that knocked the breath out of her.

Dead leaves puffed up and floated down over Kestrel's face.

"Why has she sent you?" Kestrel asked. She felt a small, sudden spark of hope. "Is Dad back?"

The dog bared its teeth. That meant no. It bit her shoelaces and began to pull. As Kestrel slid through the leaves she tried to grab a tree root, but it snapped off in her hand.

"Okay, so she wants me now," shouted Kestrel. "I'm coming!"

The dog let go. Kestrel was covered in dirt, and there was a dead leaf up her nose.

Kestrel cast one last glare at the moth. "You were lucky this time," she said sourly, dislodging the leaf with a snort.

The moth surprised her by sticking its tongue out. The black dog jerked its head in the direction of the village. Then it padded away, and Kestrel followed with a scowl.

If she disobeyed, she'd have to deal with something worse than a hundred treecreepers.

MOTHER'S WEAVE

The black dog herded Kestrel into the village, snapping at her ankles so she performed a jittery dance all the way back. It deposited her by the wolf fire before falling away and growling.

Kestrel growled back, but her heart wasn't in it. The village made her feel uneasy. The houses were wedged between trees, facing one another in a cramped circle, their roofs groaning under the weight of fallen leaves. They were made of sagging planks of wood and huge, irregular stones, and covered in thick moss as though the forest was slowly digesting them.

Many of them were empty, their occupants long since dragged away by their grabbers. The largest house had dozens of marks gouged into the outside wall. The villagers liked to keep track of how many people had been eaten by their grabbers, but the grabbers were now coming so frequently they were running out of space.

The black dog butted her legs with barely contained rage. "Okay," Kestrel said, exasperated, and tore her eyes away.

She headed toward her mother, slipping quietly between the houses. Before she rounded the last corner, she heard someone muttering and froze.

It was Ike, the candle- and soap-maker, who always smelled of the animal fat he worked with. Kestrel slowly poked her head around the corner. He was on his knees in the dirt, scrabbling around in the dead leaves, his breath hissing through his teeth.

"C'mon," he muttered urgently, dragging his hands over the ground. "Stupid pocket watch. Gotta be here, can't have lost it. It can't be—"

Kestrel slowly backed away. She was nearly out of sight when a toad issued a loud and furious croak by her feet. Ike leaped to his feet like a frightened rabbit, a scream halfway out of his throat.

"Oh," he said, cutting himself off when he saw Kestrel. "It's *you.*"

"Hi," Kestrel said, wishing her stomach wasn't squirming. Ike's face twitched as though her voice disgusted him. "Just passing by," she added lamely.

"Scram," he snapped. "This is private."

A chill went through Kestrel's bones. She knew why Ike was so desperate to find his missing pocket watch. If his grabber had stolen it, it was only a matter of time before—

Well, before he—

Kestrel edged around him, but he was already sifting through the leaves again, sweat beading on his pale forehead. *Maybe I can stop his grabber before it attacks,* she thought queasily. *At least I know it's coming.*

Ike would never openly tell Kestrel that his grabber was after him. None of the villagers would. They trusted her like ice in a bowl of hot water. Instead she had to watch for all the signs that a grabber was on the prowl—mostly, for things going missing.

As she slid past something twinkled in the corner of her eye. She let out her breath, which she hadn't realized she was holding.

"It's there," she said, pointing. "You must have dropped it."

Ike fell on the polished pocket watch and clutched it to his chest, his mouth open in a silent howl of joy.

Kestrel turned away, feeling like she was intruding on something. She was just a few steps away from her mother's house. *Ten. Nine. Eight...*

Kestrel saw the stone a moment before it hit her. She ducked and it whizzed over her head, smashing into a nearby wall.

She whirled around. Runo and his sister, Briar, were crouched in the bushes, their fingers stuffed in their mouths as they tried not to laugh. They weren't much older than Kestrel, but they were as malicious as ferrets.

"I was close that time," said Runo, nudging Briar. "Did you see her stupid face?"

Kestrel knew she could sling the stone back before they had time to blink, but she caught herself just in time. If she dared retaliate, the villagers would have the excuse they needed to permanently throw her into the forest.

"She's too scared to fight us," said Briar loudly.

"*Right*," said Kestrel, seeing red. She clenched her fists and the siblings squealed.

"Watch out," said a lazy voice behind her. "Little Kestrel's lost her temper."

Kestrel groaned inwardly. She turned around, although she already knew who it was. She was used to that sneering voice and spiteful smile.

Hannah was a couple of years older than Kestrel. She was pretty and clever and told good jokes, and everyone did whatever she said. If Kestrel was the most hated person in the village, Hannah was the most adored.

"Stop bothering Kestrel," Hannah said to the siblings in the bush, who sniggered silently. "She's far too important to bother with the likes of us. Don't you know she's the queen of the forest?"

Runo snorted so hard snot came flying out.

"Why don't you just–" Kestrel began.

"Whatever," said Hannah. "I'm going home. Have fun plotting with your mom."

"I'm not plotting anything," Kestrel protested, but Hannah had already turned tail and left with an impressive sweep of her skirt.

Runo and Briar skipped away.

"Morons," Kestrel muttered.

She swallowed the lump of shame in her throat and went to her mother's door.

Kestrel's home—her *mother's* home—was set a little apart from the others, facing the rest of the village like a sulking cat. The last time Kestrel had gone inside was to steal a fork so she could prod an interesting-looking and, ultimately, very explosive mushroom. Whenever the dog made her stay at home, she refused to remain inside and slept in the gutter on the roof instead. Although, to the horror of some unfortunate and opportunistic monsters, she slept with one eye open. And she *hated* being disturbed.

Kestrel stopped outside the door, raised her fist to knock, and hesitated.

In that instant a bedraggled, fur-covered creature shot from the trees and skidded past.

"Whaddya kill?" it shouted, thrashing around in the leaves, a fast-moving blur of teeth and claws. "Lemme geddit!"

Kestrel grabbed the weasel and tried to shove him in her pocket, but he shot straight out again and ran up her arm.

26

"Lemme geddit!"

"Shut up, Pippit!" she hissed, snatching him up again. It was like trying to hold a lump of soap. "If she knows I still have you she'll squash you flat with a frying pan!"

"Gimme blood," Pippit insisted, cycling his legs in midair. "Whaddya get?"

"A treecreeper," she said. Pippit was straining toward the trees like a bloodhound. "Will you *stop*?"

"Ribs!"

"Not now," she said, finally managing to shove the squirming weasel in her shirt pocket. He burrowed through the lining and shot out at the back of her neck, where he started washing himself. It wouldn't help, because he always looked like old flannel anyway. He was also horrible and rude and he smelled quite bad, but for some reason she couldn't fathom, Kestrel couldn't imagine life without him.

She looked around, but the black dog had gone. Unable to hold herself back any longer, she plucked Pippit from her neck and hugged him as tightly as possible.

"Urghhhh," complained Pippit, but he didn't try to run away.

"Where did you go? You were meant to be helping me," she told him crossly, still squeezing him tight. "You're my lookout, remember? That's our deal. You help me hunt, and you get to keep the gross old bones you find."

"For my nest," said Pippit helpfully.

"Sure," sighed Kestrel, releasing him. She'd found him the first time she ever went hunting. He'd been trying to drag away a giant claw, happily mumbling to himself. Kestrel had lured him into a jam jar and taken him home to study, completely unaware of the fury she was about to unleash. She still had a scar on the back of her hand. Not that it made a difference; she had dozens more, all terrible reminders of her grandma's training.

"Whaddya doing?" Pippit asked, jumping onto her shoulder. He finally seemed to realize where they were standing. "Not *her*," he said, sounding disgusted. "Not the Nasty."

"She called her stupid dog on me," Kestrel whispered. "I don't know what she wants."

"Nasty lady," he chuntered. "Nasty dog. Nasty, nasty. I'll bite 'im for you."

"He'd snap you up like a biscuit, and you know it," she said, scratching his head. Pippit purred, and something dropped from his mouth. Kestrel picked it up. It was a small silver ring, old and tarnished, covered in weasel-dribble.

"Found it inna bog," Pippit said proudly. Kestrel turned the ring over. "Did a *good*," he added, butting her with his nose.

"You did," she said, holding it up to the light. She would add it to her collection. She had dozens of things, bits of jewelry and cutlery and rotten trinkets, all from the forest. She didn't know where all the objects came from; the villagers never went that far into the trees. But every one gave her a tiny bit more hope that there was something outside this place, and people other than the villagers.

Kestrel slipped the ring into her boot and took another deep breath, then raised her hand to the door again.

"Wait!" Pippit said in her ear, making her jump.

"What?"

"Something important."

"Later," she said, exasperated, pushing his head away from her ear. The last time he said he had something important to tell her, he'd presented her with a half-chewed piece of pork rind.

"Really important," he insisted.

"*Later,*" she said, and opened the door.

The dark room was covered in an impossible tangle of thick rough wool. It stretched from ceiling to floor and wall to wall, multicolored and studded with scraps of paper, dead leaves, nail clippings, and teeth. The strands met one another in midair, tangling together and spinning away like roads on a map. Kestrel dropped to the floor and crawled through a tunnel in the middle, her throat itching from the dust. A string of someone's milk teeth, their name carved into each one, brushed against the back of her neck. Kestrel shivered. She knew what her mother kept those teeth for.

The door swung shut behind her and plunged them into gloom.

Kestrel's mother was crouched next to an empty plate.

Her coarse hair was covered in dust; she had probably been sitting there for days. The floor was littered with empty cups and bowls and the odd bit of gristle. She rarely left the house and only ate what the villagers fetched for her. Later that day someone would scuttle in and clear it up, and as a reward, Kestrel's mother might use the web of string, which she called the weave, to tell them something about their destiny.

Not that anybody in the forest had much of a destiny. It was usually to be eaten by their grabber, except for the lucky ones, who died in some other, slightly less horrible manner first.

Kestrel's mother tugged the piece of black string between her fingers, and all of a sudden the dog was in the room with them, like it had melted through the wall. It padded to her side and lay down, its eyes fixed on Kestrel. Pippit stiffened around her neck.

"Kestrel," her mother said, stretching her cold arms toward her. Kestrel couldn't help leaning back a little. "I've missed you."

"I missed you, too," Kestrel said, a little too quickly. "You didn't have to use the dog," she added, eyeing it with as much disgust as possible without actually rousing it to bite her. It returned the look. "It nearly chewed my feet off."

Her mother dropped her arms. "Nonsense," she said. "It's completely under my control. Besides, if you weren't so feral I wouldn't have to use him, would I?"

"I like being feral," Kestrel said, even though she wasn't

entirely sure what "feral" meant. "And I'm sick of it following me everywhere. Its eyes *glow*. They keep me awake all night."

"You're just like me," said her mother, smiling. "A light sleeper."

Kestrel doubted that she was anything like her mother. She couldn't even stand being in the cottage, breathing in the warm, stifling air that was filled with nothing but her mother's breath.

"I'm like Dad," Kestrel said. "We're both hunters."

Sometimes when she thought about him it felt like her heart was splitting. It was all she could do to hold the pieces together.

"He sets traps for wolves, dear," said her mother. "That's different. He creeps about in the forest, hiding from us."

"He's hiding from *you*," Kestrel said angrily. She swatted a hanging feather out of her face. Her mother flinched at the sudden movement.

Kestrel's mother was tied into the weave. When Kestrel was younger her mother had suddenly become interested in magic—obsessed, almost—and she created the weave as a way of controlling it. Now she spent all day twisting wool between her fingers and murmuring to herself. It was everywhere, pressed against the walls and knotted around the furniture, trailing through soup bowls and snaking through holes in the floor. Strands of red wool disappeared up her mother's sleeve and trailed all the way through the trapdoor in the floor. There was a cellar under the house, but Kestrel had never been down there. She guessed it was full of more wool.

"What do you want, anyway?" Kestrel asked grumpily. "It's not just to say 'hello,' is it?"

The dog gave her a warning growl and Kestrel clamped her mouth shut again. She'd gone too far. Maybe there really *wasn't* an ulterior motive. Maybe her mother did just want to see her. Her heart skipped a beat.

"I have a job for you," said her mother, cold now.

Stupid heart.

Her mother picked up a ball of wool, twisting the brown strands through her fingers. The strings closed up behind Kestrel, tangling around her ankles. Beads jangled loudly.

"A grabber has visited the woodchopper," her mother said. "I need you to deal with it."

It felt like someone had tipped a bucket of cold water down Kestrel's back.

"Scared?" her mother said, smiling craftily.

"No," Kestrel said, crossing her arms. She knew her mother didn't believe her.

"You should be," said her mother. "The woodchopper had a lot of axes. The grabber must have taken at least one of them to build its body."

Kestrel tried very hard not to think of how a grabber would use an ax. They always stole things from their victim—insignificant things at first, then objects they knew the person would miss—and used them in the worst way possible. The grabbers built themselves a body out of whatever they could find in the forest, and the things they'd stolen from their victim. An ax could be a leg or an arm. It could even be a tooth. It all depended on whatever horrendous form the grabber chose to take.

Grabbers never attacked until they'd completed their bodies, turning themselves into the one thing that terrified their victim the most. But once their bodies were complete, there was no stopping them.

Not that Kestrel hadn't tried.

"There can't be another grabber," she said. "I got one three days ago."

"The wicked never rest, sweetie," her mother said, looking up. "You know what you have to do. Follow the grabber's trail and kill it. We don't want it lurking in the forest, do we? And bring back a souvenir. It will make everyone in the village feel safer."

Her blood boiled.

"What if I don't want to?" she said defiantly.

Kestrel's mother grabbed her chin and pulled her in. Kestrel opened her mouth to protest, but her mother tapped her front tooth with a long, dirty fingernail.

"You'll do it," she said, letting Kestrel go.

Her gaze deliberately slid to a small, white tooth tied to a piece of black string. Kestrel couldn't help but look as well. She knew it wasn't just the villagers' teeth tied into the weave. There were plenty of hers, too.

And her mother wasn't afraid to use them. Kestrel had failed to catch the first grabber she'd ever hunted, and her mother had been furious. She used the tooth in a spell that twisted Kestrel's bones so far they'd almost splintered.

"Dad wouldn't make me do this," Kestrel said quietly.

"Your father chooses to be away," said her mother. She gave a sudden tug at a string above her. Kestrel went tumbling forward and was locked into a tight, bony hug. Kestrel's mother might have looked gaunt, but that didn't mean she was weak.

"I'm here for you, Kestrel," she whispered into her ear. Her breath was dry and papery. "I'm the only reason the villagers haven't thrown you to the wolves."

"They hate me because of you," mumbled Kestrel, her face squashed in her mother's shoulder. She felt Pippit slide down her back, desperately trying to get away from her mother's sharp nose. "Ow. That *hurts*."

Her mother kissed her on the cheek.

"They just don't know how much they need you," she said soothingly. "You're the only one who can hunt the grabbers. Besides," added the dusty woman, her voice dripping honey, "you need to get revenge for your grandmother. Otherwise you'll never be free, will you?"

Kestrel pulled away sharply. Her mother let her go, smiling like it was a joke.

But it wasn't.

"You've got to keep your end of the bargain," Kestrel said fiercely. "When I catch the grabber that got her, the black dog goes. And the tooth. Then I'm allowed to go wherever I want."

And then I can find a way to escape the forest, she added to herself. *I won't die at the hands of a stinking grabber.*

"It's a promise," said her mother. "But you have to find her grabber first, don't you, sweetie? It's still out there somewhere, gobbling up foxes and licking its teeth."

"I'll get it," Kestrel said stubbornly. "I'll recognize it. It's got a page of her notebook and all her jewelry."

"Of course," said her mother. "But if you hadn't let it into the house, you wouldn't have this problem."

Kestrel felt sick right in the pit of her stomach.

"You don't need to keep reminding me," she muttered, feeling hot and cold at the same time, like she was being swallowed by a fever.

It had happened years ago. Kestrel was sick of being mercilessly trained by Granmos. She was sick of being thrown down wells and tossed to the bats, tied only to a piece of rope for safety. By the time she was seven Kestrel could wrestle a wolf one-handed, but her grandma only said it wasn't good enough and thought of some other highly unusual, punishing test. Even now the thought of her grandma coming toward her, her thin lips pursed, her tarnished jewelry flashing, made Kestrel more nervous than any forest creature did.

Granmos had made her life miserable, but Kestrel felt sick that she was ever stupid and selfish enough to let her grandma's grabber into the house. That she'd actually been terrible enough to want to *kill* her.

At least Kestrel would never wake up with a knife dangling over her head again. At least she wouldn't have to worry about someone jumping out at her from behind every door.

Kestrel's thoughts fled as she saw something move at the edge of her vision. She twitched her head out of the way as a knife flew past her left ear, half an inch from lopping it off.

The knife stuck in the splintered, boarded-up door, and quivered.

"Good," her mother said, satisfied. "Your eyes are as sharp as ever."

Kestrel was wrong. The tests hadn't stopped. Her mother was always testing her, too.

"Sharp as a spoon," said Kestrel.

The weave shivered and her mother licked her lips. Kestrel automatically looked through the window. Seconds later a thin, high-pitched scream curdled the air.

"There," said her mother triumphantly.

The woodchopper's grabber. Kestrel, seeing her chance to escape, turned and pushed through the forest of string. The black dog snapped its jaws behind her, but she kicked it away and wriggled free. As soon as she was out of the house Pippit escaped from her sweater and hopped onto her shoulder.

"Which way, Pippit?" Kestrel said urgently.

Pippit spun around on her shoulder, sniffing, then strained in the direction of the woodchopper's house. People were already opening their doors, drawn by the terrible scream, but when they saw Kestrel they retreated. They knew what her presence meant.

Leaves flew up from under her feet as she ran.

The woodchopper had destroyed the trees around his house with careless, almost joyful abandon. Kestrel had always thought this was a terrible idea. The forest had a mind of its own, and nobody likes having their fingers lopped off. She raced through the predawn gloom until she could see the front of the house.

The door was off its hinges and streaks of lamplight fell out, spilling over the ground. A trail of broken crockery and bits of furniture led from the front door and into the darkness of the woods. It looked like the forest had taken a deep breath and tried to suck everything into its belly. There was even a sagging armchair with a large bite mark in it. Half the leather had been pulled off like the skin from an overripe plum. The grabber's trail was slippery with yellow grease, and it had left a deep scar in the ground, a trench that twisted heavily through the earth.

"It was big," breathed Kestrel. "It was *huge*."

Kestrel squeezed her eyes shut and tried to imagine what the woodchopper would be most scared of. That was the shape the grabber would take. That's why they stalked their victims—not just to steal their things, but to find their weak spot.

Kestrel never knew what she'd find. Grabbers built their bodies out of anything, vegetation and bones and rubbish and, very often, other animals. The result was a stitched-together mess, a patchwork of body parts and stolen objects, held together by slime and sheer willpower.

Pippit tugged her ear.

"Something important!" he said, as though he'd just remembered.

"Not now," Kestrel said.

The woodchopper had tried to run from the grabber. The grabber's trail circled the cottage several times, following the woodchopper's footprints, which stopped abruptly. Then the grabber's trail went back into the forest. It had dragged the woodchopper into the forest to eat. She had to find it quickly.

She jumped into the scar in the ground. Her heart was hammering, and she could feel a familiar nausea in her throat, but she forced it away like Granmos taught her.

"Les geddit," Pippit hissed, snapping his teeth. "Les geddit's bones!"

"Sharpen your teeth, Pippit," said Kestrel. "We're going hunting."

THE GRABBER'S TRAIL

Kestrel ran, following the scar as it curved around the wood-chopper's house and plunged into the forest.

The trees swallowed her. Even though it was daytime there was a permanent darkness, with the occasional patch of sick greenish light that made everything look ill. The trail twisted left and right, and Kestrel had to dodge foot-snagging roots and animal burrows. The birds were silent. Few creatures dared come out when a grabber was on the loose.

The trail became softer and muddier, which meant that it was fresher, and she was getting closer to the grabber. But Kestrel was struggling. The trees were so close together, she could barely squeeze past them. The grabber, despite its obvious size, seemed to have slipped through with worrying elegance.

Her feet sank into the mud, and soon she was wading almost up to her knees. Kestrel gritted her teeth and plowed on, but she knew she wasn't going to catch up like this. The grabber was too quick. Her only chance of killing the grabber was when it had finished eating, when it would be slow and sluggish. When it was too late.

"Important," Pippit said. "Something important!"

"What?" Kestrel said, exasperated.

But then she heard a rustling sound high in the trees and pushed him back into her pocket. A shower of razor-sharp leaves drifted from the sky. Kestrel heard a *whoop* of joy. Despite everything, she felt a grin unravel.

Maybe this hunt would be different.

"Finn!" she shouted. "Down here!"

A pale hand dropped down in front of her. Kestrel grabbed it and was yanked into the trees, breaking through a sheet of leaves which shattered like glass. For the first time in days she could see the pale, chilly sky.

Finn was a chaotic vision of red and brown and gold. His hair was stuck with leaves, and there were streaks of mud on his face.

"Hunting rabbits?" he said with infuriating nonchalance.

"Of course not," Kestrel said. Her heart was hammering at the thought of catching up with the grabber before it ate. "I need your help. It's too muddy to run down there. There's a grabber on the loose."

Finn stiffened, and the grin died on his face.

"Are you sure?" he said.

"Come *on*!" she yelled, fighting the urge to shake him. "We're not scared of anything, remember?"

"You only had to ask," he said, but he still didn't smile. Kestrel opened her mouth to shout again, but he took a deep breath, leaped into the next tree, and started to run. Kestrel braced herself, ignoring her wobbling knees, and forced herself to jump after him.

Then she was running, too.

Finn's world at the top of the forest was filled with light. Planks of wood stretched dizzyingly between tall trees, and the fraying rope bridges he'd built twisted between the thick trunks like bunting. There were platforms and handholds, hiding places and lookouts. The system spread for miles, from the village to the darkest parts of the forest. You couldn't always see it, but it was there—a rope here, a plank there—a highway through the trees that only Finn knew how to use.

It was like flying. Sometimes Kestrel was sure this is what life was like outside the forest—you could run wherever you wanted, and nothing could stop you.

Pippit squirmed out of Kestrel's pocket and butted her with his head.

"Later," she said shortly, pushing him back down.

They followed the trail below, pushing deeper and deeper into the forest. The sunlight began to fade as the leaves grew denser. The branches became more slippery, covered in moss and slimy weeds. Below them the trail was petering out where the grabber had picked its feet up. The soil was even fresher here, as though it had just been churned up.

There were claw marks at the side of the grabber's trail, as though the woodchopper and the grabber had struggled here. Finn saw it and stopped abruptly.

"We can't go any farther," he said. "The trees are too thin."

Kestrel had left her nerves on the ground, but they came back as she and Finn slowed down. Suddenly she didn't like the idea of being alone.

"Come down," she said. "Walk with me a bit."

"Can't," Finn said, shaking his head adamantly. He was clinging to the tree trunk. "I'll slow you down." Before she could protest he swung himself higher into the tree.

Kestrel clumsily slid down. She reached the ground and bent down to sniff the trail. There was a strong vinegary smell. It was like sticking her nose in a jar of pickles, which meant the grabber was close. She felt nauseous.

She briefly closed her eyes and tried again to picture the woodchopper's grabber. She had no idea what he was afraid of. The villagers never talked about their fears, in case it gave the grabbers ideas.

She turned away so Finn wouldn't see how nervous she was, then something hit her on the back of the head. She looked up to glare at him, then saw that he was looking pointedly at the ground.

She picked the fallen stone up. It was the size of a marble, smooth and with a hole in the middle.

"If you look through it hard enough, you can see the future," he said. "Plus, it's lucky, which you need."

Kestrel's temper flared.

"Are you saying I'm not a good hunter?"

Finn twisted his fingers together.

"It's just that I—" He stopped short and went red.

Kestrel slipped the stone into her pocket, pretending that her stomach wasn't twisting with fear. She knew Finn wasn't calling her a bad hunter.

They looked at each other for a moment, not sure what to say. Then Kestrel heard a long, low rumble in the trees behind her, like thunder. Finn twitched, as though it was taking all his power not to run the other way. Kestrel wrenched herself away, turned tail, and ran toward the noise, leaving Finn behind.

"You'd better not die," Finn called, his voice already distant.

"I never die!" Kestrel called back.

The trees flew past as Kestrel ran, their lowest branches whipping her in the face. She danced over roots like skipping ropes. A bird dropped from the trees in front of her, claws out to grab her, but she dodged before it could even open its beak. The trail went on and on, then disappeared at the edge of a cramped clearing.

She slowed to a stop, putting her hand on Pippit's head.

"Keep your ears peeled," she told him.

"Something important," he insisted.

"It'll hear us if you don't shut up," she said.

The forest was silent as Kestrel entered the clearing. Her whole body felt cold, although she told herself it was just the weather. There were great scuff marks in the earth and gouges in the nearby trees. Kestrel drew her sharpened spoon from her pocket and held it out in front of her. Pippit was looking the other way, watching for anything that might come up behind them.

The grabber had stopped here. Kestrel's stomach dropped. That meant it was digesting its meal, and she was too late to save anyone. *Again.*

They circled one of the marks in the ground, but it didn't reveal anything. Maybe the grabber was hiding under the leaves and would rise when they stood on it, enclosing them like a blanket. Or maybe it was hanging from the trees, ready to drop on their heads. Kestrel looked up quickly, but she couldn't see anything.

She slowly backed against the trunk of a huge, furrowed tree, pressing her feet into the tangle of roots. If she stayed quiet the grabber might show itself. She twisted the spoon in her hand and impulsively patted her pockets, checking for her notebook and her slingshot.

After a few minutes she said, "You still there?"

"Pippit," said Pippit.

"Good."

Another long, silent pause.

"Spoooooky," said Pippit.

"Shut *up*," she said, narrowing her eyes. She was sure they weren't alone.

Pippit suddenly went rigid in her pocket. He hissed excitedly through his teeth.

"Something *important*," he said again.

"What is it, then?" she said, exasperated. He was running up to her shoulder now, sitting there like a parrot, his bad breath next to her face.

"*Saw* grabber," said Pippit triumphantly. "Taking pickles."

"The grabber was taking pickles?" she said, growing cold.

"Pippit taking pickles. In house Grabber came-woodchopper-*umph!*"

"What did it look like?" Kestrel said desperately, ignoring the fact that he had been stealing pickles *again*.

Something jabbed her in the hip. She turned around, horrified, to see a long, pointed fingernail withdraw as quick as lightning.

"Yeah," said Pippit happily. "A lots-of-legs."

Kestrel grabbed him and threw him away from her, so he landed in the leaves with a splash. Then the grabber behind her lurched, and the roots of the tree rose up and entangled her.

THE LOTS-OF-LEGS

Kestrel shrieked and tried to lift her feet. They were trapped in the jumble of roots. The grabber hissed, its sour breath burning the back of her neck, and snapped its teeth around her hair.

Kestrel scrabbled around for her spoon while the grabber's long fingernails tore at her sweater, struggling to find a good hold on her. *Hurry up!* she screamed at herself. But it was no good—she couldn't reach her pocket. Through the panicked fog in her head, she tried to image what Granmos would do.

She wouldn't mess around with weapons.

She drove her foot backward and heard a sickening *crunch*, like teeth crushing ice, as she broke part of the grabber's body. The grabber squealed. She could see its shadow on the ground in front of her as it flailed, a terrifying, hulking blob held aloft on spindly legs.

Kestrel tried to wriggle from the grabber's grasp, but it clamped a strong hand over her mouth. Kestrel almost cried out. None of the grabber's fingers matched one another. They were long and crooked and stuck with claws from a dozen animals, grimy with dirt and rotten bits of skin.

"Pippit!" she shouted, but it came out more like a muffled grunt. The grabber's stomach rumbled, and she felt warm saliva drip down the back of her neck.

Its body tensed. Kestrel yanked herself out of the grabber's grasp and dropped to the ground, just as its teeth crashed shut on thin air.

She hadn't been standing in a jumble of tree roots at all. She was surrounded by a forest of legs, each one made from ripped-up tree roots and bones. Even worse, each foot was a hand, and each hand had ten long fingers on it, exactly the same as the ones over her mouth. Fingers covered in skin, with long, dirty nails.

Hands for feet, Kestrel thought dizzily. *Actual hands. For feet.*

The grabber roared. Kestrel grabbed her spoon, raised it above her head, and drove it into one of the grabber's feet with a furious battle cry.

The grabber screamed. The noise was high-pitched and cold and it made Kestrel's hands wobble, but the feeling only lasted a second before she squashed it away. She saw one of the grabber's hands swing toward her, and she flung herself out of the way just before its nails could catch her face. It reeled, confused by her quick reactions.

Kestrel's spoon was still embedded in the ground, pinning one of the grabber's hands down. The grabber twisted its leg and tore it free, leaving the hand pinned and still flailing.

She scrambled away from the grabber on her hands and knees, then turned to face it, her fists raised. Despite her fury and determination, the full view of the monster in front of her made her falter, just for a second.

"Ungh," she said.

It was a spider.

A massive, hairy, sharp and bristling *spider*.

It was almost twice her height. Each leg was as long as a ladder, and together they supported a fat, bloated body that hovered higher than Kestrel's head. It was covered in tatty, stretched skins that had been stolen from a multitude of bristly and slimy animals. She could see bones bulging underneath its flesh, and in some places they poked right out through the skin. An ax was embedded in its back like a jaunty accessory.

The grabber had hundreds of eyes which looked like they had been violently smushed into its face, all of them rolling in different directions. It had a jagged, zigzag mouth which didn't close properly and a collection of teeth that would make a hardened dentist faint.

Kestrel had fought plenty of grabbers, and she knew that

there was only one way to kill them. You had to get them in the heart. But her spoon was still stuck in the ground, holding down a set of wriggling fingers.

She took a deep breath. This wasn't the time to lose her nerve.

The grabber straightened its legs, raising itself high, its dozens of knees making arthritic snapping sounds.

Kestrel could hear the blood pounding through its veins. She could hear its heart thumping double-quick as it walked toward her on its creaking legs. She waited for it to come, preparing to spring.

That's when Pippit burst out of the trees, a furious, spitting, grabber-killing machine the approximate size of a glove.

"AAAH!" he screamed. He flew at the grabber and attached himself to one of its legs, digging his teeth in and growling. The grabber jerked back and snapped its own teeth, spraying the ground with a shower of loose molars.

Kestrel sped forward, thinking she could grab her spoon from the ground, but Pippit's distraction only lasted a second. The grabber staggered toward Kestrel, Pippit still attached to its knee. Its mouth was hanging open, revealing a long, dark tunnel of a throat. Its stolen organs pulsed and squirmed inside it as though they were trying to get away from the nightmarish creature. As it stamped toward her,

Kestrel fell back again, her mouth dry. It clawed the ground with its fingers and left a trail of yellow grease behind it, shaking the trees and dislodged a cascade of dead leaves. They flew around in a tiny storm, blinding Kestrel for a second, but not before she saw one spiral into the grabber's mouth and make it splutter.

Kestrel's heart skipped a beat. She knew what to do.

She reached into her pocket and felt around for a missile. Her fingers closed around Finn's lucky stone. Even then, faced with the huge monster, she felt a twinge of guilt for using his gift. Then she grabbed her slingshot, pulled the stone back, and took aim.

Pippit dug his teeth in with a furious cry. The grabber twitched and roared, and Kestrel released the stone.

It disappeared down the grabber's throat with barely a rattle. For a moment it had no effect. Then the grabber started to cough. It began as a low rattle deep in its chest, which turned into a terrible hacking sound. The grabber's legs buckled and it swayed, trying to regurgitate the stone that was lodged deep in its throat. "Les geddit!" Pippit yelled, clinging to the grabber's shaking legs.

Kestrel hurtled toward the grabber. She dodged through its jumble of legs, its snapping teeth missing her by inches again as it coughed and quivered. She reached her spoon on the other side and pulled it out of the ground, pausing only to stamp on the disembodied hand, which was trying to run away by itself.

The spoon was like an extension of her arm, and Kestrel immediately felt stronger. She drew herself up tall. The grabber turned to face her. It was wheezing, but the stone hadn't been big enough to choke it, and now it was angrier than ever.

Kestrel waited as it stamped toward her, its eyes rolling furiously. It was difficult not to back away, but she dug her feet into the ground and gritted her teeth. She was good at ignoring her instinct to run.

Hold… it…

The grabber was so close she could smell the mold on its rotting body parts. It opened its mouth, and she flung herself through its legs again so she was under its body. The grabber tried to catch her with its hands, but it was too slow. She held the spoon above her head and listened for the echo of its heart.

Kestrel drove her arm upward. The blade went in. There was a crunch of wood as its makeshift bones splintered. The grabber moaned and in an instant collapsed, and Kestrel was pushed to her knees. She tried to make herself as small as possible, hoping the grabber wouldn't crush her to the ground. Then the weight stopped pressing down, and her spoon slid out, and she opened her eyes.

The grabber was dead. It was propped up on its bent

legs, its horrible body hanging an inch above her head. She crawled out and flopped down on the ground beside it.

"Yeah," hissed Pippit, running back and forth over the forest floor, leaping over Kestrel's head in a victory dance. "Yeah! Yeah!"

"We did it," she said wonderingly, rolling over in the leaves. She'd hurt muscles she didn't even know existed, and she could hear blood pounding through her ears like rows of soldiers, but she wanted to leap up and run around the forest. She couldn't believe she'd lived to kill another grabber. "We got it!"

As Pippit ran around the clearing, picking up bits of splintered bone and gobs of who-knew-what, Kestrel got up and walked around the grabber. It was still warm, and it stank like the bottom of a bin. She grabbed the handle of the woodchopper's ax sticking from the grabber's back and pulled it out.

It left the grabber with a disgusting squelching noise. She wiped it on the ground, trying to ignore the sound of Pippit enthusiastically chewing things up. She had to take it back as proof that she'd gotten revenge and killed the grabber, or her mother would be furious.

As she dragged the ax over the ground she felt something cool on the back of her neck, like a breeze was shifting through the trees.

Then she heard it. A quick, faint thumping sound.

She held her breath and tried to pinpoint the noise. She could feel the hair on her arms rising, and in the corner of her eye she saw a shadow creep over the forest floor.

The stupid, evil, stinking monster *had two hearts.*

The grabber coughed up some phlegm from deep in its lungs. Without thinking Kestrel turned and swung the ax with all her strength, driving it into the grabber's chest with pinpoint accuracy as it loomed over her. It screamed again, its hundred eyes rolling into the back of its head, and fell down. Kestrel yanked the ax out, ready to swing again, but the grabber only twitched once more before it was silent.

Kestrel let out her breath. She watched the grabber for any sign of movement, breathing hard, but this time it was well and truly dead.

A minute later its teeth began to fall out, pattering down like rain.

"Ugh," she said, making a face. Then her shoulders slumped, and all the horrible pent-up fear left her, making her feel empty.

Pippit finished collecting trophies and returned with one of the grabber's fingers hanging from his mouth. Kestrel patted her pockets to make sure everything was still there, the slingshot and the spoon and the notebook, and remembered that Finn's lucky stone was still in the grabber's throat.

The forest was growing cool and shadowy in the aftermath of the grabber's death, and in a few minutes other creatures would start to arrive, drawn by the prospect of a free meal. Kestrel looked around nervously. She knew she should leave, but she didn't want to lose the stone.

"Lessgo," insisted Pippit.

Kestrel looked desperately at the deep, dark forest beyond the clearing, then at the grabber. They probably only had a few minutes before things started to descend on them. Cursing herself, Kestrel held her breath and reached into the grabber's mouth.

It was warm and wet and slimy. She felt around, feeling nauseous, but she couldn't reach far enough down its throat. She found a big stick on the forest floor, used it to prop the grabber's jaws open, then took a deep breath and stuck her head in its mouth.

She pushed her shoulders in and reached as deep down as she could. After a few nauseating moments of scrabbling, her fingers closed around the stone, and she nearly shouted with relief. She started to wriggle out of the grabber's mouth, but then, just for a fraction of a second, she saw something move.

Kestrel froze, her eyes fixed on the bottom of its throat. There was something down there, something moving deep inside the grabber. For a horrified second she wondered if the woodchopper was somehow still in its stomach, trying to fight his way out.

She peered deep into the grabber's innards.

Four yellow eyes flickered open and peered right back.

Kestrel screamed and tore herself away from the grabber's mouth just as the stick snapped and its jaws slammed shut. She stared at its face, her stomach squirming horribly. The eyes hadn't been human, but she'd never met an animal with those eyes before, either.

"Back?" Pippit said as Kestrel grabbed the ax.

"Definitely," she said, casting one last look at the creature.

Maybe the grabber had some new, four-eyed monster living in its stomach. It wasn't unheard of for them to have whole ecosystems in their compost-heap bodies. She didn't really believe it herself, but she didn't want to stick around and find out for sure.

Pippit was happily squirming on the ground, playing with the grabber's dismembered finger. Without a second glance Kestrel scooped him up and ran toward the trail, the ax leaving a deep and terrible scar in the earth behind her.

5

THE YELLOW EYES

Night was already curling its cold fingers around the village as Kestrel dragged the woodchopper's ax out of the forest. Pippit was wound around her neck, snoring. She staggered past the woodchopper's house, then sat down with a relieved *thump.*

She landed in a puddle and sighed.

The contents of the woodchopper's house had been piled back inside, and his hat had been nailed to a nearby tree stump. It looked weirdly jolly, as though he had gone on a break and was going to walk around the corner to retrieve it at any moment. It was one of the rituals the villagers did after a grabber attack. Sometimes, when she was half asleep, Kestrel glimpsed the nailed-up hats and thought there were disembodied heads everywhere.

The door to his house opened, and Kestrel ducked.

Hannah slowly came out and stood in the doorway,

staring at the grabber's trail, not seeing Kestrel in the gloom. Her face was white. Hannah looked around, her expression wobbling, then when she was sure she was alone she let out a choked sob.

It took Kestrel a moment to remember that the wood-chopper was her father.

The thought of anything happening to her own dad made Kestrel squirm with horror. For a second, she considered running over and giving Hannah a hug. Her legs even twitched. Then she had a vision of Hannah snarling and throwing her back into the puddle, and changed her mind.

Kestrel wished she could crawl back into the forest as Hannah continued to cry. A patch of red, spongy bloodmoss on the ground in front of her started squirming. Kestrel leaned away from it, silently willing Hannah to leave before it reached her and started eating her boots. Finally, after two horrible minutes, Hannah went back inside and slammed the door.

Kestrel sprang up just as the bloodmoss reached her toes. She edged around it and, with a final burst of effort, carried the ax toward her mother's house.

But all she could think about now was her own dad. He hadn't been back in weeks, and each absence was bigger and more worrying than the one before. He tracked and trapped wolves with a stubbornness that scared even her, and she was certain that one day a wolf would take him down. He knew everything about them, and he'd taught Kestrel all of it, from interpreting their howls to following their tracks. But it didn't make Kestrel feel like he was any safer. If anything, it made her shiver even harder when she heard the yowl that meant *hunger*.

Walt, the stoker who kept the wolf fire burning, saw Kestrel approach and froze with his great mustache bristling. His eyes traveled down the length of the ax Kestrel was carrying, to its bent and dinted blade.

"Fletcher!" he hollered. Then he started heaving logs onto the fire again, his job apparently done.

Ike Fletcher sprang from his house like an eager rabbit, crumbs falling from the front of his shirt, and pursed his horrible thin lips at Kestrel.

"Good," he said, as though Kestrel had performed a clever trick. "We're indebted to your mother."

Kestrel wanted to shout *What about me?* She turned away and stomped toward the house. Within minutes, word of her return would travel around the village, and cakes and biscuits and bowls of soup would start piling up outside her mother's door. They were scared that if they didn't thank the old woman for sending Kestrel out, she would do something terrible.

She had all their teeth, after all.

Kestrel shivered and plucked Pippit from her neck.

"Come find me later," she said. "I'm going in, okay?"

Pippit grumbled and slinked away. Kestrel raised her fist and knocked on the splintered door, which swung open under her touch.

The black dog appeared from nowhere and gripped the ax handle between its teeth. Kestrel dropped it obediently, the blood rushing back into her hands, and stepped inside. Her mother was waiting with open arms.

"I knew you'd do it, sweetie," she said with a perfect impression of warmth. "Come closer and tell me all about it."

Kestrel had to force her legs to move. She crawled through the tunnel in the weave and sat on the edge of her mother's swept-out skirt, which was as far away as she could get without being disobedient. Her mother reached out and wrapped her fingers around Kestrel's shoulders, pulling her into a bony embrace.

"It was a spider," Kestrel said into her shoulder, trying not to breathe in the sweet, cloying smell of her mother's breath. She remembered the four-eyed creature in the grabber's stomach and wondered if she should ask about it, but something told her that it wasn't a good idea. She didn't want to be accused of not finishing the job. She suppressed a shudder. "It had lots of fingers," she added lamely.

Her mother pushed her away, still holding her by the shoulders, and studied her face.

"Nothing else?" she said.

"Not really," said Kestrel, certain that her face was turning red. The harder she tried not to think about the yellow eyes, the more brightly they burned behind her eyelids. "Can I go now?"

"You're hiding something," her mother said, so softly that it took Kestrel a moment to notice the threat in her voice. "I know my daughter's face when she's lying."

"Why don't you just leave me alone?" Kestrel burst out.

With one hand still gripping Kestrel's shoulder, her mother snatched one of the candles sitting next to her and pressed it to the side of Kestrel's face. "Get off!" Kestrel yelled, trying to pry her mother's hands away.

"I'll teach you not to be rude," her mother hissed. "You think you're so strong, but you wouldn't be anything without me, you little—"

There was a clang outside the door, and the sound of something shattering. One of the villagers had dropped a bowl of soup. Her mother hesitated, then lowered the candle. Kestrel fell away from her and opened her eyes. Red splotches floated in the middle of her vision. She touched her eyelids frantically. If she didn't have her vision, she'd lose the thing that made her a good hunter.

"Remember what you are," her mother said. She had the calm, glassy voice of someone seething with rage. "You're a selfish brat who fed your own grandmother to her grabber. If your father knew, he'd never come back."

Kestrel's stomach curled.

"If you continue to be rude, I don't see why I should keep your secret," her mother continued, in that horribly flat voice. She put the candle down. "Now," she said, "let me give you a kiss."

Kestrel leaned forward, feeling like a puppet, and stiffly received a dry peck on the cheek. As she did so, she caught a glimpse of herself in a shard of mirror nailed to the wall. There was a red mark on her face and half her right eyebrow had been scorched off.

She kept her rage down with superhuman effort, and forced a smile.

"Sorry," Kestrel said lightly, but the word was sour in her mouth. "I didn't mean to forget my manners."

"There, sweetie," her mother said, looking pleased again. "It's not hard to apologize. Now won't you stay and share some food with me? I can smell cake outside the door." She sniffed the air. "And cream."

Kestrel noted, feeling slightly disgusted, that her mother's face was already shining with delight at the thought of the feast outside. "It's all yours," Kestrel said. Her stomach was growling with hunger, but she was determined not to take food from her. Not with her knowing, anyway. Getting angry drained her mother, and she always fell asleep shortly after. She slept so deeply she never heard Kestrel making off with biscuits and bowls of stew.

"Why so keen to go?" her mother asked lightly, but there

was a sharp edge to her voice. "You're not meeting someone, are you? Ike tells me you were climbing trees yesterday."

"I was alone," Kestrel said, her stomach plummeting.

"You weren't with that nasty Finnigan boy, were you?"

"No," Kestrel said weakly. But Finn's milk teeth were hanging over her mother's head, and she couldn't help looking at them. Her mother reached up and brushed her fingers over the row of them. Kestrel tried not to react, desperately ignoring the horrified lump in her throat.

"You know I can hurt anyone," her mother said.

Kestrel nodded numbly. Years ago, her mother had made her go door-to-door collecting the teeth. Now, when one of the villagers got hurt by her mother, Kestrel knew it was her own fault.

"There will be consequences if you get distracted and forget your purpose," her mother continued, staring right at her. "Which is *hunting*."

"Friendship is weakness," Kestrel said, repeating one of her mother's mantras. She could almost feel the sweat rolling down her nose. "A person shared is a person halved. I know."

Her mother continued to stare at her. What did she *want*?

"I don't want to be distracted, either," Kestrel said, desperate to make her stop. "I just want to hunt, and one day find Granmos's grabber. You *know* that."

At least it was true. Her mother finally blinked.

"You will," she said. "One day. Her grabber is still out there,

Kestrel. I see it in the weave. Just be patient, and do as I say in the meantime."

"I promise." Her feet were itching to run. "Now can I go?"

"Wait," her mother said. She eagerly touched Kestrel's arm with her long fingers. "At least stay while I eat. I know you doubt it sometimes, Kestrel, but I worry about you. I don't like to think of my daughter being hungry."

For a moment Kestrel believed that she really was concerned. Her mother looked troubled, maybe even guilty. Then she touched her missing eyebrow and shook herself out of it.

"I've got monsters to catch," she said. She was already backing through the weave. She had to find the grabber that took her grandma. She was going to get rid of the dog and find the path out of this place, so she and Finn could run away. So they could be *free*.

"If you're worried about your silly eyebrow—"

But Kestrel was already out the door.

Kestrel slid into the shadows behind the dark, soulless houses. She wanted to get across the village and find Finn, but Ike had already gathered the villagers together to look at the woodchopper's ax. The black dog had dragged it to the wolf fire for everyone to see.

The villagers were leaning in, staring at Ike so intently it looked like they were going to eat him. Several kids had crept up to the fire as well, nudging one another and whispering, delighted that their parents hadn't noticed them. Kestrel was going to slip past, but then she heard the word *grabber* and froze.

"That's when my father knew he was a goner," Ike whispered to his terrified audience, enjoying himself. Kestrel wished she hadn't stopped. Ike's dad's grabber was the first one she had been sent to hunt. Whenever she thought about it, it was so vivid she could almost smell the blood on its claws. "It was the loss of his snuffbox that tipped him off," Ike said. "He always carried it inside his coat. He woke up one day and it was gone."

"You saw it, didn't you, Ike?" Rascly Badger, the fireworks maker, said, his eyes wide.

"I watched it carry him away," said Ike, lowering his voice ever further. The villagers were deathly quiet, terrified but unable to move. Kestrel couldn't tear herself away, either. "My mother tried to stop it. Then—"

He clapped his hands and they all jumped back. Ike didn't need to say anything else. They all knew how it ended. Ike's mother had tried to stop the grabber, but it had scrunched her up and thrown her away like a ball of paper.

"Poor Alice," Rascly Badger muttered. Walt touched something in his pocket, a compulsive checking of his lucky charms. Kestrel instinctively touched the holey stone in her pocket, too, to check it was still there.

"Don't speak the names of the dead," Ike muttered. "It's bad luck."

Mardy Banbury screamed in the distance. The villagers looked at one another, horrified. Kestrel grabbed her spoon without thinking. Was it a grabber? Had one actually struck *again*? They were coming more frequently than ever before, but two in a *day*?

"You little weasel!" Mardy cried.

Kestrel put her spoon away, breathing a sigh of relief. Only one person was capable of infuriating Mardy like that.

Mardy was outside her house, wielding the paddle she used for beating her beloved wolf-skin rug. Kestrel stopped by the well, just out of sight. Mardy's fingers were hooked over Finn's collar as he struggled and squawked.

"Let me go," he howled, lifting his feet, trying to keep them from touching the ground. He was clutching a squashed, paper-wrapped package in his arms.

"Not until I've beaten some sense into you!" shouted Mardy.

Finn's clothes were covered in black feathers and his face was streaked with dirt. All the buttons were hanging off his jacket, and as he wriggled he shed an impressive collection of leaves from his hair.

"What would your parents think of you, Finnigan?" Mardy

yelled, tightening her grip so Finn choked. "What would your poor mum and dad say about you stealing my food, eh?"

"Nothing, 'cause they're dead, aren't they!" gasped Finn. "Their grabbers got 'em, 'cause they weren't clever, like me."

"Living in the trees won't help you, stupid boy," said Mardy, finally dropping him. Finn sprinted toward the nearest tree and scrambled up the trunk, shivering. "Your grabber will make itself some wings and fly!"

Hanging behind her on the wash line was her wolf-skin rug. Kestrel always felt a twinge of pride when she saw it. Her dad had hunted that wolf years ago and given the skin to Mardy as a present for curing his fever.

"If I see you anywhere near my house again I'll get the Trapper to flay the skin from your body," Mardy screeched at Finn. "He'll make a rug out of *you!*"

Kestrel snorted with laughter. Her father would never hurt another person. Finn scrambled up the tree and leaped away. Kestrel ran after him on the ground below. He beamed madly when he saw her and helped haul her up.

Kestrel, despite trying to look cross, felt giggles explode inside her. Finn snorted, too, and within seconds they were both helpless.

"You idiot!" she gasped as Finn howled. "One day she'll rip your head off!"

Finn was laughing so hard he couldn't answer. Kestrel waited for him to calm down, but her own giggles were rising in her like hiccups. They both rolled around, snorting, until Kestrel hit him on the head and he stopped.

"Cake?" he said, offering the squashed brown package.

There was an excited chirrup from somewhere in the tree, then Pippit shot out and scrabbled up Finn's arm.

Finn scratched him under the chin, and Pippit stretched out.

"Fffff," Pippit said, so overcome with adoration that he couldn't speak.

"Suck-up," Kestrel said, rolling her eyes.

They all ate fistfuls of sodden cake, letting crumbs patter onto the ground below. The day was ending and the moon was coming out, smooth and pale in the dimming sky. A cold breeze stirred the trees. Kestrel leaned back, her bones aching, enjoying the cool air on her face. For a few minutes all she wanted to do was sit down and rest. She closed her eyes and tried to imagine where the breeze had come from— maybe the sea, which Granmos had described over and over in her stories.

Those stories were the only good things she could remember about her grandma. Kestrel automatically looked down at her scarred hand. She couldn't remember where the scars all came from, but she had a vague memory of being taught to fight with a knife. She could see Granmos lunging at her again and again, her colored-rag coat flapping, her silver rings and her locket glinting as they caught the moonlight. Kestrel clenched her teeth, willing the memory away, and pushed her hands into her lap so she couldn't see the scars anymore.

Her gaze fell on the woodchopper's house instead, half-visible through the trees. She remembered Hannah, standing outside her house, staring at the grabber's trail.

"Finn," she said, opening her eyes. Finn was almost asleep. "Will you go see Hannah tomorrow?"

"No," he said bluntly. "We hate her, remember?"

"Just check that she's okay. It's her dad who got taken. Please?"

"Fine," he said. He looked up at the sky. "It'll snow soon," he added, brightening. "We can make snowballs and drop them on people's heads."

The thought of snow made Kestrel's skin prickle.

Her dad always, without fail, came back to the village before it snowed. He could smell the weather coming days in advance, and as soon as there was the slightest hint of a snowflake he returned. The forest was even more danger-ous than usual in the snow. Sometimes you were lucky and it was only a light smattering that quickly melted away, but other times it became a chilly death trap. Even Kestrel got lost when the snowdrifts were as high as her head, and there was no telling what monster would leap out at you when you couldn't see anything but vague shapes. If you were outside of the village when it snowed, you were practically asking to fall off a ledge or wander straight into the grasp of a slavering beast. That was the only reason she was back in the village now. If she had her way, she'd be stalking through the places in her grandma's notebook for days, only returning when the black dog decided it needed to check up on her.

If her dad didn't come back soon, it meant something was wrong. Kestrel looked up, praying for the weather to hold, but the sky looked ready to burst.

"Finn," she began, feeling silly.

"I didn't see him," he said awkwardly. Kestrel tried to ignore the empty ache in her ribs. "I found one of his burned-out fires the other day," he added more kindly, pulling her hair to distract her. "It was only a few hours old. So he's been around. He'll be back before the snow comes."

"Yeah," said Kestrel. "I know. It's just that . . . it's been weeks."

"Don't worry about him," said Finn, and Kestrel nodded. But she wanted to talk about him so much. She wanted to ask questions like *Do you think I'd know if he died out there?* And *What if his grabber got him?*

Finn blinked as though he'd only just seen her, then tilted his head and inspected her face. "Where'd your eyebrow go? You're all lopsided." He wriggled his own eyebrows, making them dance like caterpillars, and Kestrel snorted with laughter.

"It was my mum," she said. "Now the other kids will have something else to laugh at."

"They're idiots," he said. "They're just jealous. We have way more fun than them."

Kestrel felt her mouth curve into a smile. Finn was as different to the other villagers as Kestrel. He wasn't stuck to the ground like they were; he wasn't slowly rotting inside, turning dark and sour. He saw the sky and the sun every single day. He slept in a wooden crate, and he ate birds for dinner. His feet didn't touch the ground for weeks on end.

Pippit, who had quietly finished eating the cake and was now as fat as a balloon, burped and head-butted Kestrel's hand for attention. She felt like all she needed in the world was on the branch with her.

"Oh. I was going to tell you," said Finn, looking sheepish. "I think the kids found your burrow. They've been through your stuff, and, er..."

He tipped a pile of things into Kestrel's lap. All that remained was an old shoe, a tarnished candleholder, a broken cup, and a fork with two prongs missing. Kestrel reached into her boot and added the silver ring from Pippit, seething.

Three years of finding things in the forest, gone. She'd always thought they meant something—that they were a puzzle to solve—that they would help her understand the way out. They couldn't belong to the villagers, who would never venture into the forest, let alone carelessly drop their things They *must* have come from the outside.

And now it was ruined. Kestrel wanted to shout at the kids who had done it, but even through her cloud of anger she knew it would only provoke them to do something even worse.

"Where are we going tomorrow?" Finn asked, clearly trying to distract her.

Kestrel pulled her grandma's notebook from her pocket and felt for the dog-eared page she'd marked earlier. Her grandma's spiky handwriting crawled across the paper, sharp and black and cramped.

Granmos had made it difficult to read anything in the notebook. She'd written in zigzags instead of straight lines, or put the words back to front. She threw the letter *e* around like confetti and drew pictures in the middle of paragraphs. Kestrel hadn't made it any better. Her own additions dodged in and out of each sentence, weaving through a mess of arrows and diagrams and wonky letters. And every page contained a pencil map she'd drawn of a different part of the forest, traced over the top of the writing, as part of her attempt to make sense of its never-ending paths and infinite trees.

Kestrel flipped past pages about giant spiders *which can jump a surprisingley longe way, believe you me*; strangling ivy *whiche can take down a bear, really, I've seene it*; and face painters, whose *sweete smelle makes you sicke, and they can transform to look like someone you trust.…*

"The Salt Bog," she said, finding the page. "I've got a good feeling about it. Like something big's going to happen there." Kestrel wanted to jump up and go immediately, but it was stupid to brave the forest after dark unless you had to.

"Maybe we'll find the way out," said Finn.

"I have to find my grandma's grabber first," Kestrel reminded him. When she said the word *grabber*, Finn twitched and looked around.

"What's wrong with you?" Kestrel asked, watching him closely.

"Don't say that word," Finn snapped. "They … they might be able to hear you."

"Don't be stupid," she said. "You're not scared, are you?"

"No," he said quickly. "I'm not scared of anything, am I?"

"'Course not," she said.

Finn stared grumpily into the trees.

"I know," Kestrel said after a moment, desperate to break the silence. "Let's play a game."

"Can't we play tomorrow?"

"We've escaped the forest," she said, nudging him. "Go on."

"Okay," said Finn, grudgingly uncrossing his arms. "But we're not on the ground. I hate walking."

"Okay, we're in the sky."

In her mind the village was blowing away, and the tree

they were in was stretching toward the clouds. If she tried hard enough she could even feel the wind on her face. "We're walking in the air," she said. "We're being chased by—"

"Lightning," said Finn, and he grabbed her hand, sending a jolt of fierce joy up her arm.

"We've got to keep moving," said Kestrel. "We'll die otherwise."

"I know," said Finn, and they ran into the darkening sky, shouting, the air crackling all around them.

That night the sky was as dark as oil. The wolf fire was dull and orange, and it sent up great, dirty plumes of smoke that hid the moon. Kestrel was curled up in an old fox burrow at the edge of the village, dead leaves piled around her for warmth. She'd tried to get Finn to come down, too, but he insisted on sleeping at the top of a tree, which rocked and swayed like a ship.

Kestrel was half asleep when Pippit uttered a terrible hiss. Kestrel's eyes flicked open. Something slipped between the trees, but it was gone in an instant.

"Dad?" she said, then realized how stupid she sounded. Of course it wasn't her dad. She would hear his traps clanking from a mile off.

"What can you smell, Pip?" she asked. Pippit tugged on

her ear, urging her to stay in the burrow, but she pulled herself up and stepped toward the shadows.

She could see two small candle flames flickering just ahead of her. They were so small and dim they would be easy to miss, but Kestrel fixed her eyes on them determinedly. She walked toward them, holding her breath. She couldn't imagine why anyone would be watching her sleep, unless it was Runo and Briar, coming to play a trick on her again. She curled her hands into fists.

"Nasty," said Pippit suddenly, pulling her hair as hard as he could. "Nasty!"

"Be quiet," she said, swatting him. She was only a few yards away from the lights, but she could tell now that they weren't candles. Maybe they were glowworms, or necrotic moths.

The lights flickered. Kestrel realized with a small shock that she was looking into a pair of bright yellow eyes.

The eyes didn't blink. Kestrel found herself instinctively taking a step back. She *knew* those eyes. The lights flickered, and Kestrel jumped.

"Go!" Pippit screeched, and Kestrel jerked away.

She ran back to the village, suddenly not caring that it was the most awful place in the world. She didn't slow down until she'd reached her mother's house, and then she scrambled into the gutter as quickly as she could. She buried herself in a pile of brown leaves so only her head was poking out the top, and compulsively felt around her pockets for her notebook and her weapons.

She pressed her left pocket urgently. Something was missing.

"I can't find my slingshot," she said to Pippit. "I had it earlier, didn't I?"

"Uh-huh," Pippit confirmed.

"I must have left it in the burrow," she said, wanting to kick herself for being so careless. "I should go back and look."

"Er," said Pippit.

Kestrel chewed her thumbnail. For some reason she couldn't bring herself to move.

"Scared?" Pippit asked.

"No," Kestrel said quickly. She felt a lot better now she was in the center of the village, and she couldn't think why she'd been so afraid. "I think they were the same eyes as the ones in the grabber's stomach. But whatever it is, it's lost two of the eyes. It probably got hurt."

Pippit nodded, and Kestrel curled up under the leaves. But for some reason, all she could think about were the small yellow eyes floating in the trees.

THE BRINY WITCH

Kestrel was standing in the middle of her mother's house. The familiar scent of wood smoke and soap was so strong it made her dizzy. She surveyed the clean floorboards, the gleaming mirror, and the neat furniture. The place was huge and empty, and totally weaveless.

She heard the sharp *shrrrrk* of metal against metal and turned around to see Granmos.

Granmos was hunched over the table, sharpening her knives. She was wearing her heavily embroidered clothes under a huge, shapeless coat made of mismatched rags. Colored threads, loose with age, trailed behind her like kite tails. Her fingernails were stained red with the weird tobacco she smoked; her skin was tanned and deeply furrowed, and her hair was tufty and gray.

"This is an important part of your training, Kestrel," her grandma said without looking up, exhaling a puff of smoke from her long, curved pipe. "Surviving the forest isn't just about using weapons and being clever. It's about using this." She fixed her pale blue eyes on Kestrel and tapped the side of her head.

"Can we do it later, Granmos?" Kestrel asked. She'd been dangling from a tree all morning, and her head was pounding. She wanted to sink into the corner and go to sleep.

"Do you think the forest will wait? Do you think the wolves and the god-knows-what-else will let you pause and take a nap before they catch you?" She put the knife down and swiveled to face Kestrel properly. "Do as I say. Tell me what scares you."

Kestrel's mouth was dry. She stared at her grandma's feet.

"I'm scared of wolves," she said, somewhat truthfully.

"You can knock a wolf out with your eyes closed. Don't avoid the question."

"Ghosts," Kestrel said, scrunching her fists. "Those birds with teeth."

"Nobody likes them," her grandma snapped. "What scares *you*? What keeps you awake at night and gives you nightmares? What makes your guts shrivel?"

For a moment, Kestrel knew what she was going to tell her grandma. Then she pressed her lips shut.

"You'll use it against me," Kestrel said bitterly.

Her grandma stood up so fast the chair fell over. In one

second she'd crossed the room and grabbed Kestrel's shoulders. Then Kestrel was pressed against the wall, and her grandma's face filled her vision. She was so close that Kestrel could see the veins in her pale blue eyes, and smell her dry, sour breath. The locket her grandma always wore pressed against Kestrel's ribs, so hard she knew it would leave a bruise.

"Say it," her grandma snapped.

"Get off me," Kestrel said, wriggling desperately. Her brain was shrieking at her to run. She felt the same as when she was cornered by a slavering monster, a bundle of jangling nerves and horror.

"Tell me!" her grandma shouted, her fingers digging into her shoulders. Her mouth was open in a snarl, her yellow-stained teeth as long as wolves'. "Say it!"

Kestrel felt a short, sharp pain, and woke suddenly, drenched in cold sweat. Pippit was on her face, scratching her with his claws. She gasped and fell out of the gutter, landing in a pile of dead leaves by her mother's doorstep. Her spoon landed point-down in the ground next to her.

Pippit launched himself after her and landed on her chest, and started licking her cheeks.

The smell of Pippit's breath was a horrible way to start the day, but at least it was real. Kestrel hugged him so tightly she could have crushed him.

"Nasty?" he said, wriggling to get out.

"It was just a dream," she said, although she could still see her grandma's veiny eyes, and her heart was thumping so fast she felt dizzy. "It happened a long time ago. It's over."

Pippit tilted his head, as though he could tell exactly how awful she felt. Kestrel had never answered her grandma's question; it was the first time Kestrel had really disobeyed her. And only three days later, she let the grabber in.

She was a murderer.

The scene was printed behind Kestrel's eyelids forever. On that night, she saw the grabber approach the house. It was very tall, and very old, with a thin neck that didn't look like it should support its large skull. Its clothes barely hid the jumble of bones that poked out from its shirt. It wore some of Granmos's stolen jewelry around its neck. One of its ears was hanging by a thread, and there was a large brass key dangling from its belt.

Kestrel's grandma had always been afraid of her father. When she was young he used to lock her in the cellar. The day she became lost in the forest was the day she'd finally escaped the cellar, stealing his key as a terrible souvenir which she'd kept over the fireplace, until one day it had gone missing.

Even though Kestrel's grandma was old and her father probably long dead, the old woman had always been worried, deep in her heart, that he would come looking for her and drag her back to the cellar.

Her grabber had brought a vision of the old man back to life.

Kestrel remembered glimpsing it through the shutters. The grabber pressed his pale, wormy lips to the other side, as gently as a moth bouncing against a lantern.

That night, Kestrel slipped away from the shutters and walked toward the door.

She reached out and started to twist the handle, feeling nothing except this slow, horrible anger that pushed everything else away. All she could think of was making the constant torture stop.

She heard her grandma turn around and drop the knife she was sharpening.

"Don't!" Granmos shouted, in a voice filled with sharp, sheer panic, but it was too late. The next thing stamped guilt into Kestrel's heart every time she remembered it.

The grabber was inside, striding toward her grandma, who was frozen, and it was reaching out for her with his long, cold fingers—and then it was dragging her outside.

Suddenly Kestrel realized what she had done, and she raced after them. She could see her grandmother's face, furious with betrayal and something she'd never seen before: *fear.*

Then Granmos was gone, dragged into the belly of the forest.

Kestrel knew she was a terrible person. She was so ashamed of herself that she'd dreamed of her grandma almost every night since. But something deep in the pit of her stomach was also shamefully, horribly relieved.

She tried to tell herself that the grabber would have caught her grandma anyway, even if Kestrel hadn't let it in. But it didn't change what she had done.

"Kes?" Pippit said worriedly, licking her nose. Kestrel blinked the image away.

"Let's find some monsters," she said weakly. "We'll grab Finn and go to the Salt Bog. Can you imagine if we found the path? Or my grandma's grabber? I could kill it, and my mother would let me go. This could be the day."

Pippit looked at her skeptically. He wrinkled his nose as though he wanted to say something else, but then he thought better of it and started to wash himself.

Kestrel slipped by the houses. It was a cold morning, and most of the doors were still shut tight. As she walked she flipped through her grandma's notebook until she got to the entry about the Salt Bog, which contained lots of warnings about not going near it, absolutely not, *no matter what, understande?* There was also a description of something called the *Briny Witch* that had been almost completely obscured by mud.

"Yum?" said Pippit, spying a poisonous-looking mushroom on the ground.

"No," said Kestrel quickly, and slammed the book shut so she could keep an eye on him.

It didn't take her long to find Finn, who was hanging upside down from a tree and whistling. Pippit snickered as Kestrel crept up behind him.

"BOO!" she shouted. Finn yelped and fell out of the tree.

Kestrel laughed so hard she had to sit down, but Finn didn't join her. He made a face that meant *shut up and act normal*, and flicked his eyes at the tree. Kestrel stopped and looked up. Perched in the branches, her skirt drooping like the tail feathers of an exotic bird, was Hannah.

"What's she doing up there?" Kestrel said, astonished. She'd never seen anyone else in the trees before.

"I went to see her, like you asked," Finn muttered. "She just sort of... followed me back. She said she wanted to learn how to climb trees. It's weird. She's being *nice*."

"Where are you off to?" Hannah asked. She slid down from the tree with surprising grace, landing next to them with a tiny *thump* that barely even ruffled her skirt.

"Nowhere," Kestrel said quickly, at the same time as Finn said, "Just for a walk."

"Can I come?" Hannah asked, and without warning slid her arm through Kestrel's. Kestrel froze, her whole arm on fire. She had no idea what to do. Nobody except Finn or her mother ever touched her. She was so close she could smell Hannah's soap.

"Um," said Finn.

"Er," Kestrel said, panicking.

"Oh, goody," said Hannah, beaming. "I've been so bored. And you know what, Kestrel, I feel like we've been a bit childish toward each other lately. We should actually get to know each other."

"Yeah?" said Kestrel dumbly.

"I know I'm not the easiest person to get on with," Hannah added. "I kind of follow everyone else sometimes. I hope you don't hate me."

Hannah started walking, and Kestrel found herself trotting alongside her. She was so shocked she felt like she was going to collapse. *Maybe,* she thought, hardly daring to think about it, *we're going to be friends.*

"I left my scarf in the tree," said Hannah suddenly, and Kestrel jerked to a halt beside her.

Hannah looked at Finn unhappily.

"Uh," said Finn. "I guess . . . I could get it?"

"Could you really?" asked Hannah. Finn shrugged.

"I could do it with my eyes closed," he said.

"I bet you can't," Hannah fired back.

"I *can.*"

"Go on, then."

Finn snorted and leaped into the tree. Kestrel watched

him disappear into the branches, then jumped in surprise as Hannah grabbed her and pulled her close.

"Go away, freak," Hannah hissed in her ear. "We don't want you here."

"What?" Kestrel said, shocked.

"Finn's friends with me now."

"You said—"

"You idiot. I don't want to hang out with you. *Seriously*, how stupid can you be? Nice eyebrow, by the way."

Kestrel's hand flew to her face. She'd forgotten about her missing eyebrow. Hannah turned away and beamed just as Finn landed on the ground, the scarf tied around his head.

"Okay, if you want," Hannah said loudly to Kestrel. "I guess we'll see you later."

"Oh," said Finn, looking slightly confused. Hannah bounced up to him and grabbed her scarf.

"Come on," she said. "I found this amazing place the other day." She looked at Kestrel snakily. "See you, Kes."

"I'm coming, too," Kestrel said impulsively.

"It's fine if you don't want to," said Finn, looking insulted. Kestrel glared at him. What an *idiot*.

Hannah grabbed his wrist and pulled him away. Kestrel took a step after them, expecting Finn to protest, but he shrugged and traipsed after Hannah. Even if she went with them, Hannah would find a way to torture her all day. Kestrel turned away. She pushed into the trees, clenching her hand

85

around the holey stone she still had in her pocket, trying to fight the shame and loneliness stuck behind her ribs. Of course Hannah didn't want to be her friend. She was idiotic to think anything else.

"Why does she suddenly want Finn, anyway?" she said out loud. "He smells funny and burps all the time."

Pippit gave a muffled snigger.

"And what was wrong with him?" she added, getting more annoyed. "Couldn't he see me wriggling my eyebrow?"

"Duh," agreed Pippit.

"I'm going to the Salt Bog by myself," she continued out loud. "That's right. And if I find a way out, I'm not telling Finn about it until he stops being an idiot."

Pippit was still making snorting sounds. Kestrel stopped.

"What are you laughing at?" she said.

"Did a bad," he said.

"What kind of bad?" said Kestrel.

She reached behind her and pulled him out of her hood. Without warning, a giggle rose in her throat. It grew and grew until it cut through all her rage, and she laughed helplessly.

Pippit beamed at her proudly, a chunk of Hannah's shiny hair in his mouth.

The Salt Bog was a vast white landscape completely bare of trees. The whole place was blindingly white, carpeted in a fine layer of salt. Long paths of salt-encrusted earth twisted through the water, which was frozen in place, covered in a thick, crystalline layer of white with air bubbles rolling around underneath it.

Kestrel suppressed a shudder. It looked different in the daylight, but she'd been here before. The smell of salt brought it all back.

When she was eight, Granmos made her spend the night here alone. As soon as the sun went down ghosts had oozed from the forest and drifted across the bog. They swarmed around Kestrel all night, attempting to leech off her warmth, touching her with their long fingers and leaving frozen white patches on her skin. Kestrel was so cold she thought she might freeze to death. The ghosts tried urgently to speak to her, but their voices only came out as soft, unintelligible clattering sounds.

Granmos had promised to rescue her if she ever wanted to stop a training session, but Kestrel had always stood her ground. She would rather fight any amount of snarling wolves and starving bears than admit weakness. But that night, with the ghosts, Kestrel was terrified beyond belief. She screamed for Granmos, but the old woman had vanished. Kestrel was too scared to move, and too cold to fight, and too lost to find her way back. She curled up in a ball until sunrise, shaking, slowly solidifying under a fine layer of salt.

I taught you something important, girl, Granmos said

when she came to collect her the next morning. *You can't rely on other people to save you, no matter what they say.*

Kestrel wrapped her arms around herself, trying to shake the memory. The smell of salt made it feel too real, and for a second Kestrel expected the old woman to appear behind her. She stepped hurriedly into the bog, the back of her neck crawling at the thought of her grandma's cold eyes.

Every now and then the ground belched and released huge wafts of unspeakable smells that lingered like a guilty burp. Kestrel stood at the side of a path, picking out a route with her eyes. When she finally moved she realized that rings of salt had formed around her legs. The bog crystallized anything that stood still for too long. Every few seconds a spray of salty water burst into the air, covering everything in a fine layer of brine.

A short distance away stood a crystallized fox. You could almost think it was happily asleep, if it didn't have salt icicles hanging from its nose.

Pippit made a loud crunching sound, oblivious to the fantastic landscape. He was chewing some gray knucklebones he'd found in a puddle.

"Share bones," he offered as Kestrel shielded her eyes. "Have crunch."

"No thanks," she said, and picked him up. Something had caught her eye. Halfway across the bog was something that looked like a vast white maze, a corridor of pillars and tortured, twisted shapes. It hadn't been there the night of her training. "Let's see what that is."

The maze grew larger in front of her, but it wasn't until she reached the first twisted pillar that Kestrel realized what it was made from. It was a corridor of frozen statues, each one preserved in a thick layer of salt. There were dogs with crystals hanging from their whiskers, wolves twisted up like they had a backache, and deer with milky eyes. There were hundreds of smaller animals, too, like tiny rabbits and frogs. The roof was made of trees and plants, their white branches forming a ceiling over the animals.

Kestrel licked her lips, tasting salt. Her eyes stung.

None of these animals had ended up here by accident. They were all facing one another as though they'd been carefully arranged for viewing. She cautiously moved among the animals, one hand on her spoon, making sure not to touch anything. Even Pippit was quiet.

She turned a corner in the corridor of animals, then another, and realized too late that it was almost impossible to tell one direction from another. Everything was the same color, and she was surrounded by a wall of repeating eyes and teeth and claws. She tried to go back the way she had come, but she wasn't sure how she'd gotten in. The animals leered at her.

"I'm lost," she said to Pippit urgently, her voice low. "Can you smell your way out?"

"Salt," he said, shaking his head.

Kestrel forced herself to slow down. Getting frantic wouldn't help, and neither would the twinge of panic that was dancing in her stomach. She closed her eyes and breathed deeply.

"This way," she said.

She walked softly around the statues, looking curiously into all their faces. Kestrel was starting to enjoy herself in the Salt Bog now. Being in the maze was like wandering around someone's private museum. She gently reached out to touch the face of a frozen stag, then stopped dead, standing over a pool of water, balanced precariously on a layer of clear salt.

She wasn't alone. There was something in the water, and it was watching her.

She reached for her slingshot before remembering that it was missing. She felt a pang of dread, then squashed it down.

As quietly as possible, Kestrel stepped back onto the grass. If the thing didn't know she'd seen it, it might not bother her. She started to retrace her steps, now determined to find her way out as soon as possible, but the thing glided under the water and broke the surface in front of her.

Shards of salt flew in all directions as the bloated, damp creature rose from the depths. Kestrel backed away, but her heel broke through the surface of the bog and she almost toppled in. The creature continued to rise a few feet above the surface of the water, as though it were swimming in the air, then waded forward and down until it was standing in front of Kestrel, blocking her path.

The *it* was a *he*, a man with a bloated stomach, wet, glistening skin, and lips that were blue with cold. Small bubbles issued from his lips and nostrils as though he were still underwater. His clothes were wet, limp rags, and his beard was thick with weeds, but he had a clever face that told Kestrel he was more dangerous than any person she'd known.

Kestrel raised her spoon in front of her.

"Try it," he whispered, in a wet, blubbery voice that sounded like it was coming from the bottom of a well. He stepped toward her, moving his arms like he was pushing water out of his way, even though he was on dry land. Small blue fish darted around and through his head, vanishing into one ear and flying out the other. "You couldn't hurt me if you sliced me into a thousand fillets."

Kestrel imagined him laid out on a platter like a cold, wet fish, and shuddered. "What do you want?" she asked loudly. She made sure to look him right in the eyes, although they were so filmy and white she wasn't sure he could see her at all. She waved a hand experimentally, but his eyes didn't twitch. He was blind.

"What do *I* want?" he said in his slow, bubbly voice. "You're the one who came to visit the Briny Witch's museum. You're the one who trespassed on my collection."

91

"Some collection," Kestrel said. "It's just a pile of dead animals."

He curled his lip, showing his slippery teeth.

"If you get out of my way, I'll leave without hurting you," Kestrel said, changing tack.

The Briny Witch laughed. His hair was floating away from his face in slow, thick clumps.

"Nothing can hurt me," he gurgled. "I was dead long before my body floated into this salty pit."

Despite the fact that she was standing in front of a foul-smelling, apparently dead man, Kestrel was interested.

"Where did you float in from?" she asked. She was wary of the Briny Witch, but she didn't think he could move fast enough to surprise her. "Did you come from the outside?"

"You might call it that," said the Briny Witch in his slippery voice.

"So it's real," Kestrel breathed. Then she remembered to jab her spoon threateningly. "Tell me how to get there," she demanded.

"I can't," he said, and despite his frightful face and greenish teeth, Kestrel thought she detected a hint of sadness. "Long ago, and far away, I was on the run. I had murdered my older brother. My sister hunted me down and blinded me before throwing me into a river to drown. I floated for days and ended up here. The way I know is cold and wet, and dark and lonely. Only dead people take that route." He leaned forward and slowly glided toward Kestrel, forcing her to take another step back. "There's something in this water," he whispered. "It preserves those who drown. Take care not to go through the surface or you'll end up like me, cold and alone."

"Come any closer and my weasel will burrow into your skull and give you the worst headache you've ever had," Kestrel snarled. She plucked Pippit from her shoulder and held him out, but he was as stiff as a loaf of stale bread. "That means he's getting ready to attack," she added.

To her surprise, the Briny Witch didn't come any closer.

"You're brave," said the Briny Witch. He reached out to touch the face of a nearby frozen bear, his expression turning dreamy for a second as he ran his fingers over its muzzle. Then he dropped his fingers and his face tightened again. "Maybe you're brave enough to do a deal with me."

"I don't make bargains with the dead," said Kestrel.

The Briny Witch stepped forward, his rags floating around him. Kestrel automatically stepped back again. Her heel cracked through the salt; she was standing right above the bog. She didn't know if the Briny Witch was telling the truth about the water, but she didn't want to risk becoming a half-dead thing like him.

"It would be a fair deal," said the Briny Witch. "I can give you anything you want. I can make you stronger. I can make you prettier."

"I don't want anything like that," said Kestrel derisively. "And I like the way I look, thank you very much."

"I could even," said the Briny Witch slowly, "make you invisible."

"Why would I want that?" Kestrel asked, but a tiny part of her was already imagining all the things she could do.

"Oh, there's so much potential," said the Briny Witch, casually running a finger over the back of a fox. "Imagine what you could do to those who bully you. The village children destroyed your collection of forest trinkets a few days ago, didn't they? You could hide under their beds at night and terrify them with whispers. You could slip away from that nasty black dog that's always following you."

Kestrel chewed her lip, hypnotized by the thought.

"An invisible girl could do anything," the Briny Witch said, his voice suddenly low and silky smooth. "You could even get rid of Hannah before she steals your friend."

"Wait," said Kestrel, suddenly coming to her senses. "How do you know about that?"

"I know everything," he said. "I can go anywhere there is water. I lurk in the village well and creep through the puddles. I stream in the river with my long, grabbing fingers, and I play in the gutters where the small animals drown. I can be in any glass of water or any cup of tea, listening to you all the time. I have ears and fingers everywhere."

Kestrel imagined one of the blue fish sliding down her throat as she drank a glass of water, and shivered.

"I already know a lot about you, Kestrel," he said, his voice lowering to a hiss. "I know you have the best eyes in the forest. I want your eyes for myself so I can see my precious statues. I want to see the light shine on their faces. It wouldn't hurt a bit…."

The Briny Witch slowly raised a hand. Kestrel took a step back and gasped as cold water sloshed into her shoes.

"Get out of my way," she said, Pippit in one hand, her spoon in the other. She tried to sound as terrifying as possible.

"Not until you give me your eyes," said the Briny Witch, his mouth opening in a horrible greenish grin.

Then the Briny Witch twitched, as though he'd heard something. He paused with one hand stretched toward her. Nothing in the Salt Bog had changed, but Kestrel suddenly felt icy cold.

"You didn't tell me you had one of those," the Briny Witch said, looking panicked.

"One of what?" she asked. The Briny Witch turned around and sniffed the air frantically. Kestrel tried to see past him, but his floating rags formed a dark cloud around his body. "What is it?"

"What do you mean, what *is* it?" the Briny Witch repeated, and turned back to her, seeking her out with his blind eyes.

"That's what I asked!" she yelled, caught up in his obvious panic.

"Go!" he commanded, then hesitated before adding: "If you change your mind about your eyes, I'll be in the water."

Without warning the Briny Witch collapsed into a heap of rags and frogspawn-y slime and rattling bones, all of which slid backward into the hole he'd risen from. There was a final *slurp*, and the water closed over him. Kestrel looked around wildly, but she couldn't see anything at all, only the salt-encrusted animals.

"Thanks for nothing," Kestrel said to Pippit, who had shamefacedly gone limp in her hand. "You don't mind fighting grabbers, but as soon as you see a witch you're useless!"

She wasn't really mad, but the sound of her voice helped her feel less alone, less like something was watching and waiting in the bushes. As soon as she stopped, the icy feeling came back stronger than ever.

A nasty voice in the back of her head was telling her that she knew *exactly* what would scare something like the Briny Witch.

I'm paranoid, she thought, and took a deep breath. Her heart was fluttering nervously, even though she thought the Briny Witch's damp brain was probably playing tricks on him.

"There's obviously no path to the outside here," she told

Pippit loudly. She was too embarrassed to admit that she didn't like the way the Salt Bog made her skin crawl.

Pippit nudged her hand with his wet nose, looking worried.

"Nasty," he said. "Eyes. Follow. Agh!"

Kestrel ignored him. "We've got time for one more place," she said. "To the Pit of Doom!"

And she fled through the corridor of frozen animals to the next deep, dark place in the forest.

THE PUNISHMENT

The cold was as sharp as a paper edge. Kestrel scrunched her frozen toes and kept working, scooping handfuls of rancid fat out of the burrow where she slept. She could see the forest from here, at least. Maybe she could even spot her dad.

"Lessgo," Pippit said, shivering in her pocket. His breath made tiny puffs of condensation in the air, and his teeth were chattering.

"I haven't finished," Kestrel said determinedly.

The Pit of Doom had been nothing more than a ditch with a pile of bones in the bottom of it. According to Granmos's notebook, it had once been home to an arthritic troll with a face on both the front and back of its head. She was disappointed that she'd never gotten to see it firsthand. Its skull, with its two jaws and four eye sockets, had grinned at her from the bottom of the ditch. She'd felt like it was laughing at her attempts to find a way out. *Path?* she imagined it saying. *There's nothing like that here.*

Kestrel sighed, scooped another handful of fat out of the burrow, and threw it away. It landed with a gross splattering sound. Some of the village kids liked to sneak in and dump things there. Playing tricks on Kestrel helped establish a pecking order of the brave, and messing with the gutter was the ultimate challenge. They'd egg one another on until someone gave in. Then they got to wear this stupid badge one of them had made of wax.

"Snuh-h-h," chattered Pippit as a tiny white snowflake landed between his eyes.

"I know," said Kestrel unhappily, and looked at the edge of the forest for the tenth time. Her dad was going to freeze if he stayed away much longer.

Pippit curled himself into a tighter ball. For an animal that had come from the forest, he wasn't particularly well-equipped to deal with the cold. Kestrel wondered if she'd spoiled him.

She wrinkled her nose and scooped the last of the fat out of the burrow. Then she took her trinkets—the shoe, candle holder, cup, fork, and ring—and made sure they were hidden right at the back, under a pile of leaves.

Kestrel had half expected Finn to come looking for her by now, but he'd disappeared entirely, and Hannah wasn't in her house, either. She wondered if they were out somewhere together.

Maybe they're having a horrible time in the cold, she thought, cheering up a little bit.

That's when she heard it, far away but clear as ice. The familiar, thrilling sound of metal clanking against metal deep in the trees. The forest shivered, and Kestrel felt its worry deep in her bones. Then she saw it, almost hidden by the trees—brief glimpses of shining iron.

"Trapper!" shouted Pippit. "'E's back!"

Kestrel's dad was tall and broad, and he wore a waxed brown overcoat that made him look like a tent. Around his neck he wore strings of wolves' teeth, and the brim of his brown leather hat was studded with black claws. There were metal traps hanging from his belt, swinging into one another, their sharp teeth clashing. If you saw him in the forest you would probably run from him, because he was bristling with sharp points and trophies, and covered in great, twisting scars from the neck down.

When Kestrel reached him, he was standing by a gnarled tree, his back turned to the village, watching for something in the shadows. Kestrel crept through the dirty tendrils that were blowing from the wolf fire, her hand over her mouth to stop her coughing.

She felt suddenly shy. She almost didn't want him to turn around. He hadn't been back in such a long time, a small part of her wondered if he wanted to see her at all.

Kestrel was so close now that she was almost touching his shadow. She was still working up the courage to open her mouth when he turned around, quick as a fish in a bog, and caught her with his great paw.

"You're getting better," he said. "But it'll take more than that to catch a wolf hunter."

Kestrel wriggled out of his grasp and flung her arms around him, all her doubt melting. The top of her head barely reached his chest. He crushed her into him, and she breathed in the smell of the deep forest, the bonfires he lit way out there, the fur and the blood, and something a bit like bacon. He was the greatest wolf hunter that had ever lived, and he smelled like home.

She pulled away and raised her chin for the usual inspection. She was glad the smoke was there, so he couldn't see how much she was smiling.

"You're stringier," he said. "You don't eat enough."

"I've got to be stringy so I can hide," she fired back. He didn't need to know how much she longed for the cake and stew her mother ate. "You're so fat you have to pretend to be a rock or a boulder."

"But I get to eat wolf meat every day," he said, patting

his stomach and laughing. The sound was deep and rich, as though it came from a place made of butter.

It had been three months. Kestrel wanted him to say it. The words were hanging explosively in the air, but he just smiled in that mild way of his.

"I didn't know if you were coming back," Kestrel burst out.

"I always come back," he said, catching her in his huge paw again and scooping her close.

His presence was so big, and Kestrel so small, that it was like being an ant squashed against a cliff. She couldn't stay mad at him for more than ten seconds, even when she tried. All she wanted to do was stay like this forever, in the only place she felt safe, with her face pressed against her dad's coat.

She felt silly for doubting he'd come back. He always did.

They walked around the perimeter of the village, her dad's traps clanking all the way. Pippit was clinging to her boot, his nose wiffling excitedly. Kestrel was unused to openly strolling around. She wanted to jump back into the shadows.

"Did you find anything for my collection?" she asked, trying to hide her nervousness.

"Not this time," he said, shaking his head. "But I promise I always look."

Kestrel opened her mouth to tell him most of it had been

stolen by the village kids, but she thought better of it. She didn't want to ruin his visit. Besides, now she had Hannah's plait to add to her collection. It was even better than the silver ring.

Her dad held his traps still as they passed behind Ike Fletcher, who was peering into the well with an expression of deep distrust.

"Ike's scared of water," her dad said softly, nudging her when they were safely away from him. "He looks in there every day to check there aren't any monsters."

"I don't believe you," said Kestrel, feeling thrilled with this new piece of information. She wondered how Ike would feel if he knew the Briny Witch lurked around the village.

"Just watch him. And you see that thing inside Walt Leith's coat?"

"Yeah?"

"It's a bottle of poison. They say he's saving it for when his grabber comes."

Kestrel looked at Walt with a shiver, imagining him sitting behind his door at night, holding the bottle.

"That's how his great-grandfather died," her dad continued. "He refused to be eaten by his grabber. The old man was still alive when I was your age. He said he remembered life outside the forest. Lots of the old people claimed they weren't born here, or that the forest grew up around them."

"I bet it's true," Kestrel said, excitement squirming in her gut. It explained her feeling that the forest was a single, huge living thing, almost a monster in itself, and that it was doing its best to trap them.

"How many wolves did you get?" Kestrel asked. Her dad looked around and touched his hat, running his fingers through the claws, counting them. The gesture was so automatic it was almost a tic. He didn't believe in scarecrows and sticks to keep the grabbers away, but he always said that wearing wolves' teeth would throw grabbers off his scent.

"Since I last saw you?" The claws hanging all around his hat jangled as he slipped them between his fingers. "Fifteen. Nine gray, five black, and one silver. The last one had green eyes and one ear. It had me pinned down by the throat, but I threw it off and tossed it down a hole."

"Good move," she said approvingly. Her dad smiled like she'd said something funny.

"And what about you, little fox?" he asked, gently pushing her away so he could see her better.

A scream cut the air in half. Kestrel grabbed her spoon and brandished it in the direction of the noise, her mind already racing through the options. *A wolf? A grabber? Another horde of poisonous rabbits?*

Her dad pulled her back. Before she could protest, Mardy burst out of her house.

"Who took my rug?" she screeched. "I'll beat you to a pulp!"

Anyone who was outside stared at her. Kestrel felt her dad's hand slowly drop from her shoulder. Mardy looked around, then started to shiver.

Nobody said anything. Kestrel couldn't stand it anymore. She opened her mouth, ready to offer help, but Mardy turned and fled back into the house.

Walt, who still had a log in his hands, blinked and continued to stoke the wolf fire, as though he hadn't heard anything. Ike patted his pocket watch nervously and peered into the well.

"Why don't they say something?" Kestrel asked hotly. Her cheeks felt warm and prickly.

"They're scared, pet," he said, his voice strangely grave. He ran his fingers through the teeth a second time in a distracted, worried way.

"Has she lost it?" she asked. "Or do you think it's her grabber?"

She looked at her dad. He turned away quickly, but she saw enough to know that he was scared. His face was pale.

"What's wrong?" she asked, her stomach dropping.

"Nothing," he said, turning back to her. His smile didn't quite reach his eyes.

"You're lying," she said fiercely. "I'm not stupid."

"All right," he said. "You're only twelve. You shouldn't be hunting grabbers. And you know you can't catch them before they've eaten. They're too fast and clever."

Kestrel watched him carefully, but the look of fear had gone. Maybe she'd imagined it.

"I'm clever, too," she said. "I won't stop trying."

Her father heaved a sigh and raised his hands in mock defeat.

"I still don't know why you do it," he said. "I always hoped you wouldn't catch it from your grandma, rest her soul, but you're every bit as stubborn and restless as she was."

Kestrel dropped her head. She hated it when her dad mentioned Granmos; she felt like the truth about her death would come bursting out of her at any moment. The guilt of keeping it secret made her want to shrivel up.

But she was so used to keeping secrets. Even her training had been kept under wraps.

Your dad doesn't need to know, Granmos had said when she was little, casting Kestrel her special, hawkish look. *I tried to train him once, but he was too sensitive. Couldn't handle it. In this family, strength passes down the female side.*

"How did you grow up without being mean?" Kestrel asked. The idea of having Granmos as a mum seemed horrifying. "Didn't she scare you?"

"She wasn't so bad," her dad said. "I know she was a bit tough on you sometimes, but she only wanted to make you stronger."

A bit tough? Kestrel wanted to scream. *She threw me down a well in the middle of winter to see if I could swim!*

Sometimes, even now, when Kestrel heard an unexpected noise, she was still terrified that her grandma was about to attack her.

"Anyway, she adored you," her dad added. "Do you remember the coat she made you when you were nine? She hated sewing, but she spent three weeks making it. She couldn't wait to give it to you."

Kestrel did remember. It was an exact copy of her grandma's coat, the colorful one made of rags. Kestrel loved the coat so much she didn't take it off for weeks. She'd only gotten rid of it after her grandma died, when even looking at the coat made a knot of guilt form in her stomach. She'd left it hanging on a branch in the middle of the forest.

"I remember," Kestrel said uncomfortably.

But then she thought of her tenth birthday, and the gift she'd received from Granmos then. It wasn't nice, like the coat.

The night of her birthday Kestrel was in bed, half asleep, when something jabbed her in the ribs. She woke up to see Granmos's wrinkled face inches from her own, her crooked teeth bared in a grin.

"You see the door?" her grandma said, pointing a long, red fingernail at the front door. Kestrel's mother snored in the corner of the room, oblivious. "Have you noticed how it stares at you?"

Kestrel squinted at it blearily. Her grandma was right. The

wood was old and full of knots, and if you concentrated, they looked a little like faces.

"So?" she asked.

"Sit up," Granmos said, dragging her upright by her elbow.

Granmos used the thick smoke from her pipe and flickering candlelight to make terrible shadows dance across the walls. She hissed horrible stories in Kestrel's ear, and embellished the imaginary creatures with bloodcurdling descriptions until Kestrel was convinced that she was going to die inside the house. It didn't stop until Kestrel screamed and hid her head under the pillow.

But that wasn't the end. Granmos put her through the whole nightmare again the next night, and the next, again and again until Kestrel hadn't slept in weeks.

"Use your brain," Granmos roared. "Work out how to stop being scared!"

Kestrel wanted to run away, but she knew her grandma would come after her. She tried closing her eyes and stuffing her fingers in her ears. She tried stabbing the door with her spoon, but the faces never stopped being terrifying, and she shivered with lack of sleep.

"Where's the dog?" her dad said. Kestrel blinked and realized she'd missed half a conversation.

"Dunno," she said. It had left her alone for a while now, but she was pretty sure it wasn't for her good behavior.

They continued their circuit of the village until they came to her mother's house. The windows were shuttered, and the door was tightly closed.

"Well," he said, looking relieved, "I won't disturb her. I've come a long way and I need to rest. I'll sleep by the wolf fire."

"I'll come with you," said Kestrel. "I'll watch for wolves."

"I don't need looking after," he said, laughing.

"Whatever," Kestrel replied, turning her face away so he wouldn't see her blush. She knew the wolves wouldn't come for him here, but a tiny part of her was always waiting for him to run back into the forest when she was asleep. It wasn't that she didn't trust him, or that she thought he'd leave without saying good-bye, but—well . . .

They were almost out of sight of her mother's house when Kestrel heard the door creak open. She froze at the same time as her dad, and shared dread sloshed between them.

Slowly, they turned around.

Her mother was leaning in the doorway, whole skeins of wool trailing from her clothing and into the back of the house like umbilical cords. Seeing her make it as far as the door was a shock. Although her mother's face was unhealthily gray in the daylight, her eyes were still hard, and she looked no weaker for having left the warm belly of the house.

"Come and greet me, then," she said, like she was issuing a challenge. Kestrel looked at her dad. His face was unreadable

"Let's go," Kestrel said, and when she didn't get a response she kicked his foot. It was like striking her toes against a rock. "Dad!"

"Trapper!" her mother called unexpectedly, her voice whipping across the ground like a snake. "Afraid of your own wife?"

Kestrel's dad marched toward the house, and Kestrel's mother laughed. Kestrel threw herself after him and grabbed the back of his coat, but he dragged her along like a ship breaking anchor.

They stopped at the doorstep. Kestrel hauled herself upright and stood beside her dad, furious and streaked with dirt. "Let's go," Kestrel said urgently, wishing her dad wasn't so heavy.

He shook her off. "You know I have nothing to say to you," her dad said to her mother, his voice different from its usual slow rumble. "Don't come near me while I'm here."

Kestrel had never heard anyone speak to her like that before, and it chilled her to the pit of her stomach. "I'm here to see Kestrel."

"Are you?" her mother said, leaning in. Kestrel's dad stepped back inadvertently. "Or are you here because you're running away from something?"

"Dad?" said Kestrel, trying to pull him away.

"Whatever you think you know is wrong," he said, his voice low and dangerous.

"I know enough," her mother said.

"Stop ignoring me," Kestrel yelled, surprising them both. They looked at her for a second, the spell between them broken.

"Go and wait for me by the fire," her dad said angrily. "Now!"

Kestrel flushed red. She wasn't some little kid who could just be sent away. She opened her mouth to defy him, but he looked so thunderous that she shut it again right away.

She stomped away, giving them her best look of deep disgust. As soon as her back was turned they started again, and she ducked around the corner of another house to listen. They had lowered their voices, and she had to strain her ears to hear them.

"You're not brave enough to go back into the forest," her mother said, brushing Kestrel's interruption off like a piece of lint.

"Says the woman who hasn't left her house in five years," her dad said.

"You're so terrified you'd rather wriggle under my nose than face it," her mother retorted. "You crept back to the village like the worm you are."

Her dad leaned in and Kestrel lost sight of his face. She craned her head as far as she dared, but heard nothing but mumbles. Then her mother snapped, "Better for her that you don't make it," and slammed the door in his face.

Her dad shuddered like he'd been shot in the chest. Then he turned, and Kestrel knew that he'd lost the argument.

He strode toward the forest. Kestrel tumbled out of her hiding place. She knew instinctively what was happening.

"Wait," she said to her dad, striding after him, not bothering to pretend that she hadn't been eavesdropping. He picked up the pace, and she had to run to keep up. "Don't go. *Dad.*"

He was moving toward the trees, his traps clanking as they swung around his legs. She had to duck out of the way to stop them from hitting her.

"Where are you going?" she asked. He didn't slow down. "What did she mean about you running away from something? Dad?" A terrible thought occurred to her. "Is it your—" she hesitated, her voice was so full of dread it made him stop. She had to force the words past her teeth. "Is it your grabber?"

Kestrel's dad caught his breath, as though the word was a physical blow. Then he burst into laughter, and Kestrel felt her horror deflate like a balloon.

"I promise there's no grabber," he said.

"Oh," Kestrel said, going red. She felt stupid for being so dramatic. Nobody ever talked about their grabbers, but her dad wouldn't keep any secrets from her. The rest of the villagers would rather cower in silence if they thought they were being stalked, but not him. He trusted her.

He lowered his voice, and Kestrel leaned in instinctively.

"Truth be told, I'm tracking something," he said. "I can't let it get away from me."

"A wolf?" she said, watching his face. Despite his laughter, he still wore a haunted look.

"A big one," he said, running his fingers around his hat again. "It's been baying for my blood for years, and it would love nothing more than to take a chunk out of me. But I'll get it."

Kestrel felt a pang of worry, but her dad only smiled again. He looked over his shoulder, the claws on his hat swinging past his eyes.

"It was silly to come back. I've got to pick up the trail again," he said.

"What about the snow?" Kestrel asked, wishing it would pour from the sky.

"It won't be much," he said. "Only a scattering."

Kestrel wanted to scream at him.

"You're leaving because of her," Kestrel said, her voice icy so he wouldn't know that her heart was cracking in two. She wanted to say more, but she couldn't get the words out of her mouth. That if he loved her, he'd stay.

"I'm leaving because she'll put that dog on me," he said.

"You used to be brave," Kestrel said, the words slipping out before she could stop them. "You could squash that dog under your little finger if you wanted to, but you're too afraid."

Her dad looked like he'd been hit. Kestrel immediately felt wretched, but she couldn't take it back.

The black dog padded into sight. It paused a few yards away, baring its teeth.

"There's something I need to tell you," her dad said quietly. He looked sidelong at the dog and pulled Kestrel away. His face had smoothed over again, but she could see that he was reeling from her blow. "I'm trying to find a way to get rid of that blasted animal. If your mother won't call it off, we'll get rid of it ourselves. I have an idea, but I need to find out more, okay?"

"Okay," Kestrel whispered, her mouth dry.

"In the meantime," he said, "promise that you won't come after me. I know what you're like. Remember when you hid in my bag when you were only tiny?"

"I started laughing," said Kestrel. "You had to take me back."

"None of that now," he said. "Promise you won't come after me."

"Why do I have to promise?"

"Just making sure," he said, and hugged her tight. "Off with you now."

"Dad—"

He gave her a small shove, but his size meant that it was like being pushed by a bear. She stumbled toward the dog, which jumped up and ran a ring around her, tripping her. Kestrel jumped to her feet.

"Wait!" she yelled, but her dad was already striding into the trees, his traps clanking.

She heard a sneeze behind her and turned quickly. The villagers were everywhere, half hidden, staring through the cracks in their doors or paused in the gaps between houses. They'd all come out to listen to the argument.

Her mother was there, too, watching Kestrel from her doorway with a contemptuous look on her face.

Anger bubbled up in her, an unstoppable force that made her head hot and her hands cold.

"What did you say to him?" Kestrel growled.

She marched toward her mother with no idea of what she was going to do, but the black dog ran in front of her, blocking her path. Kestrel tried to dodge it but it was too fast, and a single nip sent her sprawling on the ground.

The dog turned to Kestrel's mother, looking for approval. Without thinking, rage still coursing through her bones, Kestrel launched herself at it with a snarl.

She landed on its back. The dog yelped, and Kestrel managed to twist one of its ears when her mother issued a short, sharp scream. The dog threw Kestrel off, running into the house, past her mother, who was holding the side of her face. Her skin was red and blotchy.

"Oh," Kestrel breathed, regret coursing through her instantly.

The villagers had come to the same conclusion as Kestrel and stared at the black dog with a newfound curiosity. They leaned out to gape openly. Even Mardy stepped outside.

Her mother blinked in shock. Kestrel's heart began to beat wildly, but she didn't move. Instead she held her breath and waited. She waited for her bones to crack, for her blood to turn into acid.

Runo and Briar clutched each other gleefully. Briar whispered something in her brother's ear, and he snorted with laughter.

Her mother twitched. Then, quick as a flash, she reached into the house and grabbed a handful of wool. A small white baby tooth was knotted into it.

Something terrible was going to happen. Kestrel bit down a cry and braced herself, waiting for the pain to begin.

Her mother knotted the wool between her fingers, trapping the baby tooth inside. Then she clenched her fist.

There was a scream from the well. Kestrel turned so fast her hair flew in front of her face. Runo was on the floor, screeching, his right leg bent at a funny angle. Briar wailed and bent down toward him, but then Kestrel's mother dropped the tangle of wool with the tooth inside, and stamped on it.

Runo shuddered, as though he'd been stamped on himself,

and screamed again. It was so long and loud it made Kestrel's teeth ache. Briar leaped back, horrified.

"Don't forget what I can do!" her mother screamed at the village. None of them dared look at her. Her voice was high and cut through the echo of Runo's sobs. She licked her lips, then stared at Kestrel.

"Mushrooms," she said. "I want food. *Now.*"

Kestrel's mother picked up the wool and stepped inside, slamming the door shut. Kestrel's legs gave way. She sat down, shaking with a horrible, curdled combination of fear and relief. The villagers disappeared into the depths of their houses. Everyone left except Runo and Briar. Briar was trying to pick him up, desperately hissing at him to move.

It took a moment for Kestrel to understand that she wasn't going to get hurt. She ran over to the well.

"Is Runo all right?" Kestrel asked breathlessly. He was clutching his leg and making terrible sniveling noises.

"Don't you dare," Briar said coldly. Her usual sneer was gone.

"I thought she'd hurt *me*," Kestrel said weakly. "I wouldn't have attacked the dog, otherwise."

"You're her daughter," Briar snorted. "You can do what you want. You'll always be safe from her." She finally dragged Runo to his feet. "But you won't be safe from us," she added coldly, turning away.

Kestrel wanted to tell Briar that it wasn't true, that her own punishment was coming later, but Briar was already leading Runo away, limping.

Kestrel stared at them as they retreated, her eyes prickling. *Stupid tears.*

She felt something scratch her leg. She bent down and picked Pippit up, trying very hard not to sniff.

"Mushrooms," Pippit reminded her. "Get mushrooms or Nasty does a bad."

Pippit was right. If her mother didn't have mushrooms in the next twenty minutes, she'd go crazy. Maybe she'd hurt someone else.

Kestrel moved quietly through the trees with Pippit clinging to her head, while he quietly muttered about mushrooms and snacks. She found a tree stump covered in quietly squirming fungi and dug around for a stick she could use to knock them off. The last time she touched them, they tried to eat her fingers.

A branch snapped. Kestrel looked up, her fingers tightening around her spoon.

"Finn?" she said doubtfully. Deep down, she knew Finn wouldn't come this far into the forest alone—at least not on the ground.

She saw something move in the trees to her right. She quickly turned to face it, taking care not to make any sound. Fifty paces away, two bright yellow eyes hovered in the air.

They blinked out immediately, as though the creature hadn't meant to be seen. Kestrel stared at the space where they had been, dread oozing through her body. She had a terrible feeling about the eyes. Were they following her? She reached for her slingshot, but her hand closed on her notebook instead, and she cursed inwardly. She kept forgetting that she'd lost it.

Kestrel fumbled for her spoon instead. She crept toward the space where the eyes had been. She could see a dark outline standing in the trees, as though the creature had turned its back. Kestrel's blood raced as she approached. Then, when she was only a few paces away, it fled, and before she knew what was happening, it was in the trees behind her instead. It was so *fast*. She whirled around to face it, but it moved again, so she could only catch a glimpse of its shadowy outline.

The creature was circling her like a wolf.

"What are you?" Kestrel snapped. "What do you *want*?"

But the creature was already gone. It had disappeared into the forest with the silence of a moth.

Kestrel slowly slid her spoon into her pocket, still staring after it. Her hand touched an empty space, and she stopped breathing. Something was missing. She checked again, touching all her pockets, then digging her hands into them. But she could feel its absence like a missing limb

Her notebook was gone. It had been there just moments

before. Kestrel looked around desperately, scanning the ground all around her, but there was no sign of it.

"Where did it go, Pip?" she said, feeling her throat constrict.

The answer was bearing down on her like a landslide. She tried not to think about it, but the answer was so big, so horrible, it was almost impossible to ignore.

The thing with yellow eyes had stolen it.

"Grurbbb," squeaked Pippit, and she couldn't suppress her thoughts any longer.

Kestrel's legs turned to jelly. She felt a huge, hollow emptiness, that horrible absence of feeling that comes before a life-changing storm. For a short second Kestrel wondered if this was a grabber she knew, one that had escaped her clutches during a hunt. But this one had no body. It was as insubstantial as air.

And it had taken her notebook.

Everything that had happened to her, every horror she had ever faced, in one heartbeat became as insignificant and tiny as a black beetle with a broken wing.

The feeling began as a slow trickle, then it turned into a flood, and within moments it was crushing her, stopping her breathing and forcing her to the ground as her heart tripped and sputtered. She lost all the feeling in her arms and legs. Her bones were bending and splitting. Her fingers were breaking one by one. Her whole body was falling apart.

Her grabber was building its body.

Kestrel was going to die.

She tried to put her hands around her fear, to squash it and destroy it, but for the first time it was too big for her and it swallowed her whole.

POWER IN TEETH

Kestrel didn't know whether seconds or minutes had passed, but slowly, piece by piece, she came back to herself. She was sitting on the ground, her knees drawn up to her eyes and her hands around her legs, staring into the dark space between her feet and the dirt. Pippit was urgently bumping his head against her face, trying to make her move.

She was furious with herself for sitting there like a stupid lump, a big, obvious target for anything that wanted to eat her. She saw the flash of a tail, growled, and lobbed a rock at the animal in the trees. It gave a satisfying yelp and ran away, squeaking like an old door.

Kestrel hauled herself to her feet. Her heartbeat had slowed, but her arms were numb and heavy, as though all the blood had been sucked out of them.

"Weak," Kestrel whispered, anger sloshing between her ribs. Granmos would be ashamed to see her sitting on the ground in the middle of the forest, shivering like a baby. "Get a grip!"

She pressed her fingers over her eyes and tried to decide what to do next. Her head was a jumble of words and pictures, each of them with a wavering yellow eye planted in the middle.

Go back to the village, moron, her head said.

"Okay," Kestrel said obediently, wondering if she was mad. She touched the place where her grandma's notebook usually was and felt another pang of shock when it wasn't there.

She walked shakily through the trees. Pippit dug his claws into her shoulder and crouched low. With every step she took, the question *what will my grabber look like?* thumped in her head, and each time she swept it away before she could think of the answer.

She asked herself what her gran would do. And she knew: Granmos would ask questions. She would gather evidence, look at her options, and decide what to do next. She wouldn't make the same mistake as the villagers, who shut themselves away when things went missing, who locked their doors and never said a word. She would pull on her big, tattered coat made of rags, light her pipe, and make a plan.

And at least Kestrel had an advantage: Her eyes were sharp enough that she'd caught the grabber lurking. Most of the villagers didn't see their grabbers at all, until the end, so it was easier for them to pretend that nothing was happening.

But you did the same thing, didn't you? said a nasty little voice in the back of her head. When her slingshot had disappeared she'd brushed it aside, but what if her grabber had it? It could have been following her for days. Even the Briny Witch had noticed that something was following her.

She shivered. Maybe she was the same as everyone else. Nobody, not a single person, had escaped from their grabber once it had chosen its final form. What if Kestrel couldn't fight hers? What if it was so terrifying that she couldn't even move?

She was scared, she was *really* scared, and she had no idea what to do. She had a choice: Kill her grabber when it had a body and came for her, or escape the forest before it could catch her.

Kestrel knew what Granmos would say. She was a hunter. Her job was to fight. Maybe this time she'd kill a grabber before it fed. But when she started to wonder what form the grabber would take, she crushed the thought immediately.

She didn't want to find out.

"I'll discover a way out of the forest," she said with false confidence. Her voice helped drive the darkness away. "I'll find my grandma's grabber, and my mum will call off the dog, and I'll be able to leave. Easy."

But even if she got what she wanted, she'd be doing something terrible. Escaping meant abandoning everyone to their own grabbers. She'd have to find her dad and persuade him to come with her. And she had to find a way out of the never-ending forest, which suddenly felt as impossible as telling a moth to carry a suitcase.

Kestrel stopped. She realized she'd been walking for too long; she should have hit the village by now. She closed her eyes and sniffed the air, but she couldn't detect the usual smokiness of the wolf fire.

"I've gone the wrong way," she said bitterly, fighting the urge to kick something. What was wrong with her? She couldn't let herself get distracted by the grabber. She closed her eyes and leaned her head against the nearest tree, and seconds later it began to snow.

"Pffft," Pippit said. "Pffft."

A thin layer of snow was already covering his fur. He shook himself, but within moments it settled back on him.

"Pffft," he said again, then looked at her so pathetically that she had to hide a snort of laughter.

"You're meant to be a fearsome hunter," she reminded him, picking him up and bringing him to eye level. He ran up her sleeve, dragging wet snow with him. Kestrel yelped and tried to shake him out, but he popped out by her neck and planted himself there with an air of satisfaction.

"Not moving," he said.

She shielded her eyes from the snow. At least she felt better when Pippit was with her. "Let's try this way."

She started walking again, but she couldn't get her

bearings. The more she tried to concentrate, the more she thought about her grabber instead. As the snow swirled around her face Kestrel began to shiver uncontrollably. Her brain was playing tricks on her. She saw the wide, bright eyes of the grabber in every chink of light that came from the stars. She saw its shadowy, unformed body behind every tree she passed. It was going to grow and twist and change—so what part of its body was her notebook going to be? What would *it* be? Would it look like—?

Kestrel stamped on the thought as hard as she could, and wrapped her arms around herself.

Seconds later Kestrel's foot plunged into a stream. She yelped and tried to step back. Something snatched at her ankle, and she slipped and landed with her chin in the water. Bits of gravel tumbled past her, catching her on the cheek and making her face sting as she floundered. Cold water sloshed through her clothes, and chunks of ice swirled around her.

"Brrr," Pippit warbled miserably as Kestrel finally scrambled to her feet, her heart pounding.

She stumbled to the other side of the stream, then hesitated and looked back at the water. She was sure something had caught her ankle on purpose. For a moment she couldn't see anything except frothy scum and swirling clumps of snow. Then the face of the Briny Witch floated into view, spinning on the surface of the water so fast she felt dizzy.

"What do you want?" Kestrel snapped, embarrassed by how relieved she was that it wasn't her grabber.

"I just wanted to say hello," the Briny Witch gurgled, sounding very far away. "Have you reconsidered my offer? You know your time's running out now."

"No," Kestrel said, stepping away. But even as she spoke she was imagining the help he could give in return for her eyes, and before she knew it the words were out of her mouth. "Can you tell me how to get rid of my grabber?"

"You can't," he said, grinning nastily.

"Fine," Kestrel snapped. "Can you at least tell me where my grandma's grabber is?"

The Briny Witch laughed, as though she'd just said something very funny, his face still swirling in the eddies of the water.

"All right," she said sourly. "Then I don't need you." She splashed her hand in the water, scattering the image of his smirking face.

Kestrel turned back and tried to retrace her steps, but her footprints were filling in with snow. She started to hurry, tripping over tree roots in her haste. She was close to screaming with frustration when she heard a high-pitched whistle above her. The sound made her heart leap into her throat, and she fumbled to reach her spoon, but Pippit dug his claws into her shoulder and chattered excitedly.

"Snacks!" he shouted, which could only mean one person.

Kestrel's heart leaped. There was a fraying rope wound tightly around a nearby tree. She scrambled up, her fingers numb with cold. She found Finn sitting in a cocoon made of blankets with a lantern wedged between his knees.

Finn's face cracked into a grin when he saw her, and despite the guilt and the deep terror lurking inside her, she felt herself do the same.

"I thought I heard you stamping around," he said as she sat down with him, knee to knee. "Why do you look so pale?"

"I'm so glad you're here," Kestrel said, the words falling out of her mouth before she could stop herself. "I've seen my—"

She was about to tell him about the grabber, but as soon as the thought crossed her mind she knew that it was a terrible idea. She could see his face now. He'd run away from her. He'd be too scared to talk to her. He didn't even like it when she mentioned her grandma's grabber.

"My dad," she said, feeling wretched.

"Gruh!" Pippit said loudly, but Kestrel clamped her hand over his mouth and pushed him into her hood.

"Did Hannah go back?" Kestrel added, eyeing the trees. Hannah was the last person she wanted to deal with right now.

"Oh, yeah. She said trees were cold and dirty." He shrugged.

"Maybe she's scared of snow," Kestrel said, feeling a tiny

bit pleased. Hannah seemed like the kind of person to hide under the bed when the snow came, just because it brought monsters like ice ghasts and poisonous white spiders.

"Not like us," said Finn

"Obviously," Kestrel agreed. She touched her pocket, only to be reminded her grandma's notebook wasn't there. Her fingers curled up with panic. It came on suddenly, with the same physical pain as a stomach cramp. She couldn't afford to take her mind off her grabber for a single moment; it could strike whenever she wasn't looking, stealing her things to make its body.

"You look like you're going to throw up," Finn said. Something about him didn't look right, but Kestrel felt too distracted to work out what.

"I'm okay," Kestrel said, pushing a piece of hair away from her damp forehead. "I'm glad I found you. We need to keep exploring."

"Let's talk about it tomorrow," said Finn, yawning.

"We can't wait!" Kestrel said insistently, making Finn jump. "The Gulping Pond's next on the list," she continued, swallowing the lump in her throat. She wondered if she sounded as panicked as she felt. "It sounds interesting. We could go now."

She could feel her heart hammering again.

"Are you crazy?" Finn said. "We'll get buried in snow We'll be eaten by ghosts. We'll drown in a bog. It's *dark*."

"We haven't been trying hard enough to find a way out," she said. "We'll never escape if we don't push ourselves."

"We are trying," said Finn, taking a shriveled plum out of his pocket. Pippit's head swiveled toward it. "We go exploring nearly every day, don't we?"

"But..." Kestrel said.

Finn stretched the blanket over his head and proffered it to her. She took it gingerly but didn't wrap it around her. She didn't like not being able to see the forest.

"We can look at your notebook now if you want," Finn said peaceably. "We can plan our route to the Gulping Pond."

"I...left my notebook in the burrow," she said lamely.

Finn looked bewildered.

"But I remember nearly everything in it," Kestrel added quickly.

"Let's just skip the exploring for a bit," said Finn. "We could build snow-wolves instead. Or hunt for more weird junk in the forest."

"C'mon, Finn," she said. "This isn't a game."

"What's the point if we're not having fun?"

"To get out!" Kestrel said frantically.

"Well, *yeah*," he said, and shoved the plum into his mouth. Kestrel felt her face crumple, and Finn blinked. "Is something wrong?" he asked.

Yes! she screamed in her head.

"No," she said, thinking the word would crack under the weight of her lie. Finn looked relieved.

"Okay," he said. "Want a plum?"

Pippit dove into his pocket headfirst. As Finn wrestled with him, trying to pull him out of his pocket before all the fruit was devoured, Kestrel looked out at the snow. Stupid, horrible tears were pricking at her eyelids again. She never used to cry at all. Granmos would be horrified. She wiped her eyes on her sleeve and gritted her teeth.

"I just want to get out of here," she said. "I've never wanted it more."

"So do I," said Finn. He'd given up trying to save his fruit. "I know we'll find it one day."

Pippit spat a plum stone out, and it ricocheted off the tree. Finn ducked his head to avoid it, and Kestrel saw him in a streak of moonlight.

She realized why Finn looked strange. He was wearing a new sweater. It was the first time she'd seen him in anything that didn't have holes, although the sleeves drooped over his hands, and it was so long he'd pulled it over his feet. Kestrel recognized it at once. It had belonged to the woodchopper.

Without warning Finn reached out and pulled her into a hug. Kestrel stiffened in surprise, then relaxed into his bony arms. It was like being hugged by a pile of twigs. She could smell wood chips and sausages. She wiped her running nose on his shoulder.

"Don't be sad," Finn said.

"Okay," Kestrel said, surprised by his grown-up tone.

A wolf's howl cut through the night. Finn jumped, knocking the lantern out of the tree so they were plunged into darkness. Pippit was on Kestrel's shoulder in an instant, his warm breath tickling her ear.

They were all frozen in silence, and Kestrel was just starting to breathe again when they heard a second howl, then a third, then countless more all merging into a violent cacophony of noise.

"They're talking to one another," Kestrel said, her blood turning cold. "They're hunting something big."

They all knew what it was even before Pippit spoke.

"Trapper!" he cried.

For a second Kestrel was frozen, her thoughts grinding to a sudden, panicked halt. Then she hurled herself from the tree, crashing through the branches until she hit the ground. She scrambled up and pounded toward the noise. She couldn't see a thing, but instinct drove her through the trees in seconds. She didn't care how many wolves there were. Her dad was in trouble.

Kestrel was just about to plunge into the thick, thorny undergrowth when the black dog ran from the shadows and launched itself at her. A huge tangle of teeth and claws and fur hit her from the side.

She landed with her left arm twisted painfully beneath her. She felt a huge, crushing weight on her chest. She screamed with rage and tried to throw the black dog off, but it dug its teeth into her elbow, right into the joint. Pippit cried out and tried to bite the dog, but it knocked him away with a single swipe.

Something crashed through the trees above them, and Kestrel saw Finn scrambling through the leaves, the blanket still caught around his ankle.

"Kes!" he called.

"Hide!" she shouted. But it was too late. The dog had already seen him.

Kestrel wriggled out from underneath the dog, but it didn't attack her again. Instead, it took another long, hard look at Finn, as though making a decision. Then it rolled its tongue around its mouth and dropped something on the ground. Kestrel held her breath. It was dark, but she could just make it out: a piece of brown cloth.

"Is that from my dad's coat?" she breathed. "Have you seen him?"

The dog picked it up again and jerked its head, as though it wanted her to follow.

"Do you know where he is?" she asked, her voice breaking. "Show me!"

The dog started to run. Kestrel had no idea why it was helping her, but she didn't have time to worry about that now. She took off after it, Finn's and Pippit's shouts fading behind them.

She followed the dog through the trees, crashing back through the stream, plowing through the deepening snow. It took her a few minutes to realize they were going back toward the village.

"Wait!" she yelled. "Hang on!"

But the dog didn't slow down, and she was afraid to lose him. She bolted straight into the village, following it all the way to her mother's door. For a moment she wondered if he was inside, if he'd fled back to the village to hide from a pack of ravenous wolves.

The door to her mother's house was already open. Her mother was sitting in the middle of the room, cross-legged, wool twined between her outstretched fingers.

Kestrel followed the dog inside, gasping for breath. The dog trotted up to her mother and dropped the piece of cloth in front of her. She inspected it, then gave a sudden, strangled cackle.

She was *laughing*.

The door slammed behind them. The dog lay down beside her mother, grinning. Only then did Kestrel realize she'd been tricked.

"Clever boy," her mother crooned, scratching the dog

between the ears. The piece of cloth dissolved into the floor. Kestrel tried to grab it, but her fingers met bare wood. "What a good idea. You've got brains, haven't you?"

The dog growled, and her mother's fingers paused between its ears. She was listening to what it was saying.

Kestrel tried to back toward the door, but the dog stood up, ready to pounce. One bite and all the blood would drain from her body.

Her mother's stare crawled all over her like a nest of ants.

"Where were you sprinting off to in the dark, all alone?" her mother asked, although it was clear from her tone that she knew exactly what was happening. "You know you're not allowed to do that. You were *supposed* to be getting me mushrooms, and you disappeared, you ungrateful wretch." She scratched the dog again, and it gave a low, happy rumble. "It's a good thing the dog keeps an eye on you. We can't have you running after wolves every time they make a bit of noise."

With every long second that oozed by, Kestrel knew the wolves' teeth could be around her dad's neck. She squeezed her eyes closed and tried to concentrate on her mother.

"Dad's being chased by them," Kestrel said, ignoring the taste of blood in her mouth. "He needs help."

"What makes you think it's a wolf?" her mother asked softly, and the truth hit Kestrel like a sack of bricks.

The wolves weren't howling because they had him by the throat.

They were celebrating because something else did.

Kestrel threw herself at her mother. The black dog barreled into her back, knocking her flat against the floor, but it didn't stop her kicking and screaming. "You saw it in the weave! His grabber is after him. And you made him go back into the forest!"

"That was his choice," her mother said dangerously. "He wouldn't be any safer in the village."

"That's a lie!" she shouted. "If he stayed here, I could have helped!"

"Lower your voice," her mother said, so calmly that Kestrel instantly went still.

"Down," her mother said to the dog, but Kestrel stayed there, her cheek pressed against the cool of the floor, her face burning.

Kestrel waited for the dog to bite her, but to her surprise, it never did.

"I'll let you go after your father, if that's what you want," her mother said. "But first you have to make me a promise."

Kestrel raised herself to her knees, spitting splinters. "Whatever you want, I'll do it."

Her mother twitched an eyebrow, looking just a tiny bit impressed.

"I asked you once if you were friends with that boy," her mother said. "You lied to me."

"So?" said Kestrel fiercely.

Her mother reached up and plucked something from the weave. She held a small incisor tooth between her thumb and forefinger, making sure Kestrel could see it properly. Scratched into the back in tiny, cramped letters was *Finnigan*.

Kestrel didn't dare move. She felt like one small breath might shatter everything.

"It would take me three seconds to stop the poor boy's heart," she said matter-of-factly. "Imagine that–he'd be sitting in a tree, with all the joy of the world in him, and suddenly..."

She held the tooth delicately, almost lovingly. Finally, after a horribly long time, her mother closed her fist around it and slipped it into her pocket.

"We'll make a real bargain, this time," her mother said. "One with consequences. You will never, ever speak to that feral boy again. You'll no longer have anything to do with him."

Kestrel stared at her. She felt dizzy. She didn't know what to say.

"I don't know how to make it any clearer, Kestrel," her mother snapped, grabbing her arm so hard Kestrel cried out. "I have his teeth, and I will *not* hesitate to remove him from this earth if you speak a single word to him!"

"Mum," Kestrel begged, trying to twist her arm away.

"In return I'll call off the dog, and you can go after your father," her mother said, calm again. "Come, now. It's not like he's a good friend. Isn't he spending an awful lot of time with the woodchopper's daughter? Sweet girl. Beautiful face." She saw Kestrel's expression and smiled wickedly.

Kestrel shook her head fiercely. "I can give you something better," she said. "I can clean and make food and—"

"I don't want anything else," said her mother. "Only to help you. Get rid of him, and you'll be stronger and more fearsome than ever."

Her mother released her grip, but Kestrel felt like she was being crushed by the tiny house. The weave was everywhere, tangled into her hair, pressed against her mouth and nose. Without thinking, she slipped her hand into her pocket and wrapped her fingers around the holey stone.

"What do you say?" her mother asked. "Are you ready to grow up and leave your childish ways behind?"

Kestrel closed her eyes and tried to force the words out of her mouth. She almost failed. Then she heard the triumphant crowing of the wolves, their howls moving farther away. She released the stone.

"Yes," Kestrel whispered.

"Show me," her mother said, tapping her own cheek.

Slowly, Kestrel leaned forward and kissed her mother on the cheek. Her skin was dry and soft, as though there was no bone beneath it. She hadn't kissed her mother in a long time. Maybe even since her grandma was taken.

"Bless you, child," her mother whispered. "We'll make a hunter of you yet."

Kestrel stepped back, suppressing the urge to wipe her lips.

"Dog!" her mother called, beckoning. "Come here!"

The black dog oozed over to her. Its ears were folded back, and its tail was between its legs. It looked as though it knew exactly what was about to happen.

"This is final," her mother said.

"I know," said Kestrel.

Her mother's fingers flew over the piece of black string, tying a huge knot in the middle. The dog jerked twice like it was being kicked, then it keeled over and lay on its side, breathing gently, its tail twitching in some kind of dream.

"Come back to me as soon as you're done," her mother said curtly, "or Finn dies anyway. Go."

"Thank you," Kestrel gasped, and fled.

Finn was waiting in the trees, a limp and sodden Pippit in his hand. Pippit twisted out of his grasp and ran to Kestrel, shooting up her leg and licking the side of her face with his tiny, sandpapery tongue.

"What happened?" Finn said worriedly, looking around for the dog. "Kes?"

"Not now," she choked, stuffing Pippit into her pocket.

"Wait!" he shouted, but she was already away, plunging into the forest again, her heart cracking in a dozen places.

Nettles whipped her legs and sharp stones pierced the soles of her boots, but nothing would slow her down. She ignored the hot, ragged pain in her chest. She had to get to her dad before it was too late. She had to kill the grabber before it took him.

She ran toward the tree-covered hill that the wolves' howls had come from. The forest grew darker and danker, the ground squelchy and moist underfoot. There was moss everywhere, and the earth smelled rich and boggy.

A wolf howled on the hill above her. Kestrel deflated. It felt like everything was leaking from her in one huge *whoosh*. The fear that she had been holding back since she left the village oozed out of every pore like little black worms.

She wished that Finn was here with her. She wished that she was back in the moment before the wolves howled, when her face was pressed into his sweater and everything felt just a tiny bit better.

Without warning she remembered what Finn had tried to say the other day, when she was after the woodchopper's grabber, and suddenly she understood.

It's just that I—

"I care about him, too, Pip," said Kestrel, feeling awful and empty. "He knows that, right?"

Pippit didn't say anything. Kestrel shook her head, took one last deep breath, and braced herself.

She was ready.

THE BLIND WOLF

Kestrel scrambled up a viciously steep hill, following the tracks left by her father and his grabber. From his deep footprints, and the ones right behind his, she could see he was being chased. The grabber had four footprints and lots of claws. Every time her dad's footprints changed direction Kestrel's heart leaped into her throat, wondering if they would suddenly disappear, if the grabber had caught up with him *here* or *here*. But they kept going, on and on, as though the grabber had kept just missing him.

Pippit sat on the crown of her head, muttering urgently under his breath.

"Bad smell," he said, unhappily scratching his head with his back leg.

Kestrel could smell it, too: a sweet, cloying scent that stuck to the back of her throat. It was getting stronger the farther they went.

The hill kept rising steeply in front of them, as though the forest was trying to climb into the sky. Kestrel stumbled to a halt in front of a thick wall of trees. A great, gulping silence fell over them. The sweetness was so thick she could almost chew it.

"Something's wrong," she whispered.

"There," said Pippit, twitching.

There was something human-shaped lurking in the shadows behind the trees, not hidden quite well enough to escape her sharp eyes. She had a dark, worried feeling in her gut, the kind that tells you it's a great time to start running in the opposite direction.

Maybe it was her father's grabber, lying in wait. Kestrel gritted her teeth and crept closer.

Suddenly, the thing dodged away from her, a long brown coat flapping through the trees.

"Dad!" she screamed, her heart racing. "Dad, it's me! It's Kestrel!"

Her dad stopped and turned. He looked at her for a second, as though he wasn't sure what to do; then he pounded toward her in his heavy boots.

"Kestrel!" he shouted, flying toward her.

"Dad!" she said when he reached her, trying to hold back a big, childish sob. She ran into his arms and he held her tightly. "I thought your grabber had you."

"I gave it the slip," he said, looking around. "It won't be gone for long. Follow me!"

"Wait," she gasped. She wanted to cling on to him just for a few more seconds, to make sure she wasn't dreaming, but he was already running.

Kestrel scrambled after him. He wasn't wearing any of the metal traps that usually swung around his waist, or the fringe of teeth that decorated his hat. He must have shed them for speed. That's why he'd lost his grabber, Kestrel thought; he was cleverer than the other villagers. A huge bubble of joy swelled inside her. And now he had her. He was going to survive.

"Where are we going?" she asked between breaths, trying to keep up with him. They slipped between two gnarled trees.

"We've got to hide."

"But we could fight—"

"Quiet, Kestrel."

The snap in his voice stung. Before Kestrel could say anything, her dad grasped her wrist. His grip was strong, and he hauled her through the trees so fast her feet barely touched the floor.

"Dad, you're hurting me," she gasped as she went flying over the rocks.

"Quickly!" he insisted.

They emerged in a small hollow. Trees crowded around it

like a wall, and dead needles made a bristling carpet on the floor. Kestrel's dad released her and bent over to catch his breath.

"Tell me what happened," she demanded.

"There's so much," he said, his face falling.

He dropped to his knees. Kestrel, her bravery crumbling, ran into his arms. She was cold and tired and any minute now the grabber would be on their trail.

"I'll get it," she said fiercely. "I'll kill your grabber before it has a chance to blink."

Her dad hugged her tight. Kestrel sagged and breathed in deeply, longing for the smell of dirt and old wool and wolf blood.

But her dad stank like rotting flowers.

Kestrel gagged. She tried to twist her face to the side, so she could breathe, but her dad's fingers dug in too tight.

"Stupid little girl," her dad said, his voice twisting in the middle, changing into something new.

Kestrel screamed. She looked up, then wished that she hadn't.

The creature she was hugging wasn't her dad; it wasn't even human. It had a bald, liver-spotted head and a blurry face that looked like a painting half rubbed out. She tried to focus on its nose, but her eyes kept sliding away from it, as though there was nothing to see. It only had the shadow of a face, a blurry jumble that was impossible to look at without feeling like you were sliding sideways.

"Let's have a look," the creature said as she struggled. It grasped her hair, peeling her away just enough that it could see her properly. "Not bad. I've, *ha*, outdone myself."

Kestrel did the only thing possible, which was to spit at it. The creature disgustedly pushed her away and wiped its face. It shrugged off her dad's brown coat, which slumped to the ground like it had fainted.

"Where's my dad?" Kestrel shouted, bunching her fists.

"The hunter?" it said. It sneered despite its lack of a discernible face. "I don't know. I just took his things."

Now Kestrel could see the creature properly. It had long, pale legs, jutting knees, and stumpy feet with ingrown toenails. Its arms were similarly long. Its fingers were twice the length of Kestrel's, and it had no thumbs. Its skin was greasy and pale like an uncooked sausage.

The weird, cloying smell should have warned her that she was walking into a trap, but she'd been stupid. Granmos had written about these creatures. The words unfurled in front of her eyes like long, spidery streamers.

Their sweete smelle makes you sicke, and they can transform to look like someone you trust. They steal body partes from you, and use it for their terrible magic, in whiche they controle youre body and minde. With an iteme of clothinge, they can wear any face for a shorte while. Be warned, for they are lazey and wille make you their slave.

"Face painter," said Kestrel. She swallowed a wave of nausea. "You're a thief and a liar. You stole my dad's coat and changed your face to look like him."

The face painter might have been grinning, but she only had the impression of countless yellow teeth.

"I could wear his face all day long if I wanted," it said. "All I need is a body part, and I'd have his looks forever. You're lucky I only borrowed his coat. Bones are much better."

"Don't you dare," Kestrel growled, boiling with rage.

The face painter snorted, and Kestrel launched herself at it. She hit the face painter square in the chest, and it fell backward with a cry.

She reached for her spoon. But the face painter grabbed her hands with surprising strength and pinned her to the ground.

"My mother will find you!" Kestrel cried, wriggling uselessly under its impressive weight. "She lives in the village, and she has an awful black dog with teeth like a mincing machine. She'll rip you apart!"

The face painter, still holding her down, looked at her with new interest.

"I've heard of her," it said. "And you're the daughter who hunts? That's, *ha,* fascinating."

"Yeah!" said Kestrel, hiding her surprise. "So you'd better let me go right now!"

The face painter grabbed her hair and tore a clump out. Kestrel yelped in pain, but then it relaxed its grip on her. She backed away quickly. The face painter twirled the strands of hair between its fingers, grinning as Kestrel ran toward the trees.

With every second that passed she knew that her dad was closer to being eaten by his grabber. Pippit poked his head out of her pocket, wiffling his nose, picking up the trail again.

The face painter muttered something under its breath, then there was a short, sharp pain between her ears as though someone had pinched her brain.

Snap.

Kestrel stumbled to a halt and looked around, blinking at the unfamiliar cage of trees. Why was she in a clearing? Where was she going? She tried to grab hold of her memories, but they slipped away like water. The last thing she could recall was talking to Finn in the tree, the snow swirling around them. Why couldn't she remember why she was here?

"Kes?" Pippit hissed.

Kestrel turned around. She saw a creature with a blank, smirking face and pale, greasy skin. She took a step back, catching a scream in her throat. The faceless creature snorted with laughter.

"What are you?" she asked sharply, but it didn't reply. Kestrel felt a bolt of panic, and marched toward it with her spoon out. "Where am I?"

She raised the spoon, but the creature snatched it away and put it in its pocket. "Don't get angry," it said. "I'm only tinkering with your brain." It twirled something between its fingers, and Kestrel recognized it as a clump of her hair.

Face painters, her grandma had said in the notebook. *They steal body partes from you, and use it for their terrible magic.* Kestrel snarled.

"Tinkering? You're using magic to steal my memory," she spat. "Tell me why I'm here!"

Pippit nipped her hand. "Trapper!" he hissed. Kestrel felt a pang of fear. Something was wrong. Something to do with her dad. But what? She had to find him.

The face painter twirled the clump of her hair in its fingers again, sneering with its empty face.

"Don't even think about leaving," it said. "If you leave this clearing I'll tie another knot and make you forget even more. I'll make you forget how to survive the forest. You'll be dead within seconds. You're my slave now."

Deep in the forest, a wolf howled and was echoed by a dozen more. The face painter grinned, tapping the spoon in its pocket, reminding her that she had no weapon.

At least, that's what it thought.

Kestrel opened her mouth and loosed a huge, teeth-shaking

howl that made the face painter clap its hands over it ears. She did it exactly how her dad had taught her, bending her voice in the same way the wolves did when they found food. It echoed through the trees and sank into the depths of the forest.

"What was that for?" the face painter snapped.

Kestrel flexed her fingers, willing the wolves to hear her. For a moment it seemed that nothing was going to happen. Then softly, something padded out of the woods behind her, its paws crunching over the ground. The breeze stirred, and she caught a whiff of something animal, something dirty and hungry and bloody.

The face painter's expression changed.

On the other side of the hollow, standing in the shadows, was a tall and bony wolf. The wolf's eyes were covered in a cloudy film. It looked half starved, and clumps of its fur were falling out. It had a slavering expression that screamed *I will eat the first thing I knock to the ground.*

The face painter silently backed away from her. Kestrel grinned triumphantly, then realized that she was standing between the wolf and the face painter, alone in the clearing.

"Oops," said Pippit.

The wolf sniffed the air, straining toward her. Kestrel scanned the ground, looking for something to defend herself with. Her eyes fell on her dad's coat, and she caught a faint whiff of blood and bacon. There was no time to question how it had gotten there. The wolf crouched, ready to pounce, whimpering excitedly.

It took a moment for the pieces to connect in her head. She grabbed the coat half a second before the wolf started running toward her and lobbed it at the face painter. The face painter caught it without thinking, bewildered.

The wolf twisted away from Kestrel in a blur of gray fur and leaped in the other direction. The face painter screamed and dropped the coat as the wolf's teeth snapped. The mangy wolf drew back, its mouth dripping red where it had sunk its teeth into the face painter's arm.

Kestrel grabbed a branch from the ground and held it in front of her, but the wolf wasn't interested in attacking her yet.

It flew for the face painter's throat. The face painter was strong and almost pushed it to the ground, but the wolf was starving and desperate and filled with fury, and it sunk its teeth into its neck.

The face painter gurgled, slumped to the ground, and fell still. The wolf dug its nose into the face painter's shoulder, then withdrew sharply, realizing it had made a mistake. It turned its attention to Kestrel. She backed away, grabbing a branch from the ground and holding it out in front of her.

"Good wolf," she said, digging her fingers into the heavy branch. Her shoulder was burning. "Enjoy your tasty treat. You don't want me. I'm just a—"

The wolf jumped. It flew toward her with its mouth open, a blur of teeth and tongue. Kestrel swung the branch without thinking. The wolf and the branch connected midair with a sharp *smack*, and the branch was knocked from her hands.

Kestrel readied herself for another attack, but the wolf was on the ground, breathing shallowly, a red patch on the side of its head.

Pippit charged over to it.

"Geddit!" he yelled, pulling out tufts of its fur.

"No!" Kestrel said, surprising herself by pulling him away.

Pippit gave her a look of pure disgust.

"It's just a mangy old wolf," she said. Really, the thought of killing something as it lay on the floor made her feel ill. Some hunter she was. "It probably won't last much longer anyway."

Kestrel leaned over the face painter's body and snatched her spoon from its hand. She ripped the clump of her hair from its fingers and pulled it to pieces, letting them fly away in the breeze.

Without warning, the face painter coughed and grabbed her ankle with astonishing strength. Kestrel screeched and tried to kick it away, but its fingers were locked tight.

"We're not done with each other yet," it wheezed. "I'm going to leave you a, *hnur*, gift. When I took your hair, I, *hnur*, saw a few things. Things you've forgotten. Shall I shake them loose?"

"Let me go!" Kestrel shouted, bending down to pry its fingers away.

The face painter grabbed her ear and pulled her head to the ground, holding her down with an iron-like grip. She struggled to get free, but the face painter inserted a long nail in her ear and wriggled it around.

"Get lost!" she yelled, wrenching its hand out.

Suddenly, the hand went limp. The face painter was dead. Kestrel jumped away and rubbed her ear, wishing she could unscrew it and wash it in boiling water.

Then she felt something like a cold stream trickling through her brain and pooling in the front of her head. Something in her head went *pop*, as though a bubble had burst.

And then she was no longer in the forest.

Kestrel was standing in her mother's house. There were cool hands on her shoulders, with red-stained fingernails and thick silver rings. *Granmos.* Kestrel looked out the window, straining to see into the dark forest.

They weren't alone. They hadn't been alone for weeks.

The shadows between the trees moved, and Kestrel caught her breath. A tall and nightmarish creature slowly emerged from them. He approached carefully, a large key swinging from his waist. Kestrel could see his yellow eyes shining like wet marbles. They were fixed on Kestrel's grandma.

"Grabber," Kestrel whispered as her grandma's stalker walked toward the house. She was gripped with the desperate urge to run away, but her grandma held her firmly in place. The grabber hadn't ever been this close before.

"That's right," her grandma whispered in her ear. "I met him a couple of weeks ago. I call him Horrow. That was my father's name. Suits him, doesn't it? Give him a wave, duck."

Kestrel raised her hand slowly, transfixed by the creature's half-dead face. It turned its head and stared at her.

Then, slowly, it raised its own hand.

And it waved back.

Kestrel opened her eyes. She was still in the face painter's clearing, but the vision had been so strong she could almost feel her grandma's hands on her shoulders.

"Kes?" Pippit mumbled in her ear. "Wot?"

"Nothing," Kestrel said, wriggling her finger in her ear. She was disturbed. It had felt so real it was almost like a memory, but she knew that she had *never* waved to her grandma's grabber. And it was impossible that the grabber had been there, fully formed, for weeks without attacking. Kestrel crumpled up the strange vision like a piece of unwanted paper and tossed it out of her mind.

"Trapper," Pippit urged, pushing his nose against her face. "Gruh!"

"Where's my dad?" Kestrel asked urgently, looking around. "What happened to him, Pip?"

Her gaze fell on her dad's coat, which was in a pile next to the dead face painter. Immediately her ear went *pop* again, and Kestrel's memory flooded back so fast she almost fell over.

She winced as she remembered falling from the tree, and the black dog standing over her. She'd followed the black dog to her mother's house and promised that she would never speak to Finn again . . . and she'd done it because something awful was happening.

In the distance, a dozen wolves howled in celebration. Kestrel felt all the warmth leave her bones.

Her dad was being chased by his grabber.

"Dad!" she yelped, dropping the coat. Panic swept over her. She had to catch up with him. Kestrel jumped over the face painter's body, making for the trees.

"Smell trail," Pippit said. "Still there. Trapper!"

"We're not too late," Kestrel said, dizzy with astonishment. "We're going to make it!"

They raced into the trees, leaving the dead monster and the stunned wolf behind them.

TERRIBLE HUNGER

Kestrel knew at once where her father had been. His footprints were stamped deep into the earth, running jaggedly from tree to tree as he tried to shake the grabber off. There were paw prints laid over the top of them, deep holes with an explosion of claw marks around each one.

But the grabber still hadn't caught him.

Her dad knew the forest too well to be easily cornered. Kestrel had never come so close to finding a grabber before it ate. She could tell from the way the grabber had weaved between the fallen trees and boulders that it was stretching the hunt out for as long as possible. She prayed it would continue to lag behind.

The trees were riddled with holes, and thick red bloodmoss covered the ground. It slid away from under her feet as she ran, revealing patches of black, wet mud.

"Noise," Pippit said, leaping to the top of a giant

mushroom. It bent slowly under his weight, and Kestrel grabbed him before he could fall off. "There!"

He was right. Kestrel had been breathing so hard she hadn't heard it, but there was a crackling sound in the trees to her right, perhaps only a hundred yards away. It was like something big was shifting its weight, purposeful and patient. Kestrel knew at once from the way the noise turned and quieted that it knew she was there.

"Do you think it's him?" she asked, dizzy with hope.

The hill flattened to a plateau. Kestrel wobbled to her feet, following the trail with Pippit in her arms. Her heart was hammering, but she made herself breathe deeply and evenly.

"Hide," Pippit said as they drew closer. He could feel the same chill in the air as her. "Run!"

"No," said Kestrel, sounding braver than she felt.

The trail was at an end. The ground was all torn up as though a great struggle had taken place, but there was no blood.

"Show yourself," she called, her voice bending and breaking, gripping her spoon. "I'm ready!"

"Kestrel!"

She heard her father's cry half a second before the shadows moved and his grabber lunged at her. She stumbled backward, surprised, and hit a tree. All she could make out was a swirling mass of teeth and raggedy fur, all pinned together with a low, rattling growl. She stabbed at it with her spoon, trying to catch its face, but it had fallen back again. It was the same color as the shadows and completely unmeasurable. Kestrel looked for a heart, an eye, anything that she could drive her blade into, but her hands were shaking, and the grabber was so big that she couldn't make sense of any of it, and the spoon was slipping in her grasp, and what on earth was she thinking anyway, fighting with a kitchen utensil?

"Kestrel!" her father yelled above her.

"Dad!" She wavered, then clenched her teeth against the tremble in her voice.

Her dad's huge hands closed around her wrist and hauled her into the tree. The grabber leaped and snapped its jaws at Kestrel's ankles, but she had already withdrawn them. Her dad was above her again, scrambling away from the grabber and onto a higher branch. Kestrel, shocked to her senses, clambered after him as the grabber took a chunk of wood out of the tree with its powerful jaws.

"What are you doing here?" her father said angrily as she hauled herself onto the branch, which creaked alarmingly under their weight.

"You promised your grabber wasn't after you," she snapped, even though it was the last thing that mattered right now.

"That was for your own good," he said, looking so furious she almost feared him more than the grabber.

"How long have you been here?" she asked, struggling to get the words out through the lump in her throat.

"Long enough to know I'm beaten," he said, his voice falling.

The grabber lunged at the tree, taking another chunk out of the wood and making it shake so hard Kestrel's teeth chattered. It drew back, paused, and lunged at the tree, then did it again, and again. As it struck over and over, Kestrel could see every bone and sinew, every piece of its terrible body.

The grabber had taken the shape of a wolf, the hugest wolf the forest had ever seen. Its backbone was a string of pearls tied together with fibrous weeds from a pond. Its paws were made from chicken bones, all clasped together with gristle from a cooking pot. Tatty fur was stuck to its ribs, partially wrapped around its innards: the lungs of a deer, the heart of a bear, and the stomach of a wolf.

Its eyes were large and white, plucked fresh and shining from something huge, with a yellow glow behind them. Its teeth were snatched from the mouth of a terrible fish, its jaws cracked from the body of an old boar. Its legs were made from shards of bark, which crackled as it moved. Its flanks were dripping with tattered rags. The grabber had risen from the belly of the forest, dragging with it all the fallen corpses it could find, taking their best and worst parts to create a body of sharp points and bristles.

"Dad," Kestrel said, trying to keep her voice light. She

couldn't stand how white and scared his face was. "You know when I stowed away in your bag?"

Her dad looked surprised. Then, to her relief, his lips twisted into a rueful smile.

"I do," he said.

"We were miles from home, but you marched me all the way back," she said, trying to keep her voice from shaking. "You didn't let go of my hand once. You were so mad none of the creatures dared come near you. I saw them cowering behind the trees."

Her father looked at the grabber again. Kestrel grabbed his sleeve and pulled him back to her.

"Look at me," she said fiercely. "I've still got the spoon you gave me. Before you marched me back you sharpened it and gave it to me. You had to tell me which end to hold. You said that if anything snuck up on me, I had to hit it hard. Do you remember?"

"You attacked a plant," he said.

"Well, yes," said Kestrel. "I thought it was a snake. But that's not the point."

"What is it, then?" he said.

"You taught me how to beat the forest," she said. "And I'm not stopping now for anything."

Her dad held her hand, his huge fingers wrapped around Kestrel's.

"That's not what I was trying to teach you," he said. "The

real moral of that story is that I'm your father, and it's my job to look after you. You have no idea how scared I was that day."

Kestrel shook her head. "I know I said you weren't brave," she said. "I didn't mean it."

"When did you get so old?" he asked.

"When you weren't looking," she said, the answer catching in her throat.

The grabber snarled and hurled itself against the tree, which shuddered with a horrible splintering sound. They both tightened their grip on each other, and Kestrel felt another white-hot bolt of fear. The grabber was drawing its attack out. She had no doubt that it could have leaped up and caught them both in its jaws by now, but for some reason it was trying to shake them out the tree. Almost as though it was having *fun*.

"Kestrel," her dad said, a new urgency in his voice. "I need you to promise you'll do something for me."

He said her name in the serious tone he only used when something very bad was happening. *Kestrel, your grandmother is dead. Kestrel, your mother and I are going our separate ways. Kestrel, I have to leave now.*

"What?" she said, dreading what would come next.

"I think I found a way to get rid of the black dog," he said. "You need to make your mother eat some bloodberries."

"What?" Kestrel said, stiffening in surprise. The grabber

ripped another piece of the tree off, and the sharp *crack* of the splintering trunk sent a cold shiver through her.

"They grow in a place called the Marrow Orchard," her dad said. His voice was low and fast. "I wanted to get them for you, but it's too late. You'll have to do it, but you can't go alone. It's heavily guarded. You need a distraction so that you can sneak in unseen."

Kestrel's stomach churned. Not the Marrow Orchard. Not that place right at the back of her grandma's notebook, on the page covered in purple fruit stains. Not the page with all those horrible drawings of teeth and bones and birds...

"I need to feed her some fruit?" Kestrel protested. "I don't see how that's going to help."

"Listen to me," he said. "If I remember what your grandma taught me, it's that the bloodberries weaken spells. The dog's one of your mother's spells, isn't it? It's got a body and sharp teeth, but it's not a real animal."

"Dad—"

"Kestrel, there are plenty of things I don't know about your mother," he said. "But I think she's hiding things. It's not just the dog you need to worry about." Sweat was beading on his forehead, and his eyes kept flicking to the grabber below them. He touched the brim of his hat with his hand.

"Like what?" Kestrel said urgently.

"I don't know what. I just..."

The tree creaked. He shuddered.

"Climb higher," said Kestrel. "Follow me. We can get away through the trees."

She glanced down at the grabber again and her heart stumbled. Its obvious hunger was making it fast and desperate. For the first time, a tiny part of her doubted she'd ever be able to kill a grabber before it struck. She was sure that this one would continue to hound her dad even if she were hacking it apart piece by piece.

"We can't run forever," her dad said gently, as though he'd read her mind.

The grabber drew back and licked its lips. It craned its neck toward them, a hundred tiny bones cracking and snapping under its stolen skin. It took a deep breath, as though it was breathing in the smell of their fear, and its nostrils flared.

"Remember the Marrow Orchard. Promise me you'll get out," her dad said. "I don't know what's outside this forest, but I'm choosing to believe it's good."

The grabber was swelling, its makeshift body creaking and snapping. It was ready. It stretched its jaws toward them, its mouth open, revealing its jumbled and rotting insides.

"I've had nightmares about this for years," her dad said, his voice strangely calm. "You always know what your grabber's going to be, deep down."

The grabber hit the tree with all its weight, making it shake so hard Kestrel had to cling to the branch. The grabber jumped again, snapping its jaws a couple of inches below them, and Kestrel cried out.

All at once she knew what she would write in the notebook, if she still had it. The words scurried over her eyelids like frantic spiders.

The forest is alive, and the grabbers are its terrible appetite.

The grabber took a deep, rasping breath that rattled its gory ribs.

"Get away from here, Kestrel," her dad said. "Run away and don't look back."

"No," she said.

She gripped her sharpened spoon in one fist and leaned over the branch. She drew in a deep breath and aimed for where she thought the grabber's heart would be. She was going to jump and land on it with all her weight. For the first time ever she would kill a grabber before it struck. Even if it killed her, too. She tensed her muscles, ready to leap.

And then it was like the world had folded in the middle. Her dad was bending over, offering himself to the grabber with his arms outstretched as though embracing it, and the grabber, in turn, was reaching for him. It was slow, too slow, and Kestrel could see every individual hair on the grabber's back in terrible detail, could see the breath rising from its throat. Her mouth opened, and she yelled as the grabber took her father's hands in its jaws and pulled him down.

He was gone in a second. Time became right again. Kestrel

screamed as the grabber crunched something, then it was leaping away, taking her father with it; and he was silent, unmoving. His life had been snatched away with less effort than it takes to blow out a candle.

Kestrel's body turned white-hot with a cry of pain. It came from the bottom of her stomach and forced its way out of her mouth, so hard she thought her jaw might break apart. Pippit bit her on the hand so she could feel his teeth on the fine bones running up to her knuckles, and that broke the spell. She pitched forward, flinging herself from the tree and landing hard in the dead leaves. She crawled after the grabber like an animal.

"Go!" Pippit hissed in her ear.

"Yes," said Kestrel, and climbed up with her hand on the spoon, toward the grabber's bloody trail. Pippit hissed in her ear.

"Wrong way! Go! Now!"

"No," she said. "I'm not going back."

"Village! Now!"

"You can go if you want," she said. Her horror was slowly solidifying into a long spike of icy rage. "I'm going to kill a grabber."

She raced after the grabber's deep footprints. It had gone around the side of the hill, not wasting any time now, leaping over twisted roots and through jutting rocks. She quickly decapitated the creepers and branches that got in her way with one clean swipe of her spoon. The grabber was just ahead, and now that it had neatly dispatched and almost completely swallowed its meal, it moved with a sense of triumph.

It was scattering things behind it, its own fine white bones and claws and teeth, as though it was falling apart. Kestrel couldn't see her dad anywhere. It seemed impossible that the grabber had swallowed him whole, but it was even more impossible that he had escaped its jaws. The grabber lowered its head, then slowed to a trot. It was bloated and triumphant. It didn't seem to know that Kestrel was almost on top of it.

The grabber stopped. It was standing right on the edge of a cliff. The ground dropped away as though the hill had been chopped in half. Far below it was a pit of green needle-covered trees coated in a thin layer of snow. Small white flakes swirled around the grabber's head. The snow had been falling all this time, and Kestrel hadn't even noticed.

The grabber's back was turned to her. It dropped something heavy on the ground and lowered its head to sniff it, its jaws damp. There was a metal trap around its leg, which it wore like nothing more than a bracelet. Kestrel gripped her spoon in her fist, shaking as she looked for a weak spot.

"Belly," whispered Pippit.

The grabber twitched at the sound of Pippit's voice. Kestrel threw herself toward the grabber, and before it had time to realize what was happening, she had driven her spoon through its ribs.

The grabber howled and thrashed. Kestrel pulled the spoon out of its body and gave it a blow to the side of the head just as it swung its jaws open to bite her, and then she shoved it toward the edge.

The grabber was heavy, but it hadn't expected her to throw her whole weight into it. It scrabbled for a hold on the ground, but rocks were already sliding away under its feet. At the last moment Kestrel grabbed hold of one of the grabber's ears, trying to stop it from falling, horrified that her father was in there somewhere. She was sick at the thought of him smashing to pieces with the grabber.

The grabber's ear tore off as the monster slipped over the edge of the cliff. Its fur, which was attached to the ear, pulled away from the grabber as it plunged over the cliff. The fur dangled from Kestrel's hand. It was Mardy's missing wolf-skin rug.

The grabber's howl was cut short as it crashed through the trees. It landed on the ground below with a sharp, final-sounding *snap*. Kestrel's legs folded and she hit the ground, clutching the rug. It took her a while to realize that she was shuddering with tears, and that Pippit was licking her cheeks.

She jumped at the sight of his face so close, his brown weasel-teeth and his eyes slightly crossed from focusing on her nose.

"Blood," he said urgently. "Move. Go."

She knew at once what he meant. The smell of blood was in the air, and now that the grabber was dead other creatures would come to see if there were any scraps left behind—first the wolves, then everything from the rust-colored dogs to the poisonous rabbits, even the fat white slugs, the ones that sucked up blood. They'd find her there, helpless and weak, and if one of them was brave enough to snap its teeth at her, they'd all have a go.

Bloodmoss squirmed quietly under Kestrel's knees, trying to worm its way over her skin and into her boots.

Kestrel pushed herself to her feet, holding on to a rotten trunk for support. She felt very sick, as though the mold had finally worked its way into her body. She wanted to sink into the earth, let the bloodmoss take her. The more the seconds crawled by, the more difficult it became to pretend that she hadn't just watched her father die.

There was a howl in the distance, followed by another, and another, until a chorus was all around her.

"The wolves," said Kestrel, her voice strangely high. "They're celebrating, aren't they?"

Pippit growled, the hairs on his back standing up.

"Move," he said. "Blood. Now."

Kestrel had very little strength left, but she knew she needed every ounce of it to make it back to the village before they found her, too. Her dad would shake her if he saw her sitting here, staring at the ground, letting herself freeze in the snow. With a huge effort she stood up, the wolf skin clasped in her hand, and sank back into the forest.

THE DRESS

Kestrel was as clean and raw as the inside of an acorn. She'd been scrubbed with soap and polished with a flannel, and her hair had been painstakingly unknotted. The rubbish she'd collected in the forest, all the twigs and tree needles, had been picked out of her hair and tossed through the window by her mother. With every part of her that was cleaned or thrown away, Kestrel felt that part of herself had gone as well. The only thing her mother couldn't strip away was the queasy feeling in her stomach.

Kestrel stared straight ahead as her mother laced her into a dress with frightening speed. Instead of the wall, all she could see was Dad slipping out of the tree, his arms outstretched for his grabber, and the grabber extending its teeth toward him.

Kestrel's mother didn't notice how quiet she was. She was in a fantastic mood. She hummed as she pulled the last pins out of the dress and tied Kestrel's hair up, her fingers dancing over her scalp like spiders.

"Perfect," she said, taking Kestrel by the shoulders and turning her around to look in a broken piece of mirror. Kestrel jumped, the image of her dad's grabber scattering.

The dress her mother had made her was long and black, with a pinched-looking bodice and a high neck. It was covered in shiny green-and-black beads, and the sleeves were done up with hard black buttons like fish eyes.

She was a raven, a cockroach, a monster.

"How does it feel?" her mother asked, her hands still on Kestrel's shoulders.

"I can't breathe," said Kestrel truthfully.

"That means it fits," said her mother, and Kestrel saw her smile in the reflection.

It was a present for being good. Her mother had pulled her into the house last night and put her in a pile of blankets, and Kestrel had let her. She had been too tired to kick and scream, to climb up to the gutter. She tossed all night, dreaming about her dad being eaten. Whenever she surfaced from sleep, it felt like the blankets were suffocating her. Then, when she'd woken up this morning, the dress was ready for her.

Kestrel gasped as her mother yanked the laces on the dress to make it even tighter. The black dog sat in the corner of the room, watching Kestrel as though it knew exactly what she was thinking.

She fixed her gaze on it and tried to look impassive. But she couldn't stop her dad's words running through her head, again and again, just like his death had run through her sleep. *Remember the Marrow Orchard. Promise me you'll get out.*

Her mother made the finishing touches to the dress, tweaking the sleeves and the collar. Kestrel stared at the battered front door, wishing she could get out. For the first time in years, she could see the faces that the knots made, the ones that Granmos had terrified her with on her tenth birthday. They grinned at her nastily through the splinters, as though they knew that she was weak.

Splinters. Kestrel blinked. When did the door become so damaged, anyway? She thought back, but she couldn't remember it looking like that when Granmos first conjured up the faces. Did something happen to it?

"You look pale, sweetie," Kestrel's mother said, interrupting her. She handed her a cup of water.

Kestrel slowly raised it to her lips, then she saw the bobbing, milky-blind eyes of the Briny Witch rotating in the bottom of the cup. She gasped and dropped it, splattering water all over the floor and soaking the bottom of her dress.

"What's wrong?" her mother asked, snatching the cup and looking inside. The Briny Witch had gone.

"Nothing," Kestrel said quickly.

Her mother watched Kestrel beadily for another few moments.

"You look good in that dress," she said finally. "You should wear nice things while you're young, while you can still get away with it."

"It's special," Kestrel said, hoping her mother couldn't detect the hint of sarcasm. "What gave you the idea?"

"I thought you'd like to look less like an animal, and more like a real girl. More like your mother."

"I do look like you," Kestrel said, turning around slowly, wanting to rip every single piece of the vile dress apart.

"I'm fully aware that certain people don't treat you with the respect that you deserve," her mother said, except she said the word *people* like most would say *scum*. "And I'm not saying it's your fault, sweetest, but you don't help yourself by charging around with dirt on your face and holes in your sweater, and certainly not by playing in the trees. But if you look more like me, who's going to bother you?"

No one, Kestrel thought. She looked terrifying. They wouldn't dare mutter about her now.

"You can even hunt in it," her mother said. "There's a place inside it for your spoon."

Kestrel wondered what her dad would think of the dress if he could see her.

"Mum," she said, her voice cracking.

"I know," her mother said, and then her arms were around Kestrel and she was being pulled to the floor. She landed in her mother's lap, dust balls scudding away from their feet. "I heard the howls from here. The whole village did."

Kestrel felt a huge sob wrack her body, then she pressed her hands over her eyes and forced it all back in.

"Let me tell you something, sweetie," said her mother, running her fingers over Kestrel's newly shiny hair. "When you're my age you learn that grieving is a waste of time. You should concentrate on the people you have left. You have me, don't you? You could move back into the house, sleep in a real bed. It's all here for you."

Kestrel buried her face in her mother's shoulder. For a moment, she imagined eating hot food by her mother's side and sleeping in the warm bed every night. It was almost comforting.

Her mother ran a finger down Kestrel's nose, then tapped it playfully. "In fact," she said, "I think this might be a new beginning for us. I know we haven't always seen eye to eye, but things will change. You're growing up."

"I guess," Kestrel said. She felt a million years old. Her mother smoothed her hair, and despite herself, Kestrel felt her shoulders relax.

For a moment she considered letting it all out. She could tell her mother that her grabber was coming. Maybe she'd even call the black dog off and let Kestrel go, and she could escape the forest before the grabber caught her. She wouldn't have to steal any berries. For a second, telling her mother everything was the perfect answer.

"I've been looking forward to us being friends," her mother said softly. "I knew you'd see sense one day. You'll never leave the forest—you belong here, with me."

Any tenderness Kestrel felt toward her mother drained away.

"What about our deal?" she asked. The words felt leaden in her mouth. "You said that when I find Granmos's grabber, you'll call the dog off for good."

Her mother froze.

"Well, of *course* that's still the deal," she said. "I've just been thinking, sweetie, that maybe you should stop trying. To be honest, I thought you'd give up years ago."

Kestrel pulled sharply away from her embrace. "What do you mean, you thought I'd give up? It is out there, isn't it?"

"Yes, darling," her mother said, annoyed. "Of course."

Doubt was worming its way through Kestrel's bones. Something in her mother's voice was wrong, and her eyes were too hard.

I think she's hiding things, her dad had said.

Kestrel tried to breathe steadily. She was burning to get up and scream, to tear down the weave with her bare hands, but she couldn't afford to lose her temper. The moment her mother thought Kestrel was going to disobey her, she'd be trapped. Kestrel slowly uncurled her fingers, and moved her lips into the shape of a smile.

She had to get the bloodberries. It might be the only way to get rid of the dog, so that she could escape the forest. Whatever her mother was hiding, Kestrel suddenly doubted she ever intended to let her go.

"I hope you haven't forgotten your promise, either," her mother continued softly. "No more speaking to that boy."

"I know," Kestrel replied as calmly as she could. How could her mother think it was that easy to get rid of a friend?

"Now," said her mother, clapping her hands so suddenly Kestrel jumped, "I want you to fetch me some apples."

"Apples?" Kestrel repeated, bewildered. Maybe she hadn't heard right.

"That's what I said, sweetie. I'm hungry."

Kestrel didn't need any more persuading. The thought of walking through the forest when her grabber was following her made her skin crawl, but there was no choice. She needed to find a way to get to the Marrow Orchard and steal the bloodberries. She obediently squeezed through the tunnel in the weave, the stiff dress cutting into her stomach, then stood up by the door.

People were murmuring outside. She pressed her ear to the wood.

"They're sacrificing trinkets to the wolf fire," said her

mother. "Ike thinks that if he has nothing for his grabber to take, it'll keep away."

"Why does he think that?" Kestrel asked.

"Because I told him so." She snorted. "I wanted to see if I could get him to burn his wretched watch. I hate the way he clutches it in his grubby hands all the time."

Kestrel didn't answer. Ike would do whatever her mother suggested. She actually felt sorry for him.

"I found this in your shirt pocket," her mother added. She opened her hand, revealing the lucky stone Finn had given her. Kestrel felt a bolt of shock, but her mother seemed to have no idea what it was. She took it gingerly and pushed it up her sleeve. "This is for you as well," her mother said. She picked up a gray bundle of fur and pushed it into Kestrel's arms.

Kestrel almost choked. It was the pelt she'd pulled from the grabber's back, made out of Mardy Banbury's wolf-skin rug. Her mother had meticulously cleaned it; the fur was unbloodied and shining. There was a clasp on its front paws, and the head was a hood with two jaunty ears on top.

"You deserve to keep the trophy this time," her mother said sweetly.

Kestrel wanted to scream with revulsion. Before she could answer, her mother reached over her shoulder and turned the door handle, shoving Kestrel outside.

A basket landed at Kestrel's feet, and the door slammed shut again.

Kestrel coughed. The air was thick with smoke, and through it she could see the wolf fire burning in the middle of the village. Ike was clutching his watch in his fist, looking miserable, surrounded by a large audience.

Kestrel picked up the basket and tried to slip past without being seen. Walt and Rascly Badger were muttering to each other, with one eye on Ike.

"Gotta lay sticks down outside your door," Rascly said. "The... *you know whats* can't walk over sticks. Or fireworks. Scare 'em off with fireworks."

"Hold your tongue," muttered Walt. "They're coming faster than ever. Don't tempt fate."

When Kestrel was almost past them, a piece of ash went up her nose and she spluttered.

"Who's there?" Mardy asked sharply. She was holding a teacup, ready to throw it into the flames. She squinted and saw Kestrel with her wolf-skin rug in her hand. Her eyes widened and she dropped the cup.

"It was *you*?" she whispered.

Hannah elbowed past Mardy to see what was happening. When she saw Kestrel her lips twitched into a nasty grin.

"You've got a nerve, showing your face after what you did," she said.

For a moment Kestrel thought they were talking about her dad, and how she hadn't been able to save him. Then she saw Runo, his leg in a splint, staring at her venomously.

"His leg's never going to be right," Hannah said, stepping toward her. Even through the smoke, Kestrel knew that she was smirking. "Are you going to apologize?"

Kestrel realized that the kids had crept all around her, standing in a wide circle, half hidden in the smoke. Something had changed. They felt brave enough to push her around in front of the adults.

At that moment the air stirred and the thick smoke billowed, making a path between Kestrel and the wolf fire. Kestrel tightened her hand around the basket, ready to swing it at Hannah. But Hannah stepped back. The villagers were staring.

Kestrel glanced down and stifled a scream. The gloom of her mother's house and the smoke had covered it before, but now that she was standing in the firelight her dress was shining like a mirror. It was made with hundreds of real beetle wing cases, glowing oily-green in the firelight. The dress crunched as she shivered. Her skin itched as though the hundreds of beetles were crawling all over her.

She knew at once that her mother had sent the breeze herself. She must be watching through a crack in the door right now, waiting to see what Kestrel would do next.

For once, she did exactly what her mother wanted.

"Heel!" she shouted confidently, and the black dog oozed out of the shadows. It trotted to her side and lay down by her feet, grinning at the villagers in a way that dogs shouldn't be able to. Kestrel felt a shiver of power. "Don't bite them," she said to the dog. "Not unless they get too close."

The dog growled. Ike pressed his watch to his chest, his hand trembling. Kestrel threw a last glare at the assembly and walked into the forest, causing the villagers to scatter around her.

No. She didn't walk. She *glided*.

She was a monstrous beetle with poison under her shell.

She was a creature made of shadows, with a terrifying hound by her side.

She was as powerful as her mother, and if anyone came near her, they'd regret it for the rest of their lives.

"You made her angry," she heard Walt tell Hannah behind her. "She'll hurt you next."

Kestrel turned to scowl at him. He stepped back quickly, but Hannah didn't flinch.

"We'll see," Hannah said.

Kestrel strode into the trees until she was sure that nobody could see her. Then she put the basket down, fighting the urge to rip the dress off, and glared at the black dog.

"You don't need to follow me," she said. "I'm only picking apples, aren't I?"

The dog raised its lip.

"If I'm not back in fifteen minutes, you can come get me," she added. "Now go lick my mother's face or something."

The dog sniffed and trotted off. Amazing. She'd actually *commanded* it.

She looked around, aware that there were a great many shadows for a grabber to hide in. Part of her wanted to run back to the house. She squeezed the holey stone in her pocket, trying to draw some strength from it, and took a deep breath.

Kestrel got to work. She shoved the basket under a bush, rolled her long sleeves out of the way, and pulled the plaits out of her hair to stop her head aching. She closed her eyes and tried to think of the maps in Granmos's notebook. Where was the Marrow Orchard?

Something nudged her leg.

"Pip," she said. "I know you're there."

Something rustled between the layers of her horrible beetle-covered skirt. Pippit dropped out of the bottom, two shiny wings sticking guiltily from his mouth.

"I saw you hide," she said.

"Food," he said sheepishly, and sucked the wings in with a *crunch*.

"Eat as many as you want," she said, trying to wriggle her shoulders. The bodice pinched under her arms when she moved. "We're going on a mission, and we've got to finish it before the dog realizes we've gone. And when we get there I need a distraction."

Pippit looked ecstatic at the thought of causing chaos.

Kestrel bent down to tighten her shoelaces, and blinked. There was a set of footprints next to her. They were fresh. One foot was bigger than the other, and turned outward slightly. She followed the footprints with her eyes. They came from the direction of her mother's house and went parallel with her own before disappearing into the trees just in front of her.

Kestrel stopped breathing. The forest was silent. Slowly, she leaned over and sniffed the footprints.

Vinegar. Just like the trail left by the woodchopper's grabber.

It's here. She saw a tiny flicker of movement in the trees and looked up, dread knotting her stomach. Something huge and person-shaped detached itself from the shadows and fled into the forest.

The grabber.

Kestrel froze, her blood curdling. She wanted to give in to her instincts and run the other way, but then years of training kicked in, and she bolted after it. It was just ahead of her, running with barely a noise, almost invisible in the gloom. As it passed through a gap in the trees she caught sight of something brown and moldering embedded in its chest, or where its chest should be. *Her grandma's notebook.* Its cover was pressed open like the wings of a huge moth, forming a solid rib cage.

"Wait!" Kestrel screamed.

The grabber melted into the shadows. It left a trail of cold air and the smell of rotting meat behind it.

Kestrel stumbled to a halt, breathing hard.

Her grabber had two feet. It was shaped like a person.

Kestrel's insides were doing belly flops as she scanned the trees. She wanted to know what form it was taking.

No—she didn't.

But she couldn't stop herself wondering.

What keeps you awake at night and gives you nightmares? What makes your guts shrivel? Granmos hissed in her memory. She could see the old woman's face as clear as day, her cruel, milky eyes threaded with angry veins as she pinned Kestrel against the wall. She could feel her silver locket pressed against her ribs, her heavy rings digging into her shoulders. *Say it!*

The forest shivered. Kestrel backed away from the footprints. She suddenly felt too close to them for comfort.

"Gruh," Pippit warbled, pushing his nose into her ear. "Nuh, nuh."

"It's not ready yet," Kestrel said. She was trying to comfort herself as much as him. She picked him up and held on to him tightly, shivering. "We have time. We'll get out. But we've got to get a head start on the dog. I think the Marrow Orchard's... this way."

"Dark," said Pippit, his nose quivering.

"We don't have time to find a lantern," Kestrel said.

She stopped short and blinked. It felt like cold water was running through her head, just like it had in the face painter's clearing.

She clapped her hands over her ears. Something went *pop*. And then she remembered.

Kestrel shuffled impatiently in her chair, the heavy book sliding around in her lap. She was meant to be learning to read, but she couldn't tell the difference between *b* and *d*. Granmos was in the corner, knitting, and her mother was twirling pieces of string between her fingers, peering at the hidden pictures inside them. She'd only begun weaving recently; the walls and the ceiling were bare. The lantern on the table cast shadows of her spidery, dancing fingers on the wall.

Kestrel allowed her eyes to wander around the room, irritated by the way her mother's elbows clicked as she weaved. She watched a tiny spider climb up the wall opposite her, scuttling over the cracks and toward the door, silently willing it toward freedom.

As she stared at the spider, Kestrel saw her mother's elbow move in the corner of her eye, and she immediately knew what was going to happen.

She leaped out of her seat without thinking, a split second before her mother knocked the lantern and gasped. Kestrel landed on the floor, her arms outstretched, and caught the lantern in her bare hands. For a moment she didn't feel anything; then the pain ripped through her fingers. She screamed and dropped the lamp.

The glass shattered and sprayed all over the floor. Kestrel shoved her blistered fingers into her mouth, trying not to cry. It took a lot to stop her mother weaving, but her hands were frozen, and she was staring at Kestrel.

"Your eyesight is even better than I thought," her mother said. She thoughtfully ran her tongue over her teeth. "There's a lot we could do with that."

Despite her scorched fingers, Kestrel felt a proud grin spread over her face. Her mother smiled back, then swept the lantern glass from the floor and carried it outside. As soon as she was out the door, Kestrel's grandma swiveled in her chair and jabbed a knitting needle at her.

"Don't you be clever in front of her," she hissed. Her voice was so venomous Kestrel backed away. "Do you understand?"

"What did I do?" Kestrel asked. She twitched as her grandma tightened her grip on the knitting needle.

"Don't question me," her grandma snapped, and slammed

the needle point-down into the table, where it quivered. Kestrel nodded dumbly.

"Your eyesight is normal from now on. Get it?"

Kestrel shook her head. Her breath was catching in her throat, and she had to remind herself that Granmos wasn't there anymore and couldn't punish her. She glanced down at her hands, almost expecting to see fresh blisters, but all she saw were the same patchy scars she'd gotten from her training. Except—

Kestrel caught her breath.

"How could I have forgotten?" she whispered.

The scars weren't cuts from training—they were burn marks. She could even remember Granmos plunging her hands into a bucket of ice water to stop it hurting.

She rubbed her eyes, trying to clear the image of her grandma's face. Questions were fighting for attention in her head, but she couldn't afford to waste time on them now.

"The Marrow Orchard," she said determinedly, trying hard to push the new memory aside.

Kestrel looked around for the black dog, then climbed up the nearest tree as fast as she could. She'd already wasted most of her fifteen minutes, but if she stayed in the trees until she was far away from the village, she might be able to keep ahead of it for a while.

The dress made movement difficult, but she managed to climb stiffly through the branches. She rained beetles on the ground below, and her spoon poked her in the leg like an accusation.

Kestrel was concentrating so hard on climbing through the trees in her stiff dress that she didn't hear the village kids talking until she was right above them. She cursed under her breath. They didn't usually come this far out.

"Her dad's dead," said a boy called Alec, as though he hadn't stopped chattering about it for the last fifteen minutes. "He got gobbled up."

Kestrel felt like her heart had been torn open. *Gobbled up?* She pressed her hand over her mouth, thinking that if she didn't, she'd scream.

The kids were all sitting on the floor. Hannah, Runo, Briar, and most of the others. Kestrel held her breath, knowing that she couldn't pass over their heads. One tiny noise and they'd all look up.

"She's got his grabber's skin," said Briar darkly.

"Let's not get carried away," said Hannah's voice directly below her. It was calm, but it carried a drop of poison. "We know she's up to something, but we need evidence. The adults won't get rid of her otherwise."

"We've got evidence, haven't we?" said Briar sharply.

Kestrel leaned over the branch, wondering if she should

drop the cloak on them and make them scream. As she moved a beetle detached itself from her dress and spiraled down onto Hannah's head, but Hannah didn't notice. The boy next to her flicked it away. Something about the gesture made Kestrel pause.

"We don't know what she really does with the grabbers. Has anyone actually seen her kill one?" said Runo.

"She's probably the one who sends 'em," said Alec, and they all gasped with a mixture of glee and disgust.

"As it happens, there is someone who can tell us," Hannah said. "Finn must know what happens when Kestrel goes after the grabbers. Right, Finn?"

Kestrel's heart almost stopped. Finn looked so different. He'd been given a brutal haircut, and there were stiff brown shoes on his feet. He sat with his legs stuck out in front of him as though he was trying to get as far away from the shoes as possible. And he'd come down to the ground to hang out with them. The *ground.* He had never done that for Kestrel.

Everyone turned their attention to Finn.

"It doesn't work like that," he said awkwardly.

"So you don't *know* that she kills the grabbers," said Hannah.

"She does kill them," said Finn. "She brings trophies back."

"Might be having a chat with 'em instead," said a girl called Erin. "Might be telling 'em who to eat next."

187

Kestrel wanted to launch herself out of the tree at them, but she clenched her teeth and stayed quiet. Finn would tell them to shut up.

"Do you help her kill them?" Hannah asked. Kestrel rolled her eyes. Finn wouldn't fall into her trap.

"I help a bit," said Finn, twisting his fingers together nervously. Hannah continued to look at him. Finn wriggled. "I mean, I don't actually see much." He looked at Hannah pleadingly. "She won't let me get close."

Kestrel was so outraged that the words slipped out before she could stop them.

"Liar!" she shouted, and everyone looked up.

"What do you mean?" Hannah asked, so unsurprised by Kestrel's presence that Kestrel wondered if she'd known she was there all along.

She opened her mouth to say that Finn had always refused to go near a grabber. He made terrible excuses, like *the trees are too slippery* or, *time to steal cake from Mardy!* He didn't even like touching the ground in case his grabber came after him. And now he was lying about it.

"Coward!" she screamed. Her voice was full of ice, but her face was burning.

Finn looked like he'd been slapped.

She strode away, violently pushing branches and twigs out of her path. They were meant to stick up for each other. Finn was *different* to the other villagers.

Wasn't he?

A few seconds later she heard Finn scramble up the tree and follow her.

"Take it back!" he shouted. Kestrel sped up. She didn't want him to see her face, or her probably red eyes. She heard Finn pause, then two thumps as he flung his shoes away. Then he was right behind her, and she knew she'd never outrun him in the trees. She stopped and turned to face him, her arms crossed.

He looked like an alien. His face was approaching clean, and he wasn't wearing any feathers. He smelled like soap. All of his *Finn*-ness had been washed away.

"Why are you friends with them?" she asked, hating how petty she sounded. Pippit was sitting on her shoulder, his hair raised, baring his teeth at Finn in solidarity. "They've bullied us for years, and now you're wearing their clothes!"

"They never bullied me," Finn said. "Now *take. It. Back.*"

"What about the time they greased your ropes and you fell out of a tree?" she said, ignoring him. "What about when they set your coat on fire? Or when they—"

"That was ages ago," he snapped. "They're different now. If you were nicer—"

"*Nicer?*"

"You know what I mean. Hannah said—"

"Hannah hates me, and she's using you to get to me," Kestrel yelled.

The dead leaves crackled on the ground below them. Pippit stiffened.

"Something important," he hissed under his breath. But Kestrel didn't have time for the other kids now.

She still had the terrible wolf-skin cloak under her arm. She threw it around herself and fastened it at the neck. Finn flinched as she raised the hood, two long, wolfish incisors dangling in front of her eyes.

"This cloak is to remind me who I am," she said savagely. "I'm a hunter. I'm going to find my way out of here. And," she added imperiously, fixing him with her coldest stare, "you can come as well, if you stop being such a monumental cowardly *idiot!*"

Finn looked at Kestrel as though she'd told him she could fly.

"You've lost it," he said. "We're never going to escape."

"You're just too scared to try," she replied coldly.

Finn clenched his fists. His face twisted spitefully.

"It was just a game," he said, deliberately slow. "There's no way out."

Kestrel gaped at him. The world was falling over. All the weeks they'd spent planning their escape—all the plans they'd made—all the *promises*. There had to be an outside. How would she escape her grabber otherwise?

"It's not a game!" she yelled. A flock of razor-winged blackbirds flew up from a nearby tree, squawking.

Finn opened his mouth again, but he was cut off by a growl. Kestrel looked down, her stomach plummeting. It wasn't the village kids below them. The black dog was staring up at them from the ground. And it had seen her and Finn together.

Kestrel tried to duck from sight, but it was too late. The dog's nostrils flared as it took them in, dribbling in anticipation.

"Finn," said Kestrel. Her mother would kill him. *She was going to kill Finn.* "You've got to run!"

"Why?" he said, backing away. "What's happening?"

"Go, you moron!" she shouted. The dog yapped. Finn yelped and scrambled away. Kestrel started running after him, but her feet got tangled in the beetle dress, and she stumbled. The dog leaped, its powerful jaws snapping around the bottom of her boot, and she plunged to the ground.

BONES IN A BOX

"Let go!" Kestrel shrieked.

The black dog had her by the shoelaces. It was pulling her through the forest at a terrific speed, panting and growling under its breath. Kestrel grabbed fistfuls of earth, but nothing could stop it.

"Kestrel!" Finn yelled in the distance, but she was moving too fast even for him. They were going toward her mother's house. It was too late.

Pippit bounded up behind her. He landed on her face and ran into her pocket. She wanted to clutch him in her arms, but all the breath was being knocked out of her by the lumpy ground.

The wolf fire had been abandoned and the path to the house was clear. The dog headbutted the door open and dragged Kestrel inside. She scrambled to her feet as the door slammed behind them, feeling like a sack of bruises.

Kestrel slammed her fists against the door, but it was

locked tight. The dog yawned, as though it had known exactly what she would do.

Everything was cold and silent. Kestrel peered into the gloom, but for the first time she could remember her mother wasn't there.

The trapdoor to the cellar was open, and there was a strange scraping sound coming from below.

"What's she doing?" Kestrel asked the dog suspiciously. The dog had planted itself in front of the door to stop her leaving, but its eyes kept flicking to the cellar. It obviously hadn't known her mother would be down there, and it didn't know what to do now.

It just growled at her instead. Pippit shuffled and nudged his way up her sleeve, where it was safe.

Kestrel trod softly toward the hole in the floor, scattering the abandoned dressmaking pins. What was it her dad said? *I think she's hiding things.* She felt a cool shiver in her spine. If her mother was hiding something, where would she keep the evidence?

The dog twitched an ear, sensing that something had changed. Kestrel took her chance. She threw herself at the trapdoor and pitched headfirst into the gloom.

She landed on stone, her arms breaking her fall. She scrambled up quickly, reached for the trapdoor, and slammed it shut just as the barking dog tried to wedge its muzzle through the gap.

Pippit snickered gleefully in her sleeve.

Kestrel waited with bated breath, certain her mother would have heard the commotion, but nothing happened.

"Mother?" Kestrel whispered, regretting her impulsive behavior. The cellar was a lot bigger than she'd imagined, spreading far away from the house and quietly absorbing any kind of noise. It was cool and crammed with leering shadows. "Are you here?"

No answer.

A candle had been left by the stairs. It illuminated the long, thin cellar, which was piled with junk and covered in soft, gray spiderwebs. It was like a museum of her early childhood. Kestrel could see her old bed, her books, her toys—everything that had been moved to make room for her mother's weave. It was all heaped against the walls, leaving a narrow passage down the middle that Kestrel could only just about squeeze through. The end of the pathway was pitch black.

As Kestrel squinted into the gloom, she heard the long, low scraping sound come from it.

She couldn't turn back now.

She stretched her arms out and moved forward, feeling her way through the shadows, although part of her was shouting to run back upstairs and take her chances with the dog. She could hear its toenails clicking on the floorboards above them as it paced back and forth.

As Kestrel walked, her fingers brushed against a patch of

wet mushrooms. She shuddered and almost moved on, but then recognized the chair they were growing on. It used to sit by her bed, back when she slept in the house.

There was something carved in the left arm.

She paused, digging the mushrooms away with her fingernails until she could see what was underneath.

There were eleven letters, cut deeply into the wood. Each one was in her own cramped writing: *C h o o s e a n a m e.*

It was as though someone had run their fingers down her back. When had she carved that there? And why? Then it happened. It began as a slow, cold trickle inside her head.

"Not now," she muttered desperately, stuffing her fingers in her ears. But then her right ear went *pop*, and the images were as unstoppable as a flood.

Kestrel was in her mother's cottage, her fingers tightly wrapped in the blanket under her. She was sitting on the bed, facing the wooden door with hundreds of faces in the wood, trying not to cry.

Smoke poured from her grandma's pipe and crawled over the door, making it look as though the faces were shifting. Shadows flickered on the walls, and Granmos issued another bloodcurdling shriek that seemed to come from the mouth of the biggest monster. Kestrel stuffed her fingers in her ears. This was one of the worst training sessions she'd ever lived through. Granmos had taken one of her fears and made it even worse.

All of a sudden, the shrieks fell silent. Her grandma sighed and leaned over. Kestrel flinched, expecting her to do something horrible, like dig her fingers into her arm.

"Putting your fingers in your ears won't help," Granmos said. To Kestrel's surprise, she patted her on the knee and smiled. "Choose a name for the faces. Make friends with them. Hadn't thought of that, had you?"

Kestrel stared at her.

"Training you is like trying to train a brick," her grandma said, shaking her head and picking up her pipe again. "Just try it, duck."

Kestrel watched the faces through the cracks in her fingers. She reluctantly fixed her gaze on the face with wide eyes and a jagged, twisting mouth as it flickered through the smoke.

"That one's called Fearn," she blurted.

"You can do better than that," Granmos said. "What else?"

Fine, Kestrel thought. She screwed her eyes up, and the face twisted into a comical grin. *Your name's Fearn,* she told it, feeling stupid. *Your job is to keep the door locked at night, to keep me safe. You're scared of... spiders. And you're allergic to toads.*

It worked. The face twisted away and sank into the wood. Kestrel latched onto the next face, her mouth dry, and the next, and the next. Soon they no longer looked like monsters. After a while she stopped seeing the faces at all, and the door was just a door.

"Good girl," her grandma said, grinning widely. Had Granmos ever been this proud of her before? "Monsters want you to be scared. Otherwise they'd have nothing. So this is your birthday present. The best piece of advice you'll ever get. Got it? Write it down somewhere so you'll remember it. Name your fears, duck, and acknowledge them."

Kestrel opened her eyes to the cold, gloomy cellar. She had an uncontrollable urge to get away from the vision. It felt so real that she couldn't convince herself it was made up.

"Wassat?" Pippit asked, nudging her with his face.

"I dunno," Kestrel said, touching her ear. She felt like she'd been privy to something important and terrible. "I think I'm remembering things. None of it makes any sense." She shivered. "My gran told me to name the things I was scared of. I carved it in the arm of the chair, so I wouldn't forget it. But I forgot anyway."

She could almost feel her grandma's fingers tickling her under the chin. She'd never given Kestrel so much as a hug before, but in the memory, she seemed ... almost kind.

And what did you do? said a nasty voice in Kestrel's head. *You let her grabber in.*

A soft clattering sound came from the next room. Kestrel stood up quickly, but her mother didn't appear. She left the old chair behind and walked toward the noise, breathing in air thick with shut-up secrets. Slowly, she passed through the doorway. There were three steps leading down, then a new space opened to the right.

The new room was full of boxes and bags piled against the walls. Her mother had her back to the steps, and she was rummaging in a large chest with another candle on the floor beside her. Kestrel had the urge to run and push her mother in, but she held herself back.

The red thread that trailed from her mother's sleeve was piled on the floor next to her, and the other end snaked into the wooden chest. Kestrel knew at once that she was intruding on something very private.

Her mother was leaning over the chest, so preoccupied with examining whatever was inside that she didn't seem to notice Kestrel behind her. Kestrel took another step forward, then another. She was so close she could almost touch her.

Kestrel held her breath, her spine aching.

The chest contained a large, dusty quilt with dozens of bumps in it. Before her mother could see her, and without knowing quite why, Kestrel reached forward and yanked the quilt aside.

Her mother jumped. She grabbed Kestrel by the wrist and

slammed the lid shut, but it was too late. Kestrel had seen the bones, long and white, wrapped in the quilt.

"Why are there bones in there?" Kestrel asked, yanking her wrist out of her mother's grasp. She backed toward the wall again until she could feel the stone pressed into her spine, desperate to put space between them.

Her mother's face was white. There were two red blotches on her cheeks, as bright as poisoned apples, and she was frozen like a rabbit in lamplight. Kestrel looked at all the boxes around her, wondering what was in them. More bones? More teeth? Something worse?

"What was in the chest?" she demanded again. Her mother was staring at her as though she'd been caught chewing up a mouse. "Tell me what you're hiding!"

"It's nobody you know," her mother said, finally finding her voice. She smoothed her skirt with shaking hands, and slowly regained her composure. "What are you doing in here?"

"The door was open," Kestrel said. She didn't have a plan other than *dive into the cellar and look*, which in retrospect was quite stupid. "The dog—"

Her mother looked up, hearing the whining of the dog above them, and her face darkened. She stamped on the candle and grabbed Kestrel by the hair, dragging her back to the trapdoor.

"Stop struggling, you brat. You'll ruin your dress."

"I'll struggle as much as I want," said Kestrel, trying to kick her mother's feet from underneath her. "I'll scream so hard everyone will think you're killing me."

"They'll be glad someone's finally doing it," her mother snapped.

She hauled Kestrel up the steps, flung the trapdoor open, and pushed Kestrel out. The dog immediately ran circles around her mother's legs, barking. Her mother put her hand on the dog's head, quieting it. She listened for a moment.

"You broke your promise about the boy," her mother hissed, baring her teeth at Kestrel. "Did you think I wouldn't find out? Do you think the consequences are *funny*?"

"Don't," Kestrel said, forgetting all about the bones in the cellar. "Please, I'm sorry—"

Her mother pushed through the weave toward the door. Kestrel grabbed her arm and tried to pull her back, but she flung it open and shoved Kestrel outside.

"You've forced me to do this," she said, stepping into the light.

She was holding Finn's tooth. Kestrel tried to grab it from her, but her mother threw her to the ground with astonishing ease.

Kestrel reached for her spoon, but her mother snatched it and flung it away.

She could see Finn at the edge of the village, one hand planted on a tree for support. She willed him to run away, but he saw Kestrel and took a step toward her. Even though he had betrayed her, Kestrel felt a sudden rush of love for him. He was petrified of her mother, and of the open ground, but he was coming to help her.

"Run!" she yelled to Finn.

"This will teach you to be disobedient," her mother said.

Her mother yanked a ball of black wool from her pocket and started tying it around Finn's tooth, preparing the spell. Kestrel tried to grab her hands, but her mother shoved her aside. Then she reached behind her and plucked another piece of string from the weave, the one with Kestrel's tooth in it, and gave it a single tug.

It felt like someone had punched Kestrel in the chest. She hit the ground with an *umph*, landing next to her spoon. She struggled to her feet, but her legs were numb and she fell over again.

Finn ran toward her. Her mother finished tying the black wool around Finn's tooth. Then she smiled at Kestrel, so sweetly she wondered if she was letting Finn go.

"Don't!" Kestrel shouted at him. "She's got your tooth!"

Her mother dropped the bundle of wool and stamped on it. Finn screamed and fell down as though he'd been crushed from above. He was on the floor, writhing like a worm, sobbing and snotty. Kestrel used all her strength to pull herself to her feet, but her mother caught her with her free hand and pushed her down again. Finn's screams grew louder.

"Stop it!" Kestrel shouted, horror bubbling in her throat. She tried to scramble away, but the dog threw itself at her back and pinned her to the ground.

Pippit launched from Kestrel's pocket like a small tornado, throwing himself at Kestrel's mother and landing spread-eagled on her face. Her mother cried out, releasing the tooth. Finn fell still as the dog snapped its jaws at Pippit. Kestrel scrambled up, snatched the bundle of wool from the ground and pried it open, rescuing the tooth inside.

Her mother hurled Pippit to the side and grabbed Kestrel. Kestrel wrenched away and, on a desperate impulse, shoved the tooth in her mouth and swallowed it.

Her mother paled. Kestrel met her mother's eye triumphantly, even though she felt a little bit sick.

"Deal with the weasel," her mother hissed at the dog, jerking her head toward Pippit on the ground. Kestrel dove for him, but the dog got there first. It snapped Pippit's tail between its jaws and began to shake him. Pippit twisted around and sank his teeth into the dog's muzzle.

The dog bit down, hard, then dropped him. Pippit skittered away, howling. Kestrel, sickened, saw that half of Pippit's tail was still in the dog's mouth.

Kestrel grabbed her spoon from the ground and faced

the dog. She readied herself to fight, but the dog was staring at her mother. Kestrel turned. There was blood trickling from her mother's nose. She took a step back into the house so she could hold on to the door frame. One of the threads from her sleeve had come loose in the struggle, and her clothes were tattered. She looked suddenly exhausted. She slowly put one hand over her face, as though nursing a terrible headache.

"Don't you have anything to say?" Kestrel asked, feeling reckless. "Aren't you even going to set the dog on me?"

"I should have gotten rid of you a long time ago," her mother said, her voice strange and low. Her fingers were digging into her cheeks.

She stumbled back into the house, slamming the door on both her and the dog. It sat down on the doorstep, looking small and alone.

Kestrel turned and ran over to Finn. She expected him to sit, groaning like Runo had, but he was just a small, limp pile on the floor.

"Get up," she said. "It's safe. *Finn*. C'mon."

He was flopped in the leaves, lying on his side with a glazed look on his face. Kestrel dropped down beside him. She saw something move in the corner of her eye and realized that the other kids had gathered around the side of a cottage to watch. Not a single one of them came to help. "It's not funny," she said to Finn, ignoring them. "Come *on*."

Nothing happened. She looked at the other kids. Runo's mouth was hanging open, and even Hannah looked pale.

"Why aren't you doing anything?" she snapped. Briar twitched, but didn't say anything. Kestrel shook Finn again, but he was as limp as a scarecrow.

"Get up, you idiot," she hissed. "I mean it!"

Finn didn't answer. She grabbed his shoulders and shouted in his ear.

"Finn!" she howled.

Kestrel's heart collapsed into itself, even though she hadn't thought it could break any further. She put her head in her hands, wailing. She couldn't cry. She could only make one long, horrified noise.

"Shut up," Finn mumbled. "Head hurts."

Kestrel stopped immediately and looked up, astonished. Finn blinked slowly, then sat and rubbed his head.

Briar was the first to move. She rushed over and dropped down beside Finn.

"What did that witch do to you?" Briar gasped at him.

"The same thing she did to me," Runo said, finding his voice. "And all because of *her*."

The kids all fixed their eyes on Kestrel.

"I tried to stop her!" Kestrel said, boiling over. "You saw me!"

"She hurt Finn because *you* wouldn't do as you were told."

"Are you serious?" Kestrel asked, striding forward. They all scattered backward, like they were scared of her. "She's the one who tortures people!"

Briar's eyes flickered to her mother's cottage, as though she was afraid Kestrel's mother might hear.

"Don't worry, Finn," Hannah said, ignoring her. She gave Kestrel a truly hateful look. "We'll make sure you don't get hurt again."

"He knows it wasn't my fault," Kestrel said. She reached out for Finn, but he flinched away. Kestrel stopped short, surprised. "Finn, tell them." He didn't respond, only looked at her blearily. *"Finn?"*

He shook his head and turned away.

"Leave me alone," Finn mumbled, touching the side of his face as though he had a toothache. "I've had enough."

Hannah and Briar picked him up, putting their shoulders under his arms, and helped carry him away.

Pippit was watching from behind a stack of wood, but as soon as he saw them go he ran up Kestrel's sleeve, whimpering. His tail was a tattered stump.

"Kes," said Pippit timidly, licking her face.

Kestrel turned her face away, trying to hide the tears that were threatening to leak from her eyes.

"Kes," he said. "Tail. Ow. Hug. Nasty!"

"Not now," she said, her voice cracking.

"Tail! Ow!"

"Leave me alone!" she burst out. Pippit froze. Sorrow and rage bubbled up together, and she couldn't stop herself.

"*Tail*," he insisted. "Ow! Help, Kes? Clever Pippit?"

"I could have stopped her by myself," Kestrel snapped. "You're the one who decided to bite her. It's your own fault your tail's gone!"

As soon as she said it, she knew it wasn't true. But it was too late to take it back.

Pippit froze, staring at her, his nose twitching as though he couldn't digest what she was saying. Then he hissed and leaped from Kestrel's hand, landing in the leaves and skittering away.

"Wait," she cried, stepping after him, trying to spot him in the leaves. It was quiet, and loneliness was already settling over her shoulders like a cloak. "Pippit! Come back!"

He was gone.

She ran after him, tripping on her skirt. She thought she could see Pippit darting ahead of her, but then he was lost, and she was alone among the black trees. Regret formed a bitter lump in her throat.

She stopped and slumped against a tree. She was alone. Completely, utterly, and irrevocably alone. Her best friend hated her, and so did Pippit. There was no one to turn to. For a second she wished her dad would come back from a hunting trip; he'd know what to do. Then she remembered he'd never come out of the woods again, no matter how bad things got.

It felt like all the air had been suddenly sucked out of her lungs. Part of Kestrel wanted to curl up on the forest floor and stay there forever.

But another part of her was trained to fight. She'd made her dad a promise, and she was going to keep it.

She dragged herself to her feet, wrapping her fingers around her spoon. Three black crows were sitting in the branches above her, kicking needle leaves at each other, but as soon as they saw her they croaked and flapped away.

Maybe she looked as dangerous as she felt.

She would do it all herself. She would find the Marrow Orchard and steal the bloodberries to feed to her mother. She would wrestle her secrets away from her, because now she was sure her cellar was crammed full of them. She would find out the truth about her forgotten memories. And finally, she would find a way out of this forest. And no one—not even her own grabber—was going to stop her.

"Bloodberries," she said, rolling the word around her mouth. It sent a shiver down her spine. She closed her eyes and imagined plucking them from the Marrow Orchard, putting them in her pocket, and bringing them home.

All she needed was a distraction, and the answer was as dreadful as the Billy Witch's laugh.

THE BRINY WITCH'S EYE

Kestrel shredded the beetle dress into hundreds of tiny pieces. Off came the tight laces, off came the cruel black buttons. She ripped huge slits in the skirt so she could move again and pulled the laces apart so there was room to breathe without being cut in half. She tore the pins out of her hair and kicked them into the bushes with the scattered beetle wings, and with every piece of the dress that she ripped her determination to win grew.

Night was already creeping through the trees. Candlelight shone through the shutters in her mother's house. Kestrel dug a hole at the edge of the forest while she waited for the light to go out, ignoring the tight, nervous feeling in her throat. She pushed the pins and beetle wings and tattered pieces of dress into the hole, then stamped earth down over the top.

She wasn't going to leave things behind for her grabber to take.

Kestrel knew it was close. The back of her neck itched, as though someone—or something—was staring at her very hard, but every time she turned around, the forest was empty. Her brain was screaming at her to run. Every second she spent hiding was a second the grabber could use to build its body. But she knew she didn't have a chance of escaping if her mother still had the black dog.

She backed against a tree and closed her fingers around the holey stone in her pocket, feeling like a snail without its shell.

"She'll go to sleep soon," Kestrel said reassuringly, watching her mother's house. For a moment, she forgot that Pippit wasn't there. The only thing listening was the cold, hard moon.

Slowly, the village shut itself up. The kids crept back into their houses in dribs and drabs. Walt threw a last log onto the wolf fire and slipped inside. Before retreating to his house, Ike crept to her mother's door and left a bowl of soup outside before scuttling away like a frightened rat.

Finally, the light flickered out in her mother's house. Kestrel pulled the hood of the wolf-skin cloak over her head and braced herself, sucking in the power in its teeth and claws.

The door was unlocked. Kestrel left it ajar so there was a

small wedge of light to see by, highlighting the long-legged spiders perambulating over the ceiling. The room was cold and filled with scuttling mice.

"Mother," Kestrel whispered, fixing her eyes on the dark shape in the middle of the room, so quietly she was only just moving her mouth. "Are you awake?"

Her mother had her head propped against her hands, her elbows dug into her knees. Her mouth was slightly open and she looked dead but for the thin whistle that came through her nose. As Kestrel had suspected, she was fast asleep. She'd been angrier today than she had in weeks, and it had exhausted her. The black dog was snoring by her side.

Kestrel crawled toward her mother and the dog, trying to make herself as tiny as possible. Her breath rattled loudly in her ears. As she picked her way toward them her elbow caught on a piece of red thread, and the whole room shivered.

Her mother grunted. The dog twitched. Kestrel bit her tongue, screaming internally, but they both fell silent again.

When she was sure they were still asleep, Kestrel swept her hands over the floor around her mother's skirt, squinting until she could see the piece of black string used to control the dog. It was next to her mother's right hand, which lay palm-up like another spider.

She tried to remember exactly what her mother had done with the string when she was tying the dog up. It had looked like a simple knot, but what if there was more to it?

Well, she didn't have a choice. As long as she did it slowly.

She reached out and touched the string. The dog shivered but didn't wake. Kestrel, with her eyes fixed on the dog, picked up the loose end and began looping it over itself, pulling it through the hole as gently as possible, her tongue sticking out the corner of her mouth.

"Steady, boy," she whispered to the dog. "I'm just putting your leash on. . . ."

The dog's eyes flicked open, lamp-yellow and accusatory. Without thinking Kestrel grabbed the string in both hands and pulled tight.

The dog let out a strangled whine and fell to the floor. Its chest was rising and falling, but it was completely, stone-cold unconscious.

Kestrel pulled the knot tighter and tighter, until it was as small and hard as an apple pip, then knotted it again and again for safety. It wouldn't take her mother very long to undo it, and she might wake soon. Hopefully it was enough.

She dropped the string and touched the dog on the head, but it didn't respond. It suddenly looked a lot smaller, lying on the floor with a look of startled consternation on its face. If it wasn't so intent on ruining her life she could almost feel sorry for it.

Almost.

Pale mud bubbled out of the Salt Bog, pushing between huge cracks in the salty crust. Kestrel tried to step as lightly as possible along the paths, but wherever she put her foot down there was a loud crunch. Every time she saw something in the corner of her eye she thought: *grabber!* and whirled to face it, only to find that it was a frozen mouse or a dead leaf blowing around. Even though she couldn't see it, she knew it wouldn't be far away. The thought of it watching made Kestrel quicken her pace, while her nerves shrieked at her to run.

She hurried toward the place she'd last seen the Briny Witch, gripping the handle of her spoon. Her plan was uncomplicated and nerve-racking. She'd find the drowned man and lure him with the promise of her eyes; then at the last minute, force him to make her invisible at spoon-point.

But the farther she walked the less clever her plan sounded. No matter how far she stuck her chin in the air or how hard she gripped her spoon, she felt more and more doubtful. What if she couldn't find him? What if he was stronger than her and pushed her into the bog? What if he had been lying and couldn't help her anyway? What if her grabber caught up with her and ate her first?

"Good evening," whispered the Briny Witch in her ear.

Kestrel jumped and flung her spoon so hard it stuck between two of the drowned man's ribs. He was standing right next to her, his hair floating around him in a slimy aura.

He looked shocked for a second, and when he opened his mouth to speak the only thing that came out was a small, round bubble of surprise. Then he gathered himself, sighed, and pulled the spoon out of his ribs.

It was covered in something like jelly. Kestrel snatched it back and the Briny Witch brought his face close to hers, his milky eyes unblinking, the fat fish circling him like slow comets.

"You know why I'm here," said Kestrel, trying very hard not to lean away from his fishy breath.

"I can guess," said the Briny Witch with his underwater voice. He moved as though he were wading through thick mud, bubbles rising from his nostrils as he spoke. "But maybe you kept me waiting too long. Maybe I changed my mind."

They stared at each other, the Briny Witch with his blind eyes that seemed to know exactly where to fix themselves. Both refused to be the first to speak. After a minute the Briny Witch smiled.

"Very well," he gurgled, an elegant fish circling his head. "What do you want?"

"Invisibility," Kestrel said firmly.

"For?"

"My eyes," she said, tightening her hand on her spoon. The Briny Witch licked his lips.

"I detect a hint of untruth," he said.

The bubbles around his head popped, and he sprang

toward her with the speed of a wolf. Kestrel lashed out with her spoon, catching him in the arm, shocked by his sudden rapidity. The blade bounced off, and it was all Kestrel could do not to drop it. The Briny Witch's hair was no longer floating about his head, and he was dripping water as though he had just stepped out of rainfall. He closed his fingers over the top of her head, holding her still, and chuckled with a noise like knucklebones rattling in a cup.

Kestrel felt water running down the side of her head and shivered.

"You're a stupid little girl," the Briny Witch said, his voice no longer wet. He sounded cruel and elegant. "You thought I was slow. You thought you could cut me to pieces and take what you wanted, and I'd simply float around like a slow, fat fish." He leaned in. "That's why you shouldn't trust strangers," he said.

"You've forgotten something," Kestrel replied, her stomach churning as his wet fingers pressed into the side of her head.

"And what's that?"

"You shouldn't trust little girls, either."

Kestrel twisted herself out of his grasp and flung herself square into his chest. They both tumbled backward, the Briny Witch's slimy rags and her toothy cloak tangling together. Kestrel tried to wrestle him to the floor, determined to pin him down and make him give her what she wanted,

214

but he was stronger than she imagined. He fought back, and they tumbled over and over, trying to wrestle each other to the ground. She reached for her spoon but the Briny Witch knocked it away. It hit a frozen badger and stuck there, point out.

She really, *really* needed to learn to hold it properly.

Neither of them realized they'd left the path until they heard the *crack*. The salt crust split and pulled apart with a long, slow sound, like ice being crushed between teeth. Kestrel felt a jolt of panic, remembering that the Briny Witch had said there was something in the water that had preserved him. It was too late. They fell through and plunged into the water, springing apart just as they were swallowed.

Kestrel remembered to hold her breath just before the water closed over her head, so cold it felt like she'd been encased in ice. The wolf-skin cloak floated up behind her, still clasped at the neck, twirling in the water as though it were alive.

Kestrel's eyes were wide open as she plunged to the bottom. The moonlight shone through cracks and holes in the salt, illuminating the bog in astonishing detail.

It was full of animals who had wandered in and drowned, but they were perfectly preserved, their fur lifting and settling with the movement of the water. Thick, blubbery blue weeds curled between them like waving hands. At the bottom of the bog there was a rotting wooden table and a set of chairs, with weeds growing up the legs. There was one place set for the Briny Witch's dinner.

The Briny Witch floated down beside her and laughed. He had no trouble opening his mouth underwater.

"I like this," he said, gurgling again. "I don't have to make deals with dead people. I'll just wait for you to drown and take what I want."

He reached out for Kestrel, and she kicked him away clumsily. He sniggered and stepped back to watch her struggle.

As Kestrel floundered for the surface red dots grew in front of her eyes, and she felt light-headed with the effort of kicking. Everything around her grew vague. In her dizziness it looked like the animals were laughing, shaking their heads as they watched. The Briny Witch settled into his waterlogged chair, waiting for her to drown and come floating down.

She faltered for a second and drifted back, barely fighting the terrible urge to take a deep breath. She should have known this would happen. Granmos always said she was a terrible swimmer, and that anything that wanted to kill her should just push her into a pond.

Kestrel started to kick. She was *not* going to prove her grandma right.

She struck for the surface with every last ounce of energy. The Briny Witch jumped up and came after her, but it was too late. Kestrel's hands broke into the air, and then she was pulling herself out of the hole and onto the path. The Briny Witch tried to grab her ankles, but she withdrew them just in time.

Kestrel spat out a particularly unpleasant-looking water-bug and pulled herself to her feet. She waited for the Briny Witch to emerge, but nothing happened.

She growled and stamped over to the hole in the bog.

"Come out, you coward!" she yelled.

The Briny Witch politely cleared his throat behind her.

Kestrel turned and grabbed his hands just as he reached for her face. They thrashed around for a few seconds before falling over, then Kestrel's right hand went through its chest, which, with him being a corpse, was wet and bloated. They both shouted in disgust as her hand touched his ribs.

"Get your hand out of my ribs," the Briny Witch snarled.

"Let my hand go," Kestrel snarled back, her fingers trapped between its bones.

"Not until I get your eyes."

"I'm not leaving until you make me invisible, and you don't get my eyes, because that's gross."

"Maybe I'll just take them!" the Briny Witch hissed.

"Maybe I'll knock your head off, and you won't need eyes!" Kestrel hissed back.

They glared at each other. Kestrel could feel his water-logged heart thumping under her fingers. Maybe if she squeezed it she could stop him altogether, but the thought of killing him with her bare hands made her shudder.

Kestrel moved her free hand to her pocket, looking for something sharp enough to hurt him with, but her fingers closed around the round, holey stone that Finn had given her.

"It won't take a second," the Briny Witch said, his hand pressing against her face. "I'll just pluck them out and pop them in."

"Wait," she gasped, her fingers scrabbling on the stone, although it came out more like a muffled gasp. The Briny Witch hesitated, then parted his fingers so she could speak. "*Wait*. I have something better than my eyes."

"So *now* you want to trade," the Briny Witch said gloatingly. "You know exactly what I want."

"You can have an eye," she said. "Just not the one in my head."

The Briny Witch peeled his hand away, probably so Kestrel could see his sneer all the better. Kestrel finally managed to pull her fingers free of his ribs.

"I have a special stone from the forest," she said before he could move again. "If you look through it, you can see the future."

The Briny Witch snorted and tried to grab the stone from her hand, but she closed her fist around it.

"I still want invisibility," she said.

"I still want your eyes," he replied quickly.

"What's the point? You know they'll rot," she said, looking at his bloated, wet body. "You live in the water. You'd go blind again in days. But stones last forever."

The Briny Witch scoffed, but she knew that she'd caught his attention. He grudgingly held his hand out, and she dropped the stone into his palm. He brought it to its mouth and licked it. Kestrel held her breath.

"You're a tricky one," he said.

Kestrel snatched it out of his hand.

"Do we have a deal?" she snapped.

The Briny Witch hesitated. The hole in his chest was leaking water, and he suddenly looked old and tired.

"Come with me," the Briny Witch said shortly.

Kestrel extracted her spoon from the nearby badger, silently apologizing, and followed the Briny Witch to the edge of the bog. She stayed well back from him, but it didn't seem like he was going to try any more tricks.

"What are you doing?" she asked suspiciously.

"Take your little victory and don't push it, or I'll change my mind," the Briny Witch said sharply. He was clearly not happy with what he was about to do.

He plunged a hand into the bog and broke the salt crust, making a big hole through which Kestrel could see gray goop.

"Please excuse me," said the Briny Witch. "This is . . . embarrassing."

He turned to the hole.

"Hurble, hurble, toil and turble," he said to the hole. He lowered his voice, as though he didn't want Kestrel to hear any more. "Fire burn, and cauldron … burble."

He waited a moment, then sighed. He seemed to know that Kestrel was laughing, even though she hadn't made a sound.

"Is this a joke?" Kestrel asked, straightening her face and folding her arms.

"They won't come unless you make a fool of yourself and sing," the Briny Witch said. "Do you have any frog spawn?"

"Er … no?" said Kestrel, thrown.

"Very well." He dug a stone out of the ground. "By the picking of these … plums," he said, "something tasty this way comes."

The bog continued to belch.

"Come out, you little idiots," the Briny Witch snapped.

Three faces bobbed out of the gray bog, round and pudgy like babies, with blue eyes and rosy cheeks. They looked livid. The largest face spat at the Briny Witch.

"Whaddya want?" it demanded, swiveling so it could look directly at them. It had the voice of an old man who smoked thirty pipes a day. "We were having a nap!"

"Yeah!" said the second and third shrilly, spinning around. Kestrel gagged as some of the bog hit her.

"Give me invisibility," the Briny Witch said. "Go on."

"Just like that?" said the biggest head. "Just give it to you?"

"I command you," the Briny Witch snapped, pushing the head under the water. "Just do it."

The other two heads cackled and disappeared after the first.

"Give me your cloak," the Briny Witch said. Kestrel stared at him, aghast. He snatched the wolf skin away from her.

"That's mine," she snapped, trying to grab it.

"You'll get it back," he said, rolling it into a ball.

"What are you doing? What *are* they?"

"Minions," said the Briny Witch, disgusted. "They're awful. I don't recommend them at all."

The bog coughed and sputtered. The Briny Witch dropped the cloak in, which hissed like water in an oil pan. Then he picked up a stick and slowly stirred the soup. Kestrel hopped from foot to foot impatiently.

"They'll take their time," the Briny Witch said. "There's no point fidgeting." He poked the soup, then sniggered. "Did you find that grabber you were looking for?"

Kestrel frowned. It looked like the Briny Witch was enjoying himself.

"My grandma's grabber? No," she said cautiously.

To her surprise the Briny Witch gave a wicked smile. He pointed at the edge of the bog, just a few hundred yards away.

"Look over there," he said, grinning.

Kestrel looked at him suspiciously, then trod carefully toward the edge of the bog. There was a large bone on the ground, half covered in dirt. She circled it slowly, peering at it from every angle. Then she felt something underfoot, looked down, and saw a slim finger bone poking out from under her boot. She drew back quickly.

She was in the middle of a bone graveyard. There were hundreds of bones on the ground, all different sizes and shapes. There were teeth as well, from huge fist-size molars to tiny incisors that could have belonged to a mouse.

Kestrel gingerly picked up a bone and inspected it. It wasn't old; it could only have been here for a couple of years. There was a thin layer of salt on the outside, enough to make it undelicious to the scavengers that lived in the forest.

The hairs on the back of her neck stood up, and not because she was being watched. Kestrel dropped the bone and looked around again. She could see other small things among the bones, like horribly familiar tarnished silver rings and the broken chain from a silver necklace.

Kestrel got up quickly, shivering as a bone crunched under her foot. She backed away until she was almost in the bog again. She could see the whole thing clearly now.

She had been standing in the remains of a dead grabber. She could even see its outline, as though it had gently lain down and fallen to bits.

And near its hip bone was a huge, bronze key.

For a moment she thought she would be sick. She *knew* that key. It was the key her grandma's grabber had stolen from her, to help make its body. And those rings—she saw them flashing on her grandma's fingers. She saw them swing toward her as her grandma surprised her with a knife in a training exercise. She stepped back, the bog swinging sickeningly around her, and put her foot down on a tarnished silver locket. She remembered it pressing against her ribs as her grandma forced her against the wall and shouted at her. The grabber had taken it all.

"It's been there a few years," the Briny Witch said conversationally. "The grabber dragged itself all the way over here, then collapsed."

Kestrel turned away from the remains, feeling ill. She couldn't make herself look at them any longer. Her grandma was among those remains, the woman who she'd helped kill. And that was her grandma's grabber. Dead. *How?*

"There must have been something wrong with it," Kestrel said, trying to ignore her racing thoughts. "That's why it died. Maybe Granmos was too tough for it."

Over in the bog, the Briny Witch sniggered.

"Think again," he said, clearly having fun. "I see grabbers crawling past sometimes. All half dead. All full up after their meals. They disappear into the forest and collapse, and they never come past again."

Kestrel put her hands over her ears, blocking him out.

"If grabbers were just lying down and dying all the time, I would have come across their bodies," she said. "I would have seen all sorts of weird things in the forest, like..."

Like silver rings. Like old shoes. Like forks and candle-holders and cups. All the trinkets she'd picked up from the forest.

Kestrel's stomach dropped. Was that why she'd never seen a grabber again after it had eaten? Did they just crumble to pieces?

She thought of her dad's grabber running toward the cliff after eating him. The image made her queasy, but now she couldn't brush aside what else she'd seen. The grabber had scattered tiny pieces of its body behind it, as though it was already falling apart. As though now that it had taken its victim, there was nothing left to hold it together.

She'd never been able to catch a grabber before it ate, but afterward, it was easier. She'd thought it was because they were bloated and slow, but what if she was wrong? What if they were already dying? It wouldn't take long for the wolves and the birds to carry away all the tasty old bones. Unless they were covered in salt, like these.

She made herself look at the bones again. The piece of paper it had stolen from Granmos—the section of her journal about the grabbers—would have long since rotted away. Now only her rings and her locket and the big bronze key were left.

"You finally got there," the Briny Witch said, seeing her face. "Your cloak's ready, by the way."

Kestrel floated toward him in a daze.

Had her mother known the truth all along?

The thought made her cold. It was a huge lie, a ground-breakingly and fantastically cruel one. It would mean that Kestrel had been risking her life hunting grabbers for nothing. It meant that her mother never had any intention of letting Kestrel go, because Kestrel would never fulfill her end of the bargain and catch her grandma's grabber. And the villagers thought they needed her mother to send Kestrel hunting, but they were all completely and totally *wrong*.

Kestrel shivered. How much of the forest had actually grown from their bodies? How many of the trees had come from an acorn that a grabber had stuck between its ribs? She looked at the nearby tree line and felt even more trapped than ever.

"One invisibility cloak," the Briny Witch said shortly.

Concentrate, she told herself fiercely. *You have a job to do.*

Kestrel forced herself to look at the cloak. It was exactly the same, if a little damp.

"Shouldn't it be invisible?" she asked, struggling to speak through the fog in her head.

"No," the Briny Witch said, turning his head toward her so quickly she was sprayed with water. She could see that he was losing his patience. "How would you ever find it?"

Kestrel reached out for it, but the Briny Witch held it over his head.

"Once it's on, it lasts for an hour," he said. "Consider this fair warning."

That was enough to get Kestrel's attention.

"One hour?" she repeated, outraged. "That's nothing!"

"We didn't discuss terms," he said. "Take it or leave it."

"How will I know it works?"

"Are you calling me a liar?" he said, his mouth widening to show his teeth.

Kestrel hesitated with her fingers around the stone. She had no reason to trust the Briny Witch, but it wasn't like she had another choice. She was now certain that her mother was lying to her, and the only way of getting rid of the dog was to destroy her spells with the bloodberries. For that, she needed the cloak.

"This stone's worth a lot to me," Kestrel said, her stomach scrunching up. She'd promised Finn she'd always keep it.

"I know," the Briny Witch said.

"So I want more," she said, knowing she was pushing her luck. "Tell me what you know about the Marrow Orchard."

"You're bold, aren't you?" the Briny Witch said. He looked,

in some small way, delighted that she'd asked. "It's no place for a stupid young girl. The Marrow Orchard will chew you up and spit out your bones."

"What about the things guarding it?"

"Bonebirds," said the Briny Witch. "They chew the body parts that get spit out."

He leered and held out his hand.

Kestrel wanted to know more, but every second she wasted bargaining with the Briny Witch was another second in which her own grabber could grow stronger. She'd have to take the chance. Kestrel took the stone out of her pocket and tossed it to the Briny Witch. He caught it eagerly and pushed it into his right eye, completely regardless of the eyeball that was already in there. It looked like he was wearing a peculiar monocle.

"Well?" said Kestrel, perturbed. "Can you see the future?"

The Briny Witch slowly inserted a finger through the hole and fiddled with it. Then he fixed Kestrel in his particularly stony gaze.

"Yes," he whispered. "I can see everything."

"What's it like?" she asked, feeling cold.

The Briny Witch didn't answer. Kestrel could feel that weird sensation on the back of her neck again, like something was watching her, and her only instinct now was to get away from the bog. She grabbed the cloak and rolled it up.

"Can you tell me the way to the Marrow Orchard?" she asked.

"That way," he said, pointing a long finger. He sounded like he wanted her to disappear as fast as possible. "Just follow the smell."

"Thank you," Kestrel said, backing away. The Briny Witch still looked deeply disturbed. "I guess I'll see you around."

"I wouldn't hold my breath," he replied quietly, gazing right through her. "In fact, I don't suppose you'll be around for very long at all."

THE MARROW ORCHARD

"Follow the smell," Kestrel muttered, her hand clamped over her nose. "Good one."

"Smell" was an understatement. After scrambling through the undergrowth for more than an hour, Kestrel had arrived at a thick, dark pond. The surface was covered in an oily skin, and every now and then something brown and greasy would lurch from the water and snap at a fly. On the other side of it, just visible through the trees, was a clearing. Kestrel was sure that it was the Marrow Orchard. The smell was coming from there, rolling toward her in thick waves.

The stink was so thick it made the air sticky, and even though it was nighttime, flies bumbled around lethargically as though they'd just staggered home from an eating contest. Even the trees around the pond were bent over like they had a stomachache.

Kestrel wondered if the forest got more and more moldy

the farther you went from the village, until the whole world just collapsed like a rotten fruit with a tiny cluster of people at its core.

She considered her options. She and Finn had never gone into this part of the forest, and it wasn't just because it was one of the last places in her grandma's notebook. Even the wolves avoided it, sensing something inherently wrong with the air. She stopped for a moment, leaned over, and spat on the ground to get the strange taste of mold out of her mouth. Her stomach was shrieking with wild hunger, but the thought of eating made her press her lips together.

A large, bloated tree had fallen into the pond, making a bridge that stretched almost the whole way across. It looked like it would fall apart under her feet. But then Kestrel looked at the thick, dark trees around the water and realized that anything could be hiding in there. Anything like–

I'll take my chances, she decided quickly, pushing the thought away. The less she allowed herself to think about her grabber, the easier it was to carry on. But it didn't stop the sick feeling in the pit of her stomach, or the sensation of eyes boring into the back of her neck.

She stepped onto the log. It sank lower in the water, and scum sloshed over Kestrel's feet. She took one step, then another, her legs wobbling. The log bobbed up and down, sending thick ripples through the oily pond. A large, brown fish slowly rose to the surface and watched her, its tail squirming.

Granmos had liked using water in her training. Once, Kestrel had woken up to find that she'd been tied to a plank and set adrift in the middle of a leech-infested pond. She had nightmares about those leeches for years, remembering the way they swarmed over her as she struggled to paddle to safety. She couldn't see a leech without thinking of her grandma and feeling sick with fear.

Maybe my grabber will be something to do with water.

But even as she thought it, she knew that it wasn't true. There was something else that she was terrified of, something a hundred times worse. As she tried to shove the thought away, she lost her concentration. Her foot slipped and she wobbled. The brown fish saw its chance and lurched at her, but she was already gone, running along the rest of the trunk and leaping to dry land. She wiped the sweat from her forehead and crept toward the clearing in front of her.

Kestrel secreted herself in the gnarled roots of a tree, then she peered over the top to get a better look.

Her stomach curled up like a piece of bacon in a frying pan.

In the middle of the clearing a ring of huge gray stones encircled a sprawling mass of fruit trees. Each stone was the height of her waist and as pitted as a rotting tooth. They were spread with moldering fruit, as though they had been used as grim banqueting tables. Twisting in and out of the stones was a wall of black thorns, each one the size and shape of a carving knife, in horrible, almost comical contrast to the bright white flowers poking out of the grass.

Despite the decay on the ground, the trees inside the ring of stones were drooping with the kind of fruit that lives in fairy tales: red, glossy apples; purple plums the size of Kestrel's fist; pears that were so huge they looked like they would burst. Suddenly Kestrel couldn't smell mold anymore.

She was almost drooling, but her common sense kicked in before she could hurl herself toward the trees.

Look again, she could hear Granmos saying, and Kestrel obeyed, still longing to feel the fruit between her teeth.

She blinked and refocused. Animals hung from the black thorns that surrounded the orchard, flat and empty as clothes hung out to dry. Foxes and rabbits and stoats had all been impaled on the spikes. All the blood had been drained from them, dripping through the gaps in the stones and soaking into the soil.

Kestrel's stomach groaned again, but not in a good way. She could see now that the grass wasn't covered in white flowers. It was strewn with bones of all sizes and shapes, white and smooth as though they had been sucked clean. There were teeth marks in most of them, like something had been happily gnawing on them for days.

It eats things, Kestrel thought, imagining that she was writing it in the notebook. *If you make it inside, it chews you up and spits out the bones.*

She was about to inch out of her hiding place when something huge and gray smacked into the ground in front of her. The creature landed a few inches from Kestrel's hiding place, turned its head, and caught a beetle from the air with a powerful crunch. The creature was the size and shape of a human, but it was thickly covered in stiff gray feathers, and it had huge, dirty gray wings.

Kestrel ducked back between the gnarled tree roots, her heart thumping. The creature gobbled to itself happily, preening.

It was close enough for Kestrel to see everything in perfect detail. Its wings jerked as though the creature only had nominal control over them. Its head, hands, and feet were bald, and it had three rows of teeth on the top and bottom of its jaws, sharp as bits of broken bottle.

Kestrel peered at the trees around the clearing. She remembered the Briny Witch's warning, and shuddered. *Bonebirds.*

Every branch had at least one of the foul creatures crouched on it, their toes hooked over the edge, arms tucked under their twitching wings. They had been asleep, but some were opening their eyes and clicking their jaws, and when they saw the bonebird that was strutting near Kestrel's hiding place they started to shuffle and chitter. Within minutes they were all in a state of high anxiety. They launched themselves from the trees and landed heavily, pushing and shoving one another out of the way as they scrambled to reach the bones on the ground.

Kestrel cursed under her breath. She'd almost run straight into the Marrow Orchard, right under the noses of the bonebirds. She hadn't even bothered to look up at the trees before doing it. She was losing her hunting instincts.

There was only one gap in the thorns through which she could reach the Marrow Orchard and some of the bonebirds were already in front of it, shuffling their wings and agitatedly biting the air. Even if she were invisible they would feel her shoving past, and she had no doubt that their teeth could cut through to the bone. The thought of getting in the way of one of the bonebird's mouths made her shudder.

The last bonebird, a thin one with particularly long teeth, landed in front of Kestrel's hiding place. It looked around, then stuffed apple after apple in its mouth, chewing noisily and spraying bits of old fruit everywhere while the others pecked at the bones.

Some of the rotten apples had rolled toward Kestrel. The bonebird hadn't noticed them, but they were still just out of her reach.

Kestrel knew that she needed those apples. If Pippit was here he'd run out and grab them, or distract the bonebirds for her. She instinctively touched the side of her face, where he pressed his nose when he was trying to tell her something, and swallowed a lump.

It was her own fault he'd gone. But it was no good thinking about it now. She shook his weasel-y face from her head and waited for her chance, but the bonebird with the apples refused to turn around again. The minutes felt infinite, and with every second that passed Kestrel was itching to leap up and wriggle her cramped toes and wave her arms.

Two bonebirds were fighting on the other side of the clearing. There was a horrible screeching sound as they tried to knock each other to the ground with their wings. The bonebird in front of Kestrel craned its neck to watch, clicking its teeth together excitedly. Just as one of the fighters let out a screech of pain, Kestrel reached out and grabbed the three apples closest to her, withdrawing just as the bonebird turned back to eat. She froze, praying that it hadn't seen her. The bonebird gazed into the tree roots, but after a few seconds it licked its lips and turned back to its feast.

Very slowly, keeping her eyes fixed on the creature in front of her, Kestrel unrolled the wolf-skin cloak. It was still damp from the Salt Bog, and it smelled like sour cheese. She felt a prick of doubt. It didn't look special at all.

She weighed one of the apples in her hand, then wriggled into a position where she could draw her arm back, feeling like she was about to do something very foolish.

She wished that Finn was here to count her down. She

wished that Pippit was by her side, ready to attack. She wished more than anything that her dad hadn't sent her here, and that she'd been able to save him in time.

But wishes wouldn't keep you alive in the forest.

Kestrel threw the apple as hard as she could.

It sailed into the clearing, high above the bonebird's head. The bonebird leaped to its feet and pelted after it without thinking, colliding head-on with three other bonebirds that had the exact same idea. One of them opened its mouth wide, unhinging its jaw for maximum effect, and jumped into the path of the apple. The fruit sailed right down its throat. It swallowed with a horrible, greedy gulping sound.

The other bonebirds in the clearing were taking an interest as well. As their heads turned, trying to work out where the apple had come from, Kestrel drew her arm back and flung the second.

It went farther this time and three more of the bonebirds hurtled toward it. They threw themselves after the fruit, squawking, snapping their teeth at the apple until it was little more than a heap of mush on the ground.

They fell back and looked toward Kestrel. They knew the apples were coming from somewhere. Kestrel felt a bead of sweat roll down her nose.

One of them started to trot toward her, its head tilted to one side. It was joined by another, and another, all three pretending not to notice one another.

She clenched her teeth.

This time she waited until they were close, then she flung the apple as hard as she could. They took off after it, screeching along with the rest of the pack, leaving a clear path to the orchard. Without a second thought Kestrel flung the cloak on and tore herself from the roots of the tree.

She ran into the clearing, hurtling toward the gap in the thorns, the cloak flapping behind her. She was faster than a greased fox. She was as speedy as a centipede diving into the floorboards, escaping the blows of a heavy book. She was going to make it! She...

Oh.

The bonebirds had already decimated the apple.

Now they were looking right at her.

They crowded around her in a ring, cutting her off and snapping their teeth. Kestrel's heart was hammering so hard she thought it would fail. The Briny Witch had lied to her. She wasn't invisible at all.

She tried to shuffle away from the bonebirds, but one of them snapped its teeth at her, and she tripped over a bone.

She landed on her chin, bit her tongue, and cried out in a mixture of pain and surprise.

Kestrel prodded her front tooth with her tongue. It was as sharp as a saw.

The bonebird in front of her wrinkled its nose in disgust

and wandered off, its legs jerking like a puppet's. One by one the others did the same, hooting and preening.

Kestrel slowly climbed to her feet and looked behind her. Heavy gray wings cast shadows over the ground.

"The forest have mercy on me," she whispered. She was a bonebird, complete with wings and teeth. Her wolf-skin cloak was gone, and instead there were feathers stuck to her body, close as a second skin and as itchy as a rash. One of the bonebirds turned back to look at her.

"Hoot," Kestrel said quickly.

It gave her a foul look and moved on.

Kestrel stood there, paralyzed by indecision. She looked at the shadow of her wings again. They fluttered nervously.

She took a cautious step forward and tried walking jerkily, even twitching her head as she made her way toward the orchard. After a minute she felt like she was getting better at it.

"Coo," she said as the ring of stones loomed up in front of her. She glanced around, but none of the bonebirds were taking much notice of her now. She flapped her arms experimentally. They didn't feel so bad. In fact, none of this was terrible at all.

Maybe, if she was honest, she was even enjoying herself a bit.

If Finn could see me now he'd be so jealous....

She grew cold at the memory of him twitching on the floor.

"Coo," she said again, trying to forget the image.

Her nerves almost got the better of her as she passed through the gap in the stones. She had to breathe in to avoid being caught by the vicious thorns that weaved between them. Inside the black tangle of spikes there were mice and squirrels and foxes, and some bigger things, too: a treecreeper, a wolf. They hung there sadly like abandoned toys.

She actually felt a bit sorry for them. Nothing deserved to end up as food for the orchard, even the nasty things that bit.

The Marrow Orchard stretched out in front of her. The ground was a carpet of tree roots, all knotted together in a huge, complicated mess. The branches were all tangled up, too, so apples were crushed together with berries and lemons were squashed against plums. Now that she was inside the stench of the place was overwhelming, like a compost heap in the sun. Most of the fruit was fat and ready to fall. Everything was sticky, and the air had the tang of blood.

The roots around her feet were slowly squirming, almost as though the orchard was wriggling its toes. She pulled her feet away from a curling root and curiously touched a cluster of plums hanging over her head. They were as warm as flesh, and they were quivering.

She snatched her hand away and looked closely at the apples next to her. They weren't apples at all. They were round and ripe and red, but they squirmed rhythmically like hearts. She stepped back, feeling nauseous. The oranges were curled-up livers, and the white berries with red veins were actually eyeballs. They swiveled to watch her pass. The trees were covered in thick, wrinkled skin.

Now Kestrel wanted nothing more than to run away, but she couldn't turn back, not if she ever wanted to get away from the black dog and escape the forest. She picked her way through the fleshy orchard, making herself look at every disgusting, quivering fruit she passed. She hoped she'd recognize the bloodberries when she saw them.

Something moved behind her. Kestrel turned quickly, withdrawing her spoon, and realized in that second that she was waiting for her grabber.

But instead, it was the bonebird whose fruit she had stolen. Kestrel glared at it, her heart tripping over itself with relief. Its head twitched and it smiled widely at Kestrel, revealing teeth stained purple with fruit. It turned and innocently plucked an apple from the tree.

Kestrel snapped her new teeth at it, warning it to stay put, and carried on.

The more Kestrel looked at the trees, the more difficult it became to see anything that might be called a bloodberry.

There were so many colors she felt blinded, and the smell was overwhelming all her other senses. She stumbled through the orchard, no longer bothering to hoot and strut. It felt like she'd been in there for days, but the slowly lightening sky told her that she'd only been in there for half an hour.

After a while she realized that the bonebird was following her again, always stopping when Kestrel did, staying just a few yards behind. Maybe it suspected something. *Or maybe,* she thought unhappily, *maybe they're cannibals.* Kestrel growled at it, but the bonebird only looked at her interestedly.

Birds, she realized, didn't growl.

She hurried on, becoming more desperate. She'd already taken too long, and she had to get out before her time was up and her disguise failed.

She pushed between two trees, kicking rotten pears from under her feet and sweeping a low branch out of her way. Her hand came back scarlet with blood. She stifled a cry, wiping her hand on her skirt, then looked up.

The tree next to her was dripping red. The thick, dark liquid oozed from cracks in its bark, forming a sticky, sweet-smelling puddle at her feet. Its branches were laden with thousands of tiny red berries, each as bright as a bead and attached to the branch by a thin red artery.

As Kestrel stepped back from the red puddle she saw that

there were creatures lying in the roots of the tree. A fox, a hare, a small bird. The fox's mouth was stained red with juice, and the bird still had one of the berries clasped in its beak. They were all deathly still.

She reached up to touch a heavy cluster of the berries. They shivered under her fingers as though they carried the heartbeat of the tree. There was almost no doubt that these were the berries she was looking for, and that they were deadly in large doses.

Her fingers hovered in the air. A question hung in front of her, her choice as delicate as a bubble. Was she really going to take them? Was she really going to feed them to her own mother?

Then she thought of Finn curled up on the floor, and her fist closed around a cluster of the berries. Before she could think, she pulled hard. They rained down on her, bouncing off her head and arms. She fished around for them on the ground, shuddering as her fingers touched the warm, bloody puddle, and stuffed them in her pockets until she couldn't carry any more.

She turned away from the tree and came face-to-face with the bonebird.

It grinned with all six rows of teeth, and Kestrel immediately knew that it could see right through her. She looked down at her feather-free arms and felt her own smooth, white teeth. The wolf-skin cloak hung limply from her shoulders.

"I can explain," she said, holding her hands up, forgetting that they were smeared red. The bonebird screamed, making the trees shudder, and before Kestrel could blink it launched itself at her in a blind frenzy of teeth.

THE FIGURE IN THE TREES

Kestrel's spoon was in her hand before she could think, its pointed edge slashing toward the bonebird.

There was blood. For a dizzying moment Kestrel thought it was her own, but then she pulled the spoon back and dislodged it from the feathered chest of the dirty gray creature, which fell away with a scream. More red liquid rained from the bloodberry tree, mixing with gray feathers on the ground and forming a big, gloopy mess.

The bonebird was surprised, but not hurt enough to run away. It clacked its jaws and flexed its neck. It was getting ready to fly at her again, and Kestrel was trapped with her back to the tree.

"I'm not afraid to use it again!" she shouted, waving the spoon maniacally.

But the smell of the Marrow Orchard, all rotting meat and redness, made her so light-headed she could barely point the spoon. She held it out in front of her, but her hands were shaking.

Weak, she thought miserably. *What kind of hunter can't kill an overgrown pigeon?*

The bonebird lunged, and Kestrel reacted too late. She tried to fight it off, but her spoon bounced off its feathered arm.

The bonebird held her tight by the shoulders, and they stared at each other for a long moment, Kestrel completely in its grasp. Then it pulled Kestrel's head toward its face as its mouth snapped open.

In the second that she knew it was going to try and bite her ear off, she also knew that if she flipped her arm like *this* and brought her leg around like *this*—

She threw the bonebird off balance, and it reeled to the side, its teeth snapping shut on the wolf-skin cloak. It tore away from her shoulders, and the bonebird cackled. Kestrel grabbed its arm and shoved it into the oozing trunk of the bloodberry tree.

It squawked and flapped and Kestrel raised her weapon again, but there was no need for the spoon now. The bonebird's back was stuck to the viscous goo coming from the tree. Its wings twitched uselessly, then it stopped and stared at Kestrel with its awful orange eyes. It was still clutching her cloak.

Kestrel wiped the spoon on her skirt. The bloody trees

shivered and the multicolored fruits pulsed on their branches. There was a new kind of quiet, the dangerous sort. The bonebird, now silent, knew it, too.

Kestrel chewed her lip. She hadn't stopped to consider the most obvious question: *What would a carnivorous orchard do if something wandered into its stomach?*

"Ohhh no," said Kestrel as she thought of the answer. "No, no, no."

The orchard was going to swallow her whole.

The bonebird started struggling again, twisting its head from side to side.

Kestrel ran. The ground sucked at her feet and rumbled as purple-and-red fruit juice pattered down from the trees.

She hadn't even thought to leave a trail, something her grandma would kill her for if she were here now. Kestrel stumbled on blindly, pushing through the plants. The ground convulsed and she nearly tripped, but she steadied herself and continued.

Kestrel saw the gap in the thorns and sprinted toward it, praying she'd make it in time. The ground tilted backward, and the fruit on the floor rolled toward the middle of the orchard. It was as though a hole had opened in the middle, and everything was being pulled into it. Racing upward, Kestrel threw herself through the thorn gap and tumbled into the bright green grass and fresh sunlight.

Kestrel turned and watched in disbelief as all the trees

leaned toward the middle of the orchard, creaking and trembling. The huge gray stones crashed against one another as the ground shifted. There was a long, low gurgling sound.

Then slowly, almost gracefully, the orchard began to unfold again. The trees uncurled toward the sky, stripped bare of their fruit. Kestrel could see that new, younger pieces were already beginning to bloom on its branches.

The orchard had devoured the bonebird and the fruit and the wolf-skin cloak and everything else inside it.

Everything was peaceful for a moment. Then the Marrow Orchard belched, and bones pattered down around Kestrel's ears.

She shielded her face until it had finished, then wiped her forehead on the back of her sleeve. She was covered in goo and sweat and pieces of half-chewed fruit. But she had the bloodberries in her pocket, and she was alive.

"I did it," she said, astonished. She'd kept her promise to her dad. She had the bloodberries. She was going to get out!

Something hit the ground in front of her in a flurry of stiff feathers and snapping teeth. Kestrel backed away as the bonebird righted itself and clacked its teeth at her.

"Hoot," said Kestrel, trying to edge around it, but she didn't have her disguise anymore. The bonebirds had all fled for the trees when the Marrow Orchard swallowed, but now they were pelting down from the sky, heavy and ungraceful. Some of them were already picking through the fresh bones the orchard had spat out, but as soon as they realized Kestrel was there, their eyes sharpened greedily. Kestrel shoved past the bonebird in front of her, but others formed a ring that blocked her from the trees.

They came rushing toward her with their wings open, reaching for her hair and her face, her arms, her skirt. One of the bonebirds grabbed Kestrel's shoulders and pulled her backward toward the thorns. Kestrel screamed in surprise, beating the creature with her spoon, but it made no difference.

She desperately drove her elbow into the bonebird's stomach and it fell aside, howling. As they snapped and pecked at her, trying to tear her clothes with their long nails, she realized that they were looking for something. *They knew what she had stolen.*

Kestrel dug into her pockets and flung a handful of bloodberries away from her. The bonebirds grasped at them as they flew past, but then they came toward her again, scrabbling and pushing. They didn't stop until Kestrel turned her pockets inside out and flung every single one of the berries away.

They scattered like marbles in the emerald grass. For a split second the bonebirds were transfixed by the bright fruit, and taking her chance, Kestrel quickly dropped to her hands and knees. She scrambled through the forest of legs as the bonebirds kicked and fought to reach her, but there were too many of them, and their wings were in the way so they couldn't bend down and grab her. One of the bonebirds snatched at her neck, but it caught its fingers on another creature's wings and the two grappled with each other, screeching.

As Kestrel fought her way through the chaos, she spotted two bright red berries out of the corner of her eye. Before the bonebirds could tell what she was doing, she grabbed them with her free hand and shoved them in her mouth.

They were cold and sour, and she gagged, careful not to bite down. She desperately wanted to spit them out, but she pushed them to the side of her mouth and continued to wriggle through the bonebirds.

As soon as she was able she scrambled to her feet, lashing out with her spoon at a bonebird's hands. The bonebird grabbed it and flung it away, but there was no time to retrieve it. She was already up, racing away from the clearing.

Kestrel ran straight across the waterlogged tree that stretched across the pond. Some of the bonebirds had followed her from the clearing, but they stopped at the edge of the water, frantically beating their wings. They were too slow and heavy to fly more than a few yards. She slowed down on the other side of the pond and looked back.

The bonebirds jeered at her, but not for long. Losing patience, they turned and flung themselves against one another. Their cries rose through the trees and made the real birds scatter.

Kestrel automatically reached for her spoon. Her fingers closed in her empty pocket. She'd had the spoon in her pocket for years, ever since her dad gave it to her. It was the last thing she had of his, and now it belonged to the Marrow Orchard.

Kestrel felt a lump in her throat, but she forced it away. She turned to look at the gap in the trees again, wanting to run back, but she knew that as soon as she returned they would chew her to pieces.

It's just a piece of cutlery, she told herself unconvincingly.

At least not everything had been lost.

Kestrel wrinkled her nose, then spat the two last bloodberries into her hand, where they shone like new buttons.

"Yuck," she said, and slipped them into her pocket. Their taste still lingered in the back of her throat.

She crept back toward the village. Mud squelched under her feet. She looked down and realized that there was a damp trail leading from the edge of the pond into the forest, as though something had been dragged out of the water.

Kestrel ignored her feeling of unease and sped up. She imagined slipping the bloodberries into her mother's food. Soup would be best, she decided—something dark and murky.

But the more she thought about it, the sicker she felt. She had no idea what the berries would actually do. They might weaken her mother's magic and get rid of the dog, but they might do more. They might kill her.

Within minutes she wanted to throw up. She must be mad. She was going to try to *poison her mother*. Her mother, who could throw her to the floor with a single twitch of her finger.

Her mother, who had raised her and looked after her.

Her mother, who had helped make her into the hunter she was today.

Kestrel stopped walking. Her heart was in her throat and she was struggling to suck air into her lungs. She was scared of what would happen if she gave her mother the berries, but she was terrified of being stuck in the forest with her grabber, too. She had to do it.

And she couldn't.

She saw something ahead of her, and froze.

The fat, greasy brown fish she'd seen in the pond was lying in front of her. The wet trail led right up to it. It had been torn open, and its bones were scattered on the ground. The air smelled sour, like a bucket of milk gone bad.

Kestrel's heart started beating at double-speed.

It was just a big animal, she told herself. *Don't think about it.* Even so, she found herself hurriedly stepping over the dead fish. She continued through the forest, following the path of squashed plants she'd carved on the way to the Marrow Orchard.

Then she saw it and stopped dead.

Someone was there, standing at the side of the path.

Kestrel bent down and pretended to tie her shoelaces, but

she was watching the person in the trees. She was lucky she'd seen them; they were half steeped in shadow, and as still as a rock.

Now she could smell something. Mold and mildew. Decay. Vinegar.

Her heart started beating so fast she thought it would fail.

It wasn't a person.

It was a grabber.

Her grabber.

Run after it! she screamed at herself, but she couldn't move an inch. She couldn't shove her fear away. It was too big for her to ignore.

She wanted to know what it was.

No, she didn't.

She *did*.

Something bright and sharp fell in front of Kestrel's face and bounced on the ground, breaking the spell.

It was her spoon.

Kestrel snatched it so fast she almost lopped her own fingers off. Before she knew what she was doing, she strode forward, fizzing with a horrible mixture of bravado and terror.

"Show your face!" she screamed, as though she were holding a saber-toothed sword.

The grabber drew in a deep breath and inclined its face toward her, just for a second. It was too dark for Kestrel to make out its features, but she saw a blob of drool fall from its lips as though it had just been offered a plate of food. Then it turned and plunged into the forest. It didn't seem scared. If anything, it seemed to be enjoying itself.

Kestrel ran after it and glimpsed her slingshot, which seemed to be propping up its head. The grabber turned between two trees. As the light caught the side of its body, she saw that it had covered itself in a tapestry of stitched-together rags, all different colors, like a bright coat. Pieces of silver caught the sunlight and gleamed. It was almost dressed like—

Don't think about it!

Kestrel stumbled into the trees, but it disappeared in an instant, leaving behind nothing but its necrotic smell. She kicked her way through the undergrowth, lashing out with her spoon, but there was nothing more dangerous than a toadstool.

Kestrel shouted in frustration and struggled back to the path. A small part of her knew that she could have gone farther, or run faster, but she stamped on the thought furiously.

"I would've gotten you," she said loudly, but she knew the grabber was gone. Her stomach was churning, and her palms were sweating. Her legs collapsed and she sat down, her fingers still curled around her spoon.

Her spoon. Weapons didn't just fall from the sky. She looked at the trees sharply.

And there was Pippit.

He was stuck to a tree, covered in the weird fruit juice of the Marrow Orchard, his fur matted and sticky, one of his eyes gummed closed.

Kestrel moved without thinking. She climbed the tree faster than she ever had before, and pried him free with both hands. Pippit was disgusting and he smelled, but he was here, he was really here, and he was hers.

She regretted every stupid thing she'd ever done to him and all the times she'd ever been careless.

Like the time she dropped him in a pot of soup.

Or the time she ran away from an angry swarm of bees and managed to leave him behind.

Or when she sat on him and didn't notice.

But he'd come back for her. He'd followed her all this way, and he'd rescued her spoon for her. She felt a rush of love so fierce she almost fell over.

"You stupid weasel!" Kestrel said, nearly sobbing with relief as they slid back to the ground. "You could've been eaten!"

Pippit glared at her with his one unstuck eye and that look told her everything she needed to know.

"I didn't mean to shout earlier," she wept, hugging him until he was as wet as a used handkerchief. "It wasn't your fault about your tail. You were trying to help."

"Gone! Tail! Gone!" Pippit wailed, straining to see his own behind.

"I'll get you another one," she said, not caring that it might be impossible. "I'll fix it."

She sniffled and wiped him on her sweater, trying to get the stickiness off.

"Gruh," said Pippit. "Got a gruh."

"It's nearly ready," she said, hiccupping. "Not yet, or it would have attacked me. But it's getting bigger. It's going to eat me soon."

She closed her eyes and saw her grabber take a deep breath, just like her dad's had before it ate him. She saw its tongue flick from its mouth as it licked its lips. It was almost as if her fear made it hungrier.

Kestrel started to wonder whose form it would take, and cut herself off immediately.

What keeps you awake at night and gives you nightmares? Granmos had asked. *What makes your guts shrivel?*

Kestrel shook her head. It didn't matter. She was going to outrun it. She would never see the grabber's face, because she would escape the forest before it caught up with her.

Say it! her grandma screamed.

"Got gruh!" Pippit said, shattering her thoughts. He jumped up and fought an imaginary grabber, weaving between its legs and biting the air. He fought so hard he threw himself over.

Despite herself, Kestrel snorted with laughter. Pippit, looking pleased with himself, jumped onto her foot.

"Go," he said. "Feed the nasty. Get ridda the dog. No more gruh!"

He was right. She was going to get rid of the dog. Then she was going to run and run, and never stop, until she came to the end of the woods.

POISONOUS PORRIDGE

The black dog was on the rampage. It tore through the houses, scattering everyone's belongings, leaving spoons and clothes and trinkets outside in its wake. Ike was on his hands and knees, scrabbling around after the things he hadn't already burned.

The dog was making a huge show of looking for Kestrel, overturning beds and tables. Every now and then it hurtled toward a villager and barked so sharply they all jumped in unison.

The dog knew Kestrel wasn't there. Neither it nor her mother were that stupid. But Kestrel knew as soon as the villagers saw her, they'd riot against her.

Kestrel crashed to a halt at the edge of the village, dread pooling in her stomach. She knew she had to show herself, and that every minute she wasted hiding in the trees, her grabber was a few steps closer. But somehow, her legs were frozen.

Pippit trembled and nudged her with his nose. "Brave," he said.

Kestrel touched the bloodberries in her pocket, took a deep breath, and stepped out from the trees.

Mardy Banbury looked up and screamed as though she'd just seen a wolf.

Kestrel realized that she must look monstrous. She was dressed in black rags, covered in cuts and bruises, and stained with a mixture of fruit juice and blood. Her hair was sticking out like she'd been hit by lightning. She was still missing part of an eyebrow. And she was so full of tension and pent-up fear that the side of her mouth was twitching.

Walt was the first to speak. "There's your girl," he rumbled to the black dog, his voice as dark as oil. "Now leave us."

The dog huffed through its nose. Mardy let out another small scream, but the black dog, instead of biting Walt's hand off, grinned.

Kestrel started walking, trying to force her legs not to shake, crossing by the well and wolf fire. It was a very long walk. Hannah was leaning against the wall of a tumbledown house, her arms folded. Only Kestrel could hear her as she passed.

"Good luck," Hannah said. Her smile was as cold as milk.

The door to her mother's house was open, the inside as dark as a grabber's belly. Kestrel paused on the doorstep, the villagers' stares scraping down her back. Without taking her eyes off the door she bent down and picked up a cold bowl of porridge that was still on the ground.

The black dog trotted up behind her, radiating excitement. Before it could push her inside, Kestrel twisted her hand and dropped one of the bloodberries into the bowl.

To Kestrel her treachery was as loud as a siren, and she waited for the dog's teeth to rip into her back, almost hoping to get it over with. But the dog did nothing except nudge her sharply with its muzzle.

The bloodberry sank beneath the spoon without a trace.

Kestrel's mother was crouched in the middle of the floor, the weave crisscrossing around her like a cage. Kestrel dropped to her knees and put the bowl down, pushing it through the tunnel in the weave.

Her mother knitted yarn between her fingers, staring into the dark, changing spaces between each pattern. Kestrel hadn't expected this. It was so silent she could hear mice under the floorboards. She waited, feeling sick, until it was clear that she had to speak first.

"I–I screwed up," Kestrel said, her voice tripping.

Silence. Kestrel squirmed.

"I lost my temper," she continued, moving just a little

closer, her throat stoppered with the thick beating of her heart. She couldn't help glancing at the porridge on the floor. "I ran away. But I can't survive in the forest by myself. I want to come home."

The door slammed behind her, making Kestrel jump. The old woman jerked a finger and a fat candle lit itself. Kestrel knew it was bad.

"You want forgiveness," her mother said slowly. She drummed her fingers against her leg. "You've disobeyed me again and again. You've repeatedly lied. Then you crept in here while I was sleeping and tied up the dog that I created to protect you. And now you want... *forgiveness*?"

Kestrel felt as though they were standing on the edge of a cliff; her mother was either going to throw her off the edge or pull her back, and neither of them knew which way it would go.

Her mother stood up. She swept through the weave, right up to Kestrel's face, the strings twisting away to let her through. She was so fast Kestrel didn't have time to move.

"Where did you run to?" her mother hissed, dropping and hooking a finger under Kestrel's chin. Kestrel wriggled.

"I don't know," she gasped, panic setting in. "I just kept going."

"You smell of blood."

"I got hurt."

"Why did you come back?"

"I need you," said Kestrel. Her mother's expression didn't change, but Kestrel thought she might have said the right thing.

Kestrel and her mother stared at each other. Kestrel felt like her lie must be plastered across her face, huge and red, but somehow she kept her face still. She wondered if her mother knew that her grabber was following her. If she did, she'd never fall for this.

"Flattery doesn't suit you," her mother said shortly. She withdrew her finger. "I suppose you do need me, don't you?"

She dropped Kestrel. "I've given you too much freedom," she said. "I should have broken all your bones the first time you disobeyed me. Maybe then you wouldn't be so arrogant."

"I won't do it again," said Kestrel shakily. She touched the bowl of porridge with her fingertips, praying her mother would notice it. It trembled with her hands.

"Look at yourself," her mother said, the corners of her mouth hard. "Look at the way you're shaking. You're as cowardly as your father."

Kestrel's arm jerked with the barely contained impulse to attack her mother. The side of her hand caught the bowl, which rattled and spun on the floor.

Her mother finally noticed the bowl, snatched it, and lifted it to her nose.

"Where did you get this?"

"It was outside," Kestrel said quickly.

Her mother slowly twirled the spoon in the bowl. Kestrel held her breath, but the bloodberry was still hidden.

"It was left for me, you greedy pig," her mother said. "From now on, you'll only eat when I let you."

She picked up the spoon, raised it to her nose and sniffed. She smiled at Kestrel.

"Delicious," she said.

Then she reached out, as quick as a snake striking, and grabbed Kestrel by the neck.

"You little witch," she said, rising, dragging Kestrel with her. She stamped on the bowl so hard it shattered. "I can smell that a mile off."

Her mother tightened her strong, bony hands. Kestrel tried speaking, but panic drowned her and she couldn't get any words out.

"Feeding poison to your own mother," she shrieked. "I was stupid to keep you as long as I did. I am going to *break* you!"

"You—need—" Kestrel gasped, struggling.

"I need what? *You?*" Her mother dropped her. Kestrel landed in a pile on the floor.

Kestrel's mother stood over her, flexing her fingers.

"You need your arms and legs for hunting," she hissed. "But you don't need a pretty face. You think the villagers hate you now? Imagine what they'll say when you only have half a *skull!*"

Her mother grabbed a piece of string above her head, the one with Kestrel's tooth tied into it. Kestrel leaped up and drove her knee into her mother's chest. Her mother doubled over, and Kestrel tore the string from her hands as she fell back.

"Dad was right to leave," Kestrel yelled, clutching the tooth in her fist. Her mother was back on her feet. The black dog advanced toward Kestrel, and she stepped back toward the door. "You tell lies to make people do things."

"You're calling *me* a liar?"

"I know the grabbers die after they've eaten!" Kestrel yelled. She hadn't meant to say it, but her fury was burning white-hot.

Her mother flinched, and Kestrel's fury grew.

"You think the villagers love you," she said. "You're wrong. They think you're an evil old hag, but they're too scared to say so. And when they see what you'd do to your own daughter, they'll hate you even more."

Her mother snorted.

"Dearest," she said, "they'll *thank* me once they've heard the truth. I'll tell them that you're the one who's brought all the grabbers to the village."

"That's a lie," Kestrel said, but for some reason, her spine had gone cold. Her mother licked her lips.

"It's no lie," she said. "After a grabber feeds, it dies. But every time you murder one, two more are born. You want to know why they're coming so fast? It's because you were too stupid to work out how they multiply. *You've* created a plague!"

Kestrel almost dropped the bloodberry. She knew her mother was telling the truth. That was why she'd seen two sets of eyes in the woodchopper's grabber. That was why they were coming faster and faster. She should have known all along, but she hadn't even tried to work it out.

Kestrel wanted to scream, but no sound would come out. Had she created her dad's grabber herself? *Was all of this her fault?*

"Thought that would wipe the smile off your face," her mother said coolly. She looked at the dog. "Rip her throat out."

The black dog bounded toward her. Kestrel stumbled backward out the door. The villagers, who had crept close to the house, scattered like birds. The dog landed on Kestrel's stomach, squashing all the air out of her and making her gasp. She pushed it off as hard as she could, sending it sprawling, and jumped up.

Within a second it was back on its feet, squaring up to her, saliva dripping from its mouth.

"Are you scared of me?" she screamed at her mother's house. "You'd have the dog kill me instead of doing it yourself?"

There was no answer. The dog crouched, ready to spring. Kestrel felt sick to the pit of her stomach.

"Don't even think about it," she growled.

The dog came toward her in a blur of teeth and claws. Kestrel flung herself out of the way, but its teeth caught her leg. She screamed and lashed out, knocking it to the side. She backed away, crawling through the dirt. The eyes of the whole village were on her, but nobody moved.

The dog leaped again, aiming for her throat. She flung her arm at it and caught it on the side of the mouth, knocking it away. A piece of her sleeve ripped off, and the dog fell over with the material snagged between its teeth. Kestrel put her hand on her spoon, waiting for it to strike again.

But the dog didn't jump right away. It got to its feet, struggling to get its balance. The piece of Kestrel's red-stained sleeve dropped from its mouth, and it wiped its muzzle on the ground as though trying to get a bad taste off its tongue.

Kestrel stared at the dog, her heart hammering.

Before the dog could get its bearings again, she quickly dug the second squashed bloodberry from her pocket. She clutched it in her fist, praying that her instinct was right. The dog looked up and licked its lips. They stared at each other, waiting for the other to make the first move.

The dog twitched, and Kestrel flung herself toward it. They met midair, teeth and fingers and black fur tangling together. Kestrel hit the ground with a rib-shaking thump. The dog was on top of her, its front paws pressed into her stomach, its colossal weight squashing her into the floor so hard she struggled to breathe. It snapped its teeth at her neck. She twisted her head out of the way just in time. With all her strength, she grabbed the dog's muzzle with her free hand.

The dog growled and tried to snap at her fingers. Kestrel brought her other hand, the one with the bloodberry, to its teeth. She forced the berry into its mouth a second before her grip gave way and the dog snapped its jaws down on her fingers.

It felt like her hand had been put into a mincer. Kestrel screamed and pulled it away. She pushed the dog off her, expecting it to lunge for her throat again.

The dog growled, but its paws slipped from her stomach, and it staggered to the side. It swung its muzzle toward her again, but now Kestrel was on her feet. She flung all her weight at the dog from above, pushing it to the ground. She held it down with all her strength as it bucked and twisted.

Finally, the dog's struggle began to fade. It snarled, kicking its legs. Another minute and it was completely still.

Hardly daring to believe it, Kestrel lifted her hands. She touched the dog's side. The bloodberry had killed it.

Kestrel rose to her feet, her eyes fixed nervously on the house.

The door didn't open. It was silent. The whole village watched, shocked that the dog was dead, knowing that there would be some kind of retribution. Then something began to move inside.

Maybe it was the glimpse of her mother's long, pale fingers wrapped around the edge of the door. Maybe it was the whiff of something sickly sweet. Maybe it was because the answer had been staring her in the face for days. Whatever it was, Kestrel knew exactly what was going to step out of the house. It made her whole body go cold with dread.

She slowly climbed to her feet and walked toward the door.

She thought about all the teeth her mother had trapped in the weave. She thought of the way her mother bossed Kestrel and the whole village around, getting them to bring her food while she sat and lapped it all up. The lies she'd told, and the memories Kestrel had lost. The bones hidden in the cellar.

I could wear his face all day long if I wanted, the face painter had said about her dad. *All I need is a body part, and I'd have his looks forever. You're lucky I only borrowed his coat. Bones are much better.*

Kestrel watched as the face painter stepped out of the house, dressed in her dead mother's clothes.

17

MOTHER

The face painter staggered to the door, leaning to one side as though the ground was tilting beneath her feet. Her head was bowed. She caught hold of the wall for support, wheezing, her hands damp with sweat.

Kestrel backed away as the creature—her mother—put a foot on the doorstep. Then another. Her body was shaking from the effort. She let go of the door frame, head still bowed to the floor, and staggered into Kestrel, trailing the weave behind her in great clumps attached to her arms and legs.

Kestrel caught her instinctively and she sagged into her arms. Then her mother looked up and Kestrel screamed.

"You clever little witch," her mother said, and fell to the floor. Her dusty hair drifted away from her scalp and formed in a ring around her. Her eyes were white all the way through, and her skin was sallow. All her facial features were trying to get away from one another, sliding around like eggs in a frying pan.

She stared at the villagers behind Kestrel. Then she snorted with weak laughter, kicking her thin, milky-white legs like a newborn child. Kestrel heard someone slump to the ground behind her.

"You're ... not my mother," Kestrel said, as though saying it would make the truth smaller and easier to swallow.

"That's only a technicality," her mother said. She had the same unthinkable, unseeable features as the face painter in the forest, but her mother's creaky voice. "I made you strong. I took care of you."

Kestrel stared at her. She didn't know what to feel. Then she thought of all the times her mother had hurt her, bending her arm, grabbing her by the throat, pushing her around, *lying* to her.

"How long have you been in my house?" Kestrel asked, finding her anger. She grabbed her mother by the collar and held her up. "Tell me, or I'll throw you into the forest!"

"You won't," her mother said. "You're too *scared.*"

Kestrel tightened her grip. The creature in her hands was small and frail, and Kestrel knew that it would be like throwing an egg to the ground.

"Don't try me," she said angrily, ashamed of her weakness.

"I didn't bring you up to be rude," her mother said, as though they were doing nothing more than drinking tea.

Kestrel dropped her, disgusted. Her mother started to get up, but her legs were as thin and weak as blades of grass, and

Kestrel held her down with her foot. She knew that the things she'd been remembering were true. And her mother—this face painter—had kept them from her.

"I know you stole my memories," Kestrel snarled. "You didn't think I'd meet another face painter. It reversed some of your magic."

But something was still stuck in the back of her head like an itch. "Unblock the rest of them," Kestrel said angrily. "Tell me what you've been hiding."

"Oh, sweetie," her mother said, shaking her head as though she were saddened by Kestrel's delusions.

"Do it!" Kestrel screamed, so loud it was like a blow. Her mother twitched, but she didn't respond.

"You wanted people to die," Kestrel choked. "You wanted the grabbers to keep picking everyone off, so we'd always be scared. So we'd keep looking after you. You sent me out to hunt, knowing I was making it worse. You turned us all into your slaves."

Kestrel could feel the anger of the village broiling behind her. The hairs on the back of her neck stood on end, as though a storm was coming overhead. She wondered who would find their voice first. She stared at the red string tied around her mother's wrist, trailing back into the house, and had a horrible idea. Her mother saw her and protectively grabbed the string, winding it around her hands.

"You should be flattered that I picked you," her mother

said. "I watched your family from the forest. I knew you could be a great hunter, with those eyes. I wanted to keep your grandma, too, but she was too difficult to work with. She wouldn't forget things."

Kestrel heard twigs snap and turned around. Ike was slowly backing away. Rascly Badger had put his hand on his knife, but he hadn't drawn it. Runo and Briar were standing with Hannah, and for the first time, they looked unsure of themselves.

"They're too scared," her mother said lightly. "What are you going to do now, sweetie?"

Kestrel couldn't stand it any longer. This woman—this *monster*—was a murderer. She'd done something with her real mother, and Kestrel was never getting her back.

Her mother suddenly grabbed her ankle, but Kestrel kicked her away with a terrible snarl that made the face painter flinch. The second Kestrel's foot connected with her mother's hand, everyone moved, as though someone had poured courage down their throat.

"You made me burn my watch!" Ike shouted, with a half-terrified, half-furious cry of rage. Mardy and Walt elbowed past each other to get to her mother. Rascly Badger thrust Runo aside to join in.

Kestrel balked as the village came toward her mother with a hundred hands. Before she could work out what to do, she was elbowed in the back of the head and pushed to the ground in the chaos. The villagers swarmed over them, burning with a horrible, bloodcurdling excitement.

"Stop!" her mother screamed at them. "Stop, or you'll all die!"

Kestrel twisted away, throwing herself at her mother through the melee. She wanted answers, and the only person who could make it happen was the face painter. Her mother was kicking the villagers with her legs, snarling and biting, but she was weakening quickly.

Kestrel crawled along the ground until she was level with her mother's wavering face.

"There's nothing left for us here," her mother hissed. "Come with me into the forest. We'll rule it all. I love you, Kestrel. I love you more than any mother."

Kestrel choked. Out of the corner of her eye, she saw Pippit dash through the jumble of legs and hands. As someone grabbed her hair, she saw him pick up the piece of red string that trailed from her mother's wrist to the house.

And Kestrel understood.

Kestrel reached out and grabbed the string from Pippit's mouth. She hesitated for half a second, her heart aching.

Then she tore through the wool with her teeth.

Her mother shrieked and stiffened. Her body jerked twice, and her legs curled inward so they looked like a broken umbrella. Then she lay completely and utterly still.

Kestrel stared at the face painter, a lump in her throat. She tried hard to remind herself that it was a murderer, and not her real mother at all. Ike shoved everyone away and held his arms out. The villagers backed away until they were behind Ike, staring with horror at the broken creature on the floor.

The face painter was stuck with half her mother's face on one side, and its own blank, featureless face on the other.

And it was dead.

Kestrel closed her eyes and shuddered with grief, trying to remember her real mother. The one who used to make beautiful dresses without beetles on them, who smiled and gave Kestrel her first story. But she could barely remember anything. For years, her real mother had been a pile of bones in the cellar.

Kestrel almost forgot where she was until she heard Ike's labored breathing. Everyone around her was staring at the face painter, waiting to see if it would move.

"Bury it," said Walt suddenly. "We can't have the body aboveground. The wolves will smell it."

"Are you mad?" snapped Ike. "Do *you* want to touch it? How do we know it's not just pretending?"

The face painter's head slowly fell to the side, making them all jump. As she watched the last piece of life leave the face painter's body, Kestrel felt something cold tickling the inside of her head.

She clamped her hands over her ears. She didn't want to remember anything else, not now. But it was too late—the face painter was dead, and whatever other memory it had hidden from her was sliding out.

Pop.

It was night, and the cottage was dark. Kestrel could feel her mother's fingers dug tightly into her neck. She struggled to get free, kicking her feet against the wooden floorboards, flailing at the strings crisscrossing the walls. But her mother didn't relent. In her other hand, she was holding a piece of string with Kestrel's tooth tied into it.

Granmos was standing against the door, her blue eyes narrow with fury.

"Are you scared yet?" her mother hissed at Granmos. "You know I'll hurt her."

"I'm never scared," Granmos said coolly, but Kestrel could see that her hands were shaking.

There was a movement at the window that only Kestrel noticed. Horrow, her grandma's grabber, was pacing around agitatedly. It was usually so calm that Kestrel waved to it every evening. She'd known it for weeks now, ever since it first came out of the forest, and all it ever did was watch Granmos. She even fed it bits of meat and bread. But Kestrel sensed that something was now deeply wrong. Something had changed.

"Granmos," Kestrel wavered.

Kestrel's mother clenched her fist around the tooth in her other hand. A world of pain exploded behind Kestrel's eyelids. She screamed. Her grandma screamed.

"Stop hurting her!" Granmos shouted.

Then the pain subsided, but sobs were forcing themselves from Kestrel's throat. Kestrel had never seen her grandma look so frightened before. Her mother licked her lips.

"After I break her bones, I'll stop her heart," she said to Granmos.

Something slammed against the door from the outside. Granmos turned to face it, drawing a knife from her pocket, but the door was already splitting in the middle, and Kestrel had to shield her eyes from a cloud of splinters.

The grabber snarled and grabbed her grandma by the throat. Her grandma tried to strike it, but it was too strong. They struggled just for a second. Then something went *snap*. Her grandma was limp, and the grabber dragged her toward the forest.

"Granmos!" Kestrel screamed, but the forest was dark. They were gone.

Kestrel opened her eyes and gasped for air. It was all real. She knew it.

She'd never let the grabber in.

Kestrel reeled under the weight of a dizzying, almost

tangible relief. The terrible memory of her opening the door for Horrow was a fabrication, something the face painter had stuffed in her head. Her false memory immediately felt absurd, less real even than a dream. Finally, she could breathe again.

She tried to scrape all the new memories together, but she didn't know how they fitted into one piece. Only one thing gave her hope: Her grandma had been able to hold her grabber off for weeks. But something had changed at the end to make her grabber attack. Something to do with Kestrel.

"I don't understand, Pip," she whispered, clutching him. Her face was damp, and she realized her eyes were streaming. Even through her relief, she couldn't stop thinking of the terrified look on her grandma's face. "What does it mean?"

Walt and Ike had been prodding the face painter's body with a long stick, but now they looked up as though they had only just remembered Kestrel was there.

"How long has it been living here?" Ike asked sharply.

"She was probably working with it," Hannah said behind her.

A wave of fury crashed over Kestrel's head. Fury at what had happened to her mother and her grandma. Fury at the face painter, for tricking them. Fury at the villagers, for being complicit in it all.

"Shut up," she said quietly.

"What?" Hannah said. Kestrel turned to face her and the villagers, her fists clenched.

"You heard me," she said. "All you've ever done is hide and whisper, telling one another how terrible I am, and you're still doing it now!" She stepped forward, and several of them automatically backed away. "At least I tried to stand up to my moth- the face painter," she snapped. "You just kept feeding it, and making it stronger, and doing everything it said, and helping it by torturing me. Because you're all *weak*."

Kestrel stopped to take a breath. She could feel their disbelief rising off them. None of them seemed to know what to do.

In the end, she didn't have to say anything.

"You were its servant," said Hannah softly. "*You* were the one who made it strong."

Kestrel lashed out without thinking. She caught Hannah in the face, leaving a long scratch down her cheek. Hannah screamed. Kestrel grabbed Pippit and scrambled away as the villagers fell on her. She swam through her mother's fallen hair and crooked arms as everyone roared and tried to grab her.

"Go!" shouted Pippit.

Kestrel didn't have a plan.

She stood up, ran, and threw herself to the hungry forest.

THE GRABBER

The villagers came after her, hurling abuse, many of them braving the clutches of the forest for the first time in their lives. Kestrel ran until she was sure that she'd lost them, but she could still hear their voices curling through the trees.

So she stumbled on. Deep in her heart she knew that she wouldn't find an end to the forest. It was too cruel and clever to let her out.

She crashed through the undergrowth and fell over, gasping for breath. The forest was plunged into silence. Kestrel got up, feeling ill. Something wasn't right.

She'd only heard silence like this when a grabber was on the loose.

She heard a long, ragged breath in the trees.

"Hello?" she whimpered.

No answer. She looked around, a silent scream building inside her.

Her grabber was standing behind her. It was waiting for Kestrel to notice it. Beetles crawled over its shock of gray hair and squirmed under its coat, which was made of different colored rags. The grabber breathed in deeply, its whole body swelling until it seemed that it would burst at the seams.

Bile rose in Kestrel's throat. She meant to back away, but the grabber had her caught in a strange kind of gravity, and she found herself rooted to the spot. She was drowning in panic. It was stuck in her throat and swamping her lungs. The air was too thick to breathe.

She was going to die.

The grabber reached toward her, its fingers wriggling in anticipation.

Its hands didn't match. One was small and elegant, thick with tarnished silver rings—the rings she'd found in the Salt Bog, the ones that had belonged to her grandma. The other was the bluish, waterlogged hand of the Briny Witch. The holey stone Kestrel had given him was jammed on its middle finger. Kestrel's heart did backflips when she imagined what it would have taken to kill the half-drowned man.

Its back was slightly hunched, but it was larger, much larger than Granmos had been, as though the old woman had been stretched in all directions. It had dipped its hands in blood to mimic her grandma's permanently stained nails.

The grabber shivered in recognition when Kestrel met its eyes.

You always know what your grabber's going to be, deep down.

Kestrel couldn't speak. She could barely move. The grabber took one step forward, and its tongue darted out to lick its lips. Kestrel finally regained control of her legs, and she took one step back, then another. The grabber waited a moment.

Then it lunged.

Kestrel turned and fled, plunging back into the trees with no idea of her direction, or where she was going, only that she had to get away from her grabber. The forest came back to life, trying to catch her with its teeth and nails. Wild dogs danced behind Kestrel, snapping their jaws, and shining blackbirds crashed around her head as she ran through the grasping trees. She ran into a tangle of thorns which dug into her clothes and her hair. She ripped them away in a blind panic, hardly noticing them tear her hands, and looked for a way around them.

The grabber wasn't behind her anymore; it was coming from her right, as though it was herding her somewhere. She could hear it coming toward her, crushing branches under its feet. Kestrel's legs were shaking so hard she could barely run anymore, but she finally got free of the thorns and stumbled on.

A tiny, desperate part of Kestrel wished the grabber would just get it over with. Why couldn't it just attack her? She knew it was chasing her like this for a reason, but her thoughts were shouting over the top of one another, and she couldn't make sense of them. All she knew was that she had to get away.

Suddenly, without any noise at all, the grabber was in front of her with its arms outstretched. Kestrel screamed and swerved to the side. She fell over a branch and hit the ground with a bone-crunching oomph, and the grabber stepped toward her. It wasn't even out of breath.

Kestrel was ready to roll over and plead with it, but a creaky, familiar voice rang through her head.

Get up, you stupid girl. Run.

Granmos's voice was as clear as ice. Kestrel obeyed numbly. She dragged herself to her feet again and sprinted, just as its claws closed over where her head had been. The grabber was only surprised for a second; then it was a moment behind, running swiftly through the trees, immune to the screaming animals and the shadows. Kestrel would never outrun it. It would never tire.

Just when it seemed that there was nowhere left to go, nothing left to try, Kestrel heard her grandma's voice again.

Think! Granmos snapped, just like she had when Kestrel was training, a hundred times over. *How did I stop my grabber?*

Kestrel tried to squash the dozen clamoring voices in her head, the ones screeching at her to give up. She forced them into the dark space at the back of her mind where she'd hidden everything else, her huge fears and her sorrow, and made herself concentrate.

But she didn't know how Granmos had kept her grabber from eating her for so long. She'd died anyway, alone and frightened, sucked into the belly of her monster. Her grandma, who had never been scared of anything in her life.

Fear had gotten the better of her. Kestrel stumbled over a stone in surprise. The thought was so huge it was almost blinding. She leaned over and gasped for air, then staggered on, desperately turning it over and over in her head.

That's it! her grandma urged.

The grabber had eaten Granmos when she was scared. That's what changed—she was scared that Kestrel was going to be killed.

That's why her grabber had been drooling as it watched her emerge from the Marrow Orchard. That's why her dad's grabber had spent so long dragging the chase out, making him even more terrified.

Kestrel swept thorny branches out of her way, gasping for breath. The grabber was so close she could almost feel its breath on the back of her neck, but she knew that she was on the brink of something important. Her grandma had been trying to tell her something about fear. What had she told Kestrel the night she defeated the faces in the door?

Monsters want you to be scared. Otherwise they'd have nothing.

There was a loud *crack* behind Kestrel. She dodged to the side, her lungs burning, trying to lose the grabber just for a second. Just so she could *think*.

If grabbers fed on fear, all Kestrel had to do was stop being scared. That was the answer, right?

But she couldn't control it. She tried to shut it away, like she always did, but she couldn't stop her heart bursting through her chest, her breath swelling in her throat. She was too full of terror. The more she tried, the harder it felt, until she thought she was going to shatter into a million pieces.

The grabber drew nearer, crushing things underfoot.

Kestrel put her foot down on a rotten log and fell over. Pippit pressed himself closer to her head, hissing.

"Run," he squeaked, pulling her hair.

With a huge effort, Kestrel grabbed him round the middle and pulled him off her head. It felt like she was wrenching one of her limbs off.

"It doesn't want you," she said. "Stay safe, okay?"

Pippit tried to dig his nails into her hand, but she flung him away as hard as she could. He landed in a pile of leaves, and before he could get his bearings Kestrel found a last burst of energy and sprinted.

She swerved into an overgrown thicket. She flung herself against the trees, but they were too close together for her to get through. Their roots were tied together, their branches knitted over her head like a roof. Except for some gently glowing fungus, it was very, very dark.

Kestrel gasped for breath as she scrabbled at the trees, but there was no way through. The forest was plunged into a deep, cold silence that made the back of her neck tingle. It knew the grabber was about to feed. She could feel it in her bones, a deep shiver of unnamed dread, the sensation of a universe that had shifted slightly from its axis.

Kestrel turned around.

The grabber was so close she could see the seams of its skin, the cracks in its splintered bones. Its lips curved upward, giving Kestrel time to appreciate its hideous smile.

It had her grandma's blue eyes, the same canny intelligence. It had her grandma's expression, too, like she was staring right through you, rummaging around in your head and discovering every shameful secret you had. The grabber twitched when Kestrel did, flexing its fingers at her quickening heartbeat, and licked its lips. It was enjoying itself.

Kestrel tried one more time to crush her fear. She tried to pack it into a tight ball and hide it inside her stomach, but there was nowhere left to put it. Every piece of training her grandma had given her, every single thing she'd done to teach her not to be scared, was useless. Kestrel scrambled through her memories for something that would help, anything. But nothing could squash a terror this big.

The grabber took a deep breath. Kestrel tightened her grip on her spoon, sweating, her throat burning with horror. She had to fight it. There was no other way.

The grabber lunged, and Kestrel met it.

It was heavier than a well-fed wolf. Its bones might as well have been made of stone, and its hands slapped against Kestrel's shoulders so hard that she was knocked backward. They crashed into the trees so hard it felt like her spine had cracked in half.

Kestrel brought her knee up, just like she'd been taught. She shuddered as it crunched into the grabber's bones, then the grabber pulled away with a surprised snarl. Kestrel squared up to it, brandishing her spoon, but the grabber had already recovered.

They reeled around the clearing, crashing into branches and squashing mushrooms until they were both speckled with fungus and glowing like the night sky. Kestrel was getting weaker. She couldn't push it away anymore.

Kestrel twisted her body, determined to drive her shoulder into its chest, but it knocked her over with a single swipe of its hand and pinned her to the floor.

The grabber bared its teeth like a hungry dog. Its face was so close to Kestrel's that she could see through its stolen eyes, into the bright burning space in its skull. She tried to drive her spoon into the grabber, but it twitched its head away and she missed, again and again. It was grinning.

Kestrel fell still, and the grabber licked its lips.

It lowered its head further, until she could see the moss stuck between its teeth. Kestrel stared at it, nauseated by the smell emanating from its body, her face wobbling with horror. It was dribbling, enjoying the smell of her fear, but that only made her more terrified. All the courage had gone from her body. She couldn't even lift her spoon.

The grabber's face was perfectly her grandma's, from the crooked teeth to the cold, blue eyes.

Kestrel gave an involuntary sob. She was going to live her nightmare one last time. The one where her grandma was pinning her down, screaming at her, just as she had done when Kestrel was little.

Tell me what you're afraid of!

Kestrel shrank away from the grabber, from the veins in its eyes to the terrible expression on its face, and the snarl on its lips. She could hear her grandma again, as clearly as though she were there.

Tell me what scares you! her grandma screamed. *Say it!*

Something cracked inside Kestrel. She was weak and full of terror, and she couldn't keep it to herself anymore.

"I'm scared of you, Granmos," Kestrel blurted, the words coming out in a sob. "You're what I'm most afraid of."

Her words hung in the air, full of shame and defeat. But there was something else, too. It took Kestrel a second to realize that she felt lighter, like she'd dropped a pile of stones from her arms. And just for a second, she felt a tiny bit stronger.

She opened her eyes, shuddering, determined not to die like a coward.

But instead of eating her, the grabber hesitated. As though she'd done something it didn't expect.

As though speaking to it had changed something.

Kestrel thought quickly, hardly daring to hope that she'd done something right. Why wasn't it eating her?

"Do you like the truth?" Kestrel asked, her mind racing. "Is that it? Do you like hearing how much my grandma . . ." The words got stuck in her throat. The grabber licked its lips. Kestrel forced them out. "How much she . . . scared me?"

Saying those words felt like expelling poison from her body. The grabber's eyes flickered, almost as though it was panicking. Kestrel's mind raced on, all the voices condensing into a single stream of thought.

She knew she was getting close to the truth; it was there, in her head, just out of reach. Kestrel searched through her memories, desperately trying to stick everything else together. What had Granmos said about her own grabber? Had she told Kestrel anything useful?

The grabber looked at her sharply, as though she was about to do something it wouldn't like.

Kestrel took herself back to the cottage, standing by the window with her grandma behind her, hands on Kestrel's shoulders, murmuring in her ear.

I call him Horrow, Granmos said.

"Horrow," Kestrel said aloud. Excitement rose slowly through her body like a fever. "She gave it a name. And she told me to choose a name for the faces in the door, to help me stop being afraid of them. And then she tried to make me name the thing I was most scared of. It's all about names. She wanted me to work it out by myself, but I wasn't listening."

The grabber lunged. It shoved her into a tree again without warning. Kestrel hit back furiously, and this time she caught it in the arm, leaving a deep red line in its skin.

"That was for my stealing my notebook," she said. She lashed out again, and this time she caught its fingers. "That's for taking everything else."

The grabber snatched the spoon from her hand and dropped it to the ground.

She was trapped. They both knew that the grabber was stronger. It twirled a lock of her hair around its fingers and sucked it into its mouth, pulling her in until her ear was right by its head. It drew its lips back, so she could see every single one of its razor-sharp teeth.

Kestrel put the final piece together in her head, and for a moment her brain was filled with a universe of noises and the bright, sharp fragments of a million words. In the huge, terrible chaos, one of them settled quietly behind her eyes, making her shiver.

"I know how to stop you," Kestrel said. She could tell from its expression that she had everything she needed to destroy it. All it took was that one word.

It hung between them like a knife on a thread. Kestrel gathered her courage one more time.

"Your name," she said, her heart thrumming like a beetle trapped in a box. "Is Granmos."

DON'T BE AFRAID

For one heart-stopping moment the grabber's breath rattled against her cheek. Kestrel turned her face so she could meet its eyes, and they stared at each other, the grabber with barely disguised shock, as though she had driven a spoon through its ribs.

She was so close to its face she could see the veins in its eyes, and through its tiny black pupils, a pinprick of yellow light. Then it parted its jaws and a damp hunk of her hair fell out.

"That's right," said Kestrel, exhaling. If she moved too quickly the fragile air would shatter, and the grabber might change its mind. "I'm just going to back away, slowly...."

She slid from its grasp. It let her go, but its eyes followed her, as though it was waiting for her to try and escape. She had no doubt that it could have her between its jaws in a second if it chose.

Kestrel edged around it until she was standing in the

middle of the clearing. The grabber slowly turned so it was still facing her. Her heart was beating wildly in her chest, but it wasn't just fear anymore; there was something like excitement, too.

"Good," she said softly.

"Kestrel!" a voice yelled.

Kestrel looked up sharply. Finn was clinging to a branch above her, pressed flat against the bark like a frightened cat. Between the village and the mushroom-speckled grove he'd managed to procure several tatty feathers and decorative streaks of dirt.

Pippit was attached to Finn's head, hissing and spitting at the grabber like a demonic hat.

"Finn?" Kestrel was shocked. "What are you doing?"

The grabber's neck bones creaked as it looked up at Finn.

"I'm saving you," said Finn through gritted teeth. His fingers were dug into the branch as though he was forcing himself not to run away. "Get up here *now*."

The grabber was looking at Finn with interest, but it wasn't moving. Kestrel noticed that it inflated and deflated like a balloon every time she took a breath. Strands of her hair were still caught around its teeth, and they fluttered with the airflow from its nostrils.

"I've got it under control," she said after a moment, sounding more confident than she felt.

"It'll eat you!" Finn said hysterically.

"It won't," said Kestrel, looking at the grabber. She had an idea, but she wasn't entirely sure it was going to work. "It won't eat me. Will you, Granmos?"

The grabber's face didn't change, but she could tell that it was listening.

She took a step forward. Her grabber blinked and stepped back, so the distance between them remained the same. Kestrel slowly walked around its side. The grabber stepped away from her, but it turned its body so it was still facing her. They slowly circled each other as though they were practicing a dance.

"Come down, Finn," Kestrel said.

There was a long, hesitant pause. Then she heard a *thump* as Finn slid to the ground. He was still clinging to the tree trunk, ready to disappear into the branches like a squirrel. "I've worked it out," she said as they continued their slow, tense dance. She started to move a little faster, and the grabber matched her. Pippit bared his teeth, his fur standing on end.

"Worked what out?" Finn said, wobbling.

"I think they feed on your fear," Kestrel said. "So to stop them from eating you, you've got to take away their food source."

"Kes, get away from it now," said Finn. "Get up the tree before it's too late."

"That's what they want," Kestrel said. "They *want* you to

run away. That's why they make themselves look terrifying, and spend so long chasing you. But if you turn around and look at it—if you make it yours by naming it—"

"What are you saying?" Finn asked, his voice wavering. "Are you saying I can stop my grabber coming for me?"

"I don't think you can," she said. Granmos's eyes flickered in confirmation. "You can't kill it, because another two will be born. If you get scared, it'll take you anyway. It's just *there*."

Maybe you were never really safe. Maybe your grabber was always waiting for an opportunity to snap you up.

"What... for good?" Finn asked, looking sick.

Kestrel stopped moving and drew herself up tall. She had to try something.

"Give me my notebook, Granmos," she said, holding her hand out. Her fingers were shaking, but she couldn't change her mind now.

Granmos stared at her.

Kestrel felt a tiny flicker of doubt. Her grabber moved toward her, teeth snapping together.

"Granmos!" she shouted. To her relief it fell still, its face sagging. Kestrel tried to recover from her surprise. "Just give it to me," she said firmly.

Granmos just stared at her, curling its top lip. Kestrel had seen that expression a million times before on the black dog. She knew what it was waiting for.

No way, she thought, but after a few seconds the grabber

still hadn't moved, and she knew she didn't have a choice.

"Please," she said.

Granmos slowly curled its lips back. Its jaw widened until its mouth was almost the size of its face, its eyes pushed to somewhere near the back of its head, its skin wrinkling into great piles. Kestrel could see all the way down its throat. The back of its head was thin enough to let some daylight through, and its insides were made of gray jelly.

Granmos made a low grunting sound like marbles rattling in a glass jar.

Kestrel reached down its throat, shuddering. It was warm. Her wrist brushed the grabber's tongue and its mouth quivered, its vicious teeth straining to snap shut; but its jaws held open, and Kestrel made herself keep going until her elbow was resting against its teeth. Her hand touched the gray jelly. She closed her eyes, feeling disgusted, and pushed her hand farther down. Finally, her hand met the notebook.

She curled her fingers around it and pulled. The notebook, gray and phlegmy, came up from the grabber's stomach.

Granmos's mouth snapped shut. Kestrel looked it in the eye.

"Thank you," she said, and Granmos rearranged its teeth into a yellow grin.

"That didn't just happen," said Finn as Pippit sniffed the pages.

She pressed the notebook into Finn's hands. He opened

it and stared at the familiar black writing, now smeared and covered in goo.

"What now?" he said, his voice trembling.

Kestrel felt her heartbeat quicken. She had an idea.

The grabber had stalked her for days. It had learned as much about her fears as it could. So why shouldn't it have learned anything else? Why wouldn't it know what she *wanted*, too?

"Can you help me escape?" she asked it.

Granmos closed its fist, and its lips twitched into something like a cunning smile.

Kestrel breathed out slowly. If there was a way out, nothing would stop Kestrel getting there if there was a grabber by her side.

"We can . . . leave?" Finn said. Kestrel thought he looked a bit green.

"I think so," she said, filled with a mixture of excitement and dread. "Finn, we're finally getting out!"

Granmos moved as quickly and as silently as a bird. It suddenly swung its arm, its mouth wide open, and smacked a huge, pale hand into Finn's chest. He went flying and hit the ground so hard the trees shivered.

Kestrel turned to face her grabber, teeth bared in fury. Finn wailed until Pippit nipped him on the hand.

"Don't you dare hurt my friends," Kestrel snapped at Granmos. "I mean it."

295

The grabber snarled at Finn. He jumped to his feet and backed against a tree.

"Why don't you like him?" Kestrel said angrily. "He's coming with us, okay?"

The grabber started toward Finn again. He shrieked and scrambled up the tree.

"Stop!" shouted Kestrel, and it halted. Its expression was frosty.

"It won't let me come," said Finn. He looked horribly relieved.

"But—"

"It's fine," said Finn, climbing to his feet. "We can live here. You, me, and Pip. Even … *that* can stay, if it has to," he added, looking at Granmos with disgust. "We don't ever have to go near the village. We can live in the trees. We'll be so happy we won't want to go outside anyway. I mean, are there even trees outside the forest?"

"Don't say that," Kestrel said desperately. "We'll all go with Granmos. The three of us. Won't we, Pip?"

"Kes?" Pippit said, looking distressed. "Kes? Stay here?"

Kestrel felt like a black hole had opened inside her. She stared at him, and he started to wash himself agitatedly.

"Pip?" she said, although she already knew his answer.

She knew that Pippit belonged in the forest. He probably came from generations of weasels who had lived here all their lives. And Finn had never wanted to leave. All the times they'd been looking for the way out, he'd been treating it like a game.

"It's fine," she said quickly, turning away so they wouldn't see her face.

"You're not going by yourself, are you?" said Finn in disbelief.

Kestrel looked at the tops of the trees. By tilting her head back, she could stop the water that had started coming out of her eyes. The cool air scraped across her cheeks. She could hear the sea in her ears again, the faraway, mythical wash of water.

"Yeah," she said when she'd summoned up the courage. "I'm going."

"So that's it," Finn said coolly, his face closing up. "Even though there might be nothing there, and you might die."

They looked at each other. Something had changed in the last few moments. There was an awkwardness between them, a strange, sharp newness. They both seemed much older than before. Or maybe, Kestrel thought, the feeling had been growing there for a while and she'd only just seen it.

"Take my notebook," she said. "Tell the villagers what you know. They'll listen to you. Make them understand about their grabbers."

Finn rubbed his dirt-streaked face.

"They won't want me back," he said.

"You have to stop stealing cake," Kestrel said. "But they'll take you in. Mardy always liked you, deep down. Start by burning my mother's house. Nobody else will be brave enough to go near it, and they'll trust you after that."

"Really?" he said.

"They might even put you in charge," she said. "They need someone who's braver than them."

Finn and Kestrel stared at each other. Then Finn jerked forward, pulling Kestrel into a hug.

"I'm sorry my mother hurt you," she said quietly, hugging him back. "And I shouldn't have been mad about Hannah. I guess I was a bit . . . you know . . ." She swallowed the word "jealous," but they both knew it was there.

"I shouldn't have let the others tell lies about you," Finn mumbled. "And I should've worked out your grabber was coming and been there when your dad—er." He gulped the last word down, too.

Pippit buried his face in Kestrel's ear.

"Something would've eaten me by now, if not for you," Kestrel said to Pippit.

"Nah," said Pippit. "Kes crunch, Pip munch." He nipped her ear. "No go?"

"I can't stay," she said, feeling wretched. "If I don't do it now, I might not be brave enough again."

"Pffft," Pippit said, nuzzling her ear with his warm nose. A lump rose in Kestrel's throat.

"Look after Finn for me. He'll look after you, too."

"Bye, Kes," Pippit mumbled. "Find good snacks."

"Love you, Pip," she whispered as Finn pulled away. "You too, I guess," she added lightly. Finn laughed and wiped his nose on his sleeve.

"Maybe you'll leave as well, one day," she said.

Finn nodded uncertainly.

They heard the distant sound of shouting. It was coming from behind them, curling through the forest, a dozen voices mixed with the snapping of branches. Kestrel could hear Ike's voice floating above the others.

"I'll talk to them," Finn said unexpectedly. He tightened his hands around the notebook, looking suddenly determined. "You won't have to worry."

"Thanks, Finn," Kestrel whispered.

He turned away quickly, with Pippit still attached to his shoulder, and hesitated. For a bright, aching second Kestrel wondered if he was going to say something else. Pippit looked at her over his shoulder. But then Finn grabbed a branch and swung himself into the tree. The last thing Kestrel saw was Finn's feather-stuck hair and Pippit's face crumpling. Then the trees closed around them, and they were gone.

Kestrel suddenly felt very, very alone.

Granmos put its hand on Kestrel's back. She turned around, blinking tears away.

"Take that coat off," she demanded, trying to hide the wobble in her voice. "My grandma made a coat like that. It should stay here, where she is."

Kestrel wished her grandma were here right now, so she could wrap her arms around her and tell her that she understood why she put Kestrel through all that training. That it had saved her life. That it really had made her stronger. And that, despite everything, she missed her.

Granmos smiled wonkily and oozed its way out of the coat, drawing its arms in and letting it slide down its back and onto the ground. Kestrel caught her breath. Its body was a great jumble of rubbish from the forest, wonky stick-ribs twined with choking ivy, crabby red apples growing in a necklace around its neck. There were birds' eggs in its stomach and ferns in its chest and thin, translucent mushrooms growing on its organs. A row of seashells undulated behind its ribs.

Kestrel knew what they were right away, because they were exactly like the ones in her grandma's notebook, but bigger. She heard the sea roar in her ears and shuddered. So it *was* real.

Granmos's body was as deep as the forest, its eyes as far away as the stars. Kestrel wondered, with dizzying uncertainty, if it was even possible to escape the forest without your grabber. The idea of a secret path, snaking through the trees and toward freedom, suddenly seemed childish. Maybe the forest would only release you if you defeated it in other, more difficult ways.

"All right," Kestrel breathed, feeling tiny and insignificant. "I guess this is it."

Granmos, old and stately, with a skirt made of bones and teeth, held out its tiny, elegant hand. It—*she*—was perfectly still but for the slight wheeze of her breath and the green beetle in the center of her chest, which slowly opened and closed its wing cases like a beautiful brooch. Granmos still wore an approximation of her grandma's face, old and wise with crooked teeth. Kestrel could almost smell the pipe smoke. Her eyes were fixed on the forest, but they quickly flicked sideways to Kestrel. She was waiting.

The last pieces of regret fluttered in Kestrel's chest like so many bits of paper. She was full of holes, and she didn't think she'd ever be able to fill them in.

But maybe that didn't have to stop her.

She took one last look at the empty forest, the trees still swaying where Finn had swung through them, and turned back to her grabber.

She hesitantly took Granmos's hand. The grabber's fingers closed gently over her own. Kestrel knew she was standing with the most dangerous creature alive. She knew that one day, if she wasn't strong, it would find its appetite again. And she knew that if she took one more step, her life was going to change forever.

Kestrel nodded. Granmos smiled. Together, speckled with the light of a thousand mushrooms, they turned and faced the endless forest.

ACKNOWLEDGMENTS

I want to thank everyone who made this book possible, starting with all the awesome people at Dial Books for Young Readers and, in particular, the wonderful Stacey Friedberg, editor extraordinaire. Thank you also to my friends and writerly colleagues, whose cheerleading and proofreading skills have saved me countless times; and to my parents and sister, for shouting about my monster-ridden stories to anyone who will listen.

And lastly—but probably most importantly—bottomless thanks (and... apologies?) to the people in my life whose mannerisms and quirks I have shamelessly pilfered. Sorry, they were just too good.